MARY CRAWFORD

Heart Wish

HIDDEN BEAUTY BOOK 9

COPYRIGHT

Published on November 14, 2017, by Diversity Ink Press and Mary Crawford. Author may be reached at MaryCrawfordAuthor.com.

ISBN: 978-1-945637-48-3

Cover by Covers Unbound

HIDDEN BEAUTY SERIES

Until the Stars Fall from the Sky

So the Heart Can Dance

Joy and Tiers

Love Naturally

Love Seasoned

Love Claimed

If You Knew Me (and other silent musings)
(novella)

Jude's Song

The Price of Freedom (novella)

Paths Not Taken

Dreams Change (novella)

Heart Wish (100% charity release)

Tempting Fate

The Letter

The Power of Will

HIDDEN HEARTS SERIES

Identity of the Heart

Sheltered Hearts

Hearts of Jade

Port in the Storm (novella)

Love is More Than Skin Deep

Tough

Rectify

Pieces (a crossover novel)

Hearts Set Free

Freedom (a crossover novel)

The Long Road to Love (novella)

Love and Injustice (Protection Unit)

Out of Thin Air (Protection Unit)

Soul Scars (Protection Unit)

OTHER WORKS:

The Power of Dictation

Use Your Voice

An Everyday Guide to Scrivener 3 for Mac

Vision of the Heart

DEDICATION

To those who find the lost.

CHAPTER ONE

KENDALL

I pinch the bridge of my nose as I concentrate on the words being spoken on the other end of the phone. Instinctively, I know that this case is going to take a toll on me. It hits a little too close to home. I listen to her sob for a few moments before I gently interrupt, "Mrs. Livingston, thank you so much for calling Locate My Heart. I'll set up a file for Bethany and your grandson, Asher, as soon as I get my computer turned on. I just walked in the door."

Pausing my racing thoughts to listen, I reply patiently, "Of course, Bethany couldn't make the call herself. Being questioned by the police is a daunting thing. I understand. Tell your daughter-in-law to rest as much as she can. Asher will need her when he is found."

I place my purse on my bookshelf and try to turn

on my computer, but the cord on my headset is too short. Instead, I open a file drawer and pull out a brand-new baby-blue file, indicating yet another lost male child.

I fix the headset I've knocked askew and flex my neck. I am anxious to get started, but I know this is a crucial bonding step, and I don't want to rush her. "I need to get this file together. You have my email address. If you think of anything else or if any news stations send you any surveillance footage, please forward it on to me. I appreciate your help with this. Hopefully we'll be able to drum up lots of public-interest in your grandson's case." Mrs. Livingston sobs some more before she thanks me for my help. "It's the least I can do to help ma'am. We'll do our best to bring your grandson home. I'll be in touch if there are any developments."

I'm so exhausted after I remove my headset, I am tempted to lay my head on my desk and take a nap. Colette walks by my desk and slides a cup of fragrant cinnamon tea under my nose. "That sounded rough, Kendall. Is this case going to be as awful as it sounds?"

I jump when Colette speaks. I've been so focused on my conversation with Mrs. Livingston, I completely forgot my supervisor was here. Colette is working on the same grant I am. It's due in a few days and we're still collecting data. With this breaking case, the grant will have to take a backseat. I adjust my glasses and pull my long hair off my neck as I nod. "Unfortunately, this one is a real puzzler in every sense of the word. It's not shaping up to be your typical parental abduction. Bethany Livingston was shopping at a discount store for a particular type of binky for her son, Asher Edwin Livingston — age two months, three weeks old. Bethany stopped to go to the restroom and change his diaper. She laid him on the changing table and turned around to get wipes from her diaper bag. While Bethany's back was turned briefly, someone hit her over the head, pushed her down, swooped in, and took Asher off the changing table. She never saw what hit her."

"Who called it in?" Colette anxiously clicks the open-and-close mechanism on her ink pen.

"Phyllis Livingston she is Bethany Livingston's very concerned mother-in-law. Her son, Edwin Livingston, is a court reporter in Judge Abram's courtroom. They are in the middle of a trial today. Mrs. Livingston and her husband took Bethany and their grandson to the store to try to find some of his favorite pacifiers. They wanted to give her some space because she was feeling a little insecure. Mrs. Livingston was feeling bad for hovering all the time. She went back into the store to look around for new dish towels while her husband shopped for sporting goods at a different store. Mrs. Livingston said her daughter-in-law ran out of the bathroom and screamed hysterically. That's when Phyllis called the police. The police summoned the paramedics because Bethany Livingston had a goose egg on her head."

Colette grimaces. "Let me guess … they didn't believe the mother?"

"Well, according to Phyllis, the questioning of Bethany was intense," I reply as I turn on my computer.

"Figures. That's how it always goes. They seem to suspect the family first. Do we have anything to support an AMBER Alert?"

I shake my head. "There's no reliable description or

license plate number available. We don't have much to go on. The mother is so distraught that she doesn't even remember what her son was wearing today. It's some kind of onesie — but she can't remember if it's got trains or dinosaurs on it."

"Tell me we at least have pictures of the baby?" Colette shakes her head in dismay.

"We will — as soon as my computer boots up. Phyllis Livingston is sending me some pics from her cell phone."

"That's a start, I suppose," Colette sighs.

"Do you mind if I send the pictures to you? I could use some help to make flyers because I have a gut feeling time is especially important for this case."

"Works for me. I can take a break from grant writing for a bit. I miss front-line work"

Settling into my workspace, my brain is spinning with all the things I need to do as I click on my email program. When I do, ominous music blares through my speakers and an enormous skull-and-cross-bones icon fills the screen, making me jump.

"What the heck is that?" Colette stops in her tracks.

"I don't know. I was just trying to open my email program when this appeared." I look for a way to shut the stupid thing off. Finding none, I unplug the speakers.

"Oh Crap! Is it one of those virus thingies? How do we get rid of it?" she asks.

At first, I am shocked to put two and two together until Colette starts asking questions. Suddenly, I recall a news story I saw about ransom-ware. As the realization hits, I whisper in a shaky voice. "Who'd want to attack Locate My Heart? We're a nonprofit agency. We do nothing more than reunite families. Who could hate that?"

"You are much more of a computer person than I am. I barely know how to operate my flip phone. I don't even own one of those smart phones. I don't know the first thing about our computer system. On television, everyone always knows who to call in these situations, but I don't know anybody. It's not like I know the guy who makes Microsoft computers and the guy who invented Apple computers is dead. Who exactly does one call for this kind of thing?" Her voice raises even higher. "I don't have to remind you, we have a grant due in just a couple days. That grant is 55% of our operating fund. Without it, we are sunk. If they wipe out our data, we are toast. We can kiss our program goodbye."

"Colette, take a deep breath. You are going to give yourself a stroke. Because of the nature of the information we have here, I back it up to the cloud several times a day, so our data is very secure. It's not the data I'm so worried about — it's our ability to operate day to day."

"I don't know what in the world all this has to do with the weather. Just do whatever you need to do to salvage all of our computer stuff. We have an active case we need to start."

"Okay, I'll do what I can do. I'll start with local law enforcement. I'll see what they suggest. I want to make sure I'm not making a bad situation worse," I say as I pick up the phone and start to dial.

"Who are you calling?"

"Tyler Colton. He's my local law enforcement contact at the Sheriff's Office. He should be able to tell me where to start. I should give them a heads up about the threat, don't you think? Other local businesses might find themselves in the same boat."

Colette scowls at me and clicks her pen. "Tread with caution. I'm still not sure which of the local LEOs we can trust. We've had a contentious relationship in the past. Tyler may not support our mission."

"I understand that, but he's the only contact I've got at the moment."

"I hope it goes well. I have a healthy wariness about law enforcement types, as you well know. I'll let you deal with them. In the meantime, I'll run home and see how much of the grant data I've got in hard copy. I just don't trust computers. Maybe I had good reason."

"Perhaps you're right. Either way we need to figure it out. We have to get Asher's picture in front of as many people as possible. Come to think of it; I think I'll just head to the Sheriff's department myself. Perhaps we can issue our media package from there."

• • •

An officer barely older than a high-schooler escorts me back to Tyler's office. Ty is frowning at something on his computer screen. When I knock on his door frame, he looks at me and smiles. "Hey, Kendall! You are a bright spot in an otherwise dismal day."

"You might not say that when you hear what I have to say," I admit as I lower myself into the chair opposite his desk.

"Oh, so this isn't a personal visit? That can't be good."

I sigh. "It's not. Regardless of how you look at it, it just isn't."

Tyler pulls a legal pad out of a drawer and opens it to a clean page. He grabs a pen out of a ceramic cup on his desk. "Okay, you might as well start at the beginning. Given the nature of your job, I'm not sure I want to hear this today, but I guess it needs to be done."

"Unfortunately, you're right. The problem started out with a report of a missing child. A woman by the name of Mrs. Livingston called to tell me that her grandson was snatched today from a local discount store."

"Several of our deputies were dispatched to that call. That's the one that took place in the women's restroom, correct?"

"Yes, the baby's name is Asher Edwin Livingston. He's three months old."

"Were you able to get any pictures of the child?"

"Funny you should mention that, because that's the second reason for my visit. When I turned on our computers to open Mrs. Livingston's email, I received a notice that our computers are being held hostage unless we pay ByteLadyJusticeWhereItHurts a million dollars."

"What? That's just crazy. You guys are a nonprofit organization. How do they figure you have that kind of money? Do they even realize how you guys help us get the word out about missing kids and how you support families in crisis?"

"I was hoping you could tell me the answer to that. I didn't even think agencies like Locate My Heart were targets for these cyber-terrorists. I've seen news stories about these organizations, but I thought they went after big companies with deep pockets, not companies like ours."

"It seems like everyone is a target of crime these days. I don't suppose you remember the exact wording of the threat?"

"I took a picture with my cell phone. Will that work?" I answer as I push my phone across the desk toward him. "The news report I saw said not to click on anything if you got a threat. As soon as the window popped up, I didn't touch anything on my computer. I came right over to you."

Tyler runs his hand through his short-cropped hair. "I'm sure the forensics folks will appreciate that. Unfortunately, most of the folks that specialize in cyber-crimes are away at training up in Portland sponsored by the feds."

I slump down in the chair, feeling defeated. "What am I going to do? I've got to get the alerts out about Asher. You know how this business works — time is of the essence. Every minute we waste puts that child in exponentially more danger."

"I'll call Andy in here and see if she can contact Mrs. Livingston and get her to send the pictures to our department. We'll try to send out the alert from here instead of Locate My Heart."

"Andy?" I ask, unfamiliar with the name.

"Officer Andrea Angelica Garcia is one of our newest officers. She specializes in cases involving children. She goes by Andy. I think you'll like her a lot. She's passionate about helping children."

"Sounds good. We can use all the help we can get now because not having a computer system has completely crippled my ability to help. Colette is fit to be tied because we're in the middle of applying for a grant from our chief source of funding."

"I have another friend who might be able to help. You remember my good friend, Aidan O'Brien, who did the fundraising concert for you guys a few years back?"

"How could we possibly forget? He raised thousands of dollars for us. We're so grateful for his help; it allowed us to purchase upgraded computer equipment and software to perform age progressions on missing children."

"Yeah, that's him. Anyway, Aidan uses a company called Identity Bank to vet all of his security. They employ a ton of former agents and military types. One of the guys who works for both Aidan and Tristan is a computer whiz. Jameson helped Aidan track a cyber-stalker. I can contact him and see if he's willing to help out."

"Locate My Heart probably doesn't have the funding for that kind of thing. Private computer consultants are very expensive." I sigh. "As Colette's executive assistant, I know the inner-workings well enough to know we can't afford it."

"Don't worry about it. Tristan often does this kind of thing for free," Tyler says as he picks up the phone.

"Andy, could you come to my office, please," Tyler

instructs. He turns to me. "Andy will take care of you while I work on the rest of this. Thanks for coming. It means a lot to me that you trust our working relationship enough to reach out."

"Thank you for offering your resources. I'm sure Asher's family will be grateful."

CHAPTER TWO

JAMESON

I ADJUST MY BLUETOOTH mic as I stare at my iPad. I try to disguise my frustration as I watch my supervisor, Tristan, explain what he wants me to do over the pixelated video call. I'm still having trouble wrapping my brain around what he's asking of me. Scowling, I ask again, "Are you sure you want me to do that? We are getting dangerously close to having to pay a penalty on our current job. When we get hired for these military contracts, they don't mess around — especially when we're called in to fix someone else's screw up."

Tristan nods. "I know. I sign those contracts, remember? You guys don't have anything left on the job Kinsey can't handle. She doesn't have as much experience as you, but she's a darn good programmer. I need your skills over at Locate My Heart."

Unfortunately, I don't look away from the camera quick enough, and Tristan catches my eye roll. "Problem?" he asks sharply.

I grimace. "Honestly? Yeah, I have a problem with

places like that. To me, they're no better than those late-night fortunetellers who come on TV and charge you hundreds of dollars per minute to read from a lame script."

"Why do you say that?" Tristan asks with a scowl.

"They're a bunch of scam artists. Crooks who give families that are already in crisis, and suffering the worst possible pain imaginable, false hope. These places string them along for their own enrichment. They don't do anything that the police and the FBI can't do. Yet, they insert themselves into an already-complicated situation and make it worse. Organizations like Locate My Heart are the worst type of predators. They are like modern-day snake oil salesman."

Tristan shakes his head and smirks. "Geez Jameson, why don't you tell me how you really feel?"

"Just being straight with you, man."

"Let me tell you what I know," my boss's expression grows somber. "This was before you started with us, but Aidan did a charity concert for Locate My Heart. We did a full security workup on them. They passed with flying colors. They have one of the smallest administrative budgets we've ever seen in a charity and they never charge families for their services. Colette Stephens started Locate My Heart after her son, Jasper, was kidnapped, and she couldn't get anyone to listen to her because she and her husband were going through a divorce. Everyone assumed her husband kidnapped her son. It never was her husband — it was a deranged schizophrenic who had some delusion that her child belonged to him. Because the police assumed that it was Colette's husband, no one bothered to look for the child for several days. By the time they started looking for Jasper, it was too late."

"You can believe what you want to, but nobody does something nice for the sake of being nice. That's not how people work. There's always some sort of private agenda. Eventually, the truth will come out. When it does, don't say I didn't warn you."

"Okay, whatever you say. I'm a nice guy and I am going to send my best computer expert to solve their computer problem. Since you happen to be my best computer guy, you're going to go. I'll have Kinsey finish up what you're doing. Pack your bags. You're going to a small town outside of Salem, Oregon."

I smirk at Tristan. "You're lucky that old saw isn't true. I guess you can go home again. I suppose my folks will be happy to see me."

"Oh, that's right. You're from Oregon, aren't you?" Tristan asks. "Anywhere close to Salem?"

"I grew up in Cottage Grove. It's south of Eugene. I'll just rent a car. Hopefully I'll have time to pop in to see them once I figure out what's going on at the job site."

"You've been working a few months straight, why don't you take some days off after you've finished up with Locate My Heart? You haven't seen your family in a while — not since the last time you worked for Aidan, right?"

"Yeah, I consulted on that stalking case with Logan. That was a weird one. I'm glad Tasha is doing okay now."

"Time is of the essence here. They've got a missing infant case they're working. Do you want me to send a plane for you, or do you want to take a commercial flight?" Tristan asks.

I know Tristan has money to burn, but questions like that always take me off guard. I blow out a breath to stall as I try to come up with an answer which doesn't sound rude. "No, that isn't necessary. I'm already in Seattle working on the military contract, so it's not far to Salem. By the time you get your planes here from Florida, I could be down there. I'll just go to Sea-Tac and hop on a shuttle."

"Are you sure? I could lease a private plane out of Seattle."

"Tristan, it's fine. If you could've seen the planes I had to fly on when I was in the military, regular coach is no big deal. If you want to do anything, donate the money you would've used to fly a private plane to legit agencies that look for missing children. They could use the money more than I need a private flight."

"Consider it done. Be sure to use your corporate credit card when you book your flight. Call me when you land in Salem. Your contact at Locate My Heart is Kendall Kordes, and you'll be working with Tyler Colton at Sheriff's Office."

"Affirmative. I've dealt with Tyler before. I will check in later."

<hr>

When I walk into the Sheriff's office, the receptionist escorts me to the doorway of the conference room with her finger to her lips in a gesture of caution to be quiet. As soon as I look inside, I see why. Tyler, standing next to a giant poster of an infant dressed in a tiny baseball jersey, is explaining the circumstances of the disappearance to a room full of reporters, some with video cameras pointed at him. Next to him is someone I assume to be the baby's grandmother. When Tyler finishes speaking, the grandmother pleads for the baby's return. I wonder why the parents aren't making this plea. A reporter must have read my mind, as she asks the same question. Tyler replies, "The mother is so overcome with grief and anxiety that she's being treated at the hospital, and her husband is currently attending to her."

Tyler vividly paints a picture of the pain the family is experiencing, and I'm transported to another time and place. I remember placing scratchy, unreliable phone calls from overseas to my mom while she tried to cope with the pain of a missing child. The doctors told me my mother had cardiogenic shock otherwise known as 'broken heart syndrome'. She came precariously close to dying. We almost lost my brother and my mom on the same day. I pray the same thing doesn't happen to this family.

After Tyler wraps up the press conference, he walks over to me and shakes my hand. "Hey, Jameson, it's great to see you. I never got a chance to properly thank you for your help on the Tasha Keeley case. Your work saved my forensic team tons of time. Hers was one of the weirdest cases I've seen in a while."

"No problem. I'm just glad Tasha has such a great support team around her and was able to cut ties with her abuser."

"Thanks for getting here so quickly. I guess we were fortunate you were on this coast."

"I suppose so. I have to be honest. I'm not a big fan of this assignment."

"Really? I've worked with both Colette and Kendall before. They're good people. Locate My Heart does great work."

"If they do, they are the exception to the rule. In my experience, most of the groups like this are all like virus-ridden vultures that take advantage of families when they are at their most vulnerable. Psychics, search and rescue groups, and media representation — they all want a piece of you."

"Old wounds?" Tyler asks insightfully.

"You could say that. My little brother disappeared when I was serving overseas. Nobody wanted to believe that he didn't disappear voluntarily. In all these years, no one really looked for him. They just wrote him off as an angsty teenager who didn't get along with his parents. I never figured that was fair to my brother or my parents. Since I was already out of the house and serving Uncle Sam, I didn't have much say in it."

Tyler looks at me with his mouth agape. "You know that your boss is one of the preeminent locators of missing people in the whole nation, right? What does Tristan say?"

I shrug as I avert my gaze and study the floor. "Actually, I haven't shared this part of my past. I didn't want to look like I took the job because of the personal perks. I wanted Tristan to hire me for my skills. I didn't want to seem like I was desperate for the job because of what it could offer me."

Tyler studies me for a second before he shakes his

head in disbelief. "I take it you and Tristan haven't had one of his famous inspirational talks."

"Inspirational talks?"

"You know, the one where he takes you on a tour of his whole facility and tells you how he got started when he was barely out of elementary school? He goes into his whole background and explains why he started the business and his whole business philosophy."

"No, I guess I haven't heard the speech. When I came on board, Tristan was in the middle of a crisis. We haven't slowed down much since. I haven't had the formal introduction."

"May be worth your while to take a few moments to have Tristan tell you the whole story next time you're back in Florida. It might give you some insight into the man you're working for." Tyler explains. "At any rate, I know for a fact that Tristan would support helping you search for your little brother."

"Yeah? Why is that?" I follow Tyler down the hallway.

Tyler turns and looks at me with a puzzled expression. "Tristan started Identity Bank in large part so he'd have the resources to help his mom find the little girl she gave up for adoption when she was in college. I thought everyone who worked for Identity Bank knew."

"I guess not everyone. Tristan has a sister?" I ask, trying to hide the surprise in my voice. Although I'm not close friends with Tristan, I figure I should know him well enough to know something like that.

"The way I understand it, after he found her, his

sister passed away during a routine operation. His mom raised her grandson as her own."

I roll my shoulder as I mutter, "Oh, that explains a lot. I always wondered why Elliott was so much younger than Tristan. It'd be rude to ask so I just kept my mouth shut and figured it was none of my business."

"That's funny. Tristan's private about most areas in his life, but that's one of the few areas he discusses because it's part of the talk that he gives when he asks for donations to Elliott's House and the programs related to it. He has a condensed version of his life story that he tells investors to let them know how important it is for kids who have lost their parents to have a place to grieve and receive specialized counseling and meet other kids who are in the same situation."

"That's kinda cool. I see flyers for Elliott's House around work, but I'm not usually included in that side of things, so I haven't really looked into it. That's a great way to honor his sister."

"The more you learn about your boss, the more you'll understand that many of the things that Tristan does are over-the-top and epic. That's one of the reasons we all respect him so much. Tristan and his wife, Rogue, are special folks." Tyler leans forward and peeks his head in an open doorway. He leans back and says, "Oh, great. Kendall is here."

We enter a small conference room. On one side of the room is a two-way mirror and on the other side of the room is a set of TV monitors. I see pictures of a baby boy flashing up on the screen. It strikes me again how tiny the baby is. There's nothing in his little gummy grin or in his warm brown eyes with long eyelashes which hints at the terrible tragedy that happened today. In that picture, he looks like the world's calmest, happiest baby.

I take a moment to study the woman in front of me. Her long, blonde curls have slid off the side of her graceful neck as she hunches over a file, intently reading. She doesn't even seem to notice us in the doorway even though we were talking. Finally, Tyler clears his throat softly.

The woman jerks her head and hastily removes her glasses and stashes them in her jacket pocket. "Sorry, I didn't know you were there. I was searching the reports for some clues. Regrettably, I didn't find any." She points to her pile of notes. "Of course, it would help if I knew what I was looking for. I can't believe no one saw anything."

I glance at Tyler. "No security footage? I thought this incident took place at some sort of strip mall."

Tyler sighs. "You'd think with today's technology we'd have better luck, but on this day, the camera gods were not with us. They are remodeling the store where it happened. While they prepared to paint, they took down all the security cameras around the restroom. In the parking lot next to the entrance to the store, someone recently hit the pole with their car and took out the power source to the only operational camera in the whole parking lot. The business beside the store recently went out of business, and the one on the other side of that store had a computer malfunction and lost its hard drive. We're flying blind. No one can remember seeing anything out of the ordinary. One clerk remembers hearing a baby crying, but she also reports that the baby's cries did not seem unusually sharp or distressed, so she paid them no mind."

"I don't know how Isaac and Tristan did this, but I have copies of the police report your officer took, and I have reviewed them. You know what stuck out to me? The mother-in-law's statement that she left her daughter-in-law alone in the bathroom with the baby. I don't personally have any kids, but I know my mom. She wouldn't allow that kind of thing, even if she were trying to spare my wife's feelings or something. I think I read somewhere that Asher had colic and cried all the time. That's the reason they were searching the city for that special kind of pacifier thingy, right?"

The blonde looks up at me and nods. "I guess they were looking for a blue Soothie. Apparently, the little guy got used to it when he was in the NICU and he doesn't like to take anything else. They were all feeling pretty desperate. I guess Bethany hasn't been getting much sleep."

"The whole thing just doesn't make any sense. If the baby was screaming, why wouldn't the mother-in-law stick around to help out?"

Tyler nods at me. "That struck me as odd as well. Most moms would welcome another hand in the bathroom."

"It just seems to me like someone in the family should have had more common sense — that's all I'm saying," I comment as I take a seat. I throw my briefcase on the table and start to dig out my files. Out of the corner of my eye, I see the woman bristle.

"Believe it or not, it's not always about common sense. Sometimes, things happen that are so far out of your comfort zone and realm of experience you can't even imagine that they're happening to you. You might think you'll know how to deal with that kind of thing, but trust me you don't," she insists hotly before she takes a gulp of what passes for coffee in this place. She grimaces and then looks away. She swallows hard and takes a deep breath. "You can't know what its like to have your child disappear."

After a few moments Kendall adds, "I presume you're from Identity Bank. Are you going to help me put the brains of my operation back together so that I can get back to work? I have a little boy who is counting on my ability to do my job. Right now, it's as if someone has blindfolded me and tied both hands behind my back and placed me on a roller coaster in another state. I need the files on my computer and to be able to send out emails to the appropriate people. We've got to get the ball rolling. I can't be held hostage like this. I know it's not the same as what Asher is going through, but being held as a virtual hostage isn't fun either."

"I understand." I lean back and cross my ankle over my knee.

"I don't think you do," she mutters as she focuses on the file. She flips a few more pages in the file and then looks up at me as she rubs her temples. "Honestly, I don't know what they want. We certainly don't have any money. The coffers of Locate My Heart are very lean. Anyone who looks at our website would know that. We post our balance sheet online every three months. We are completely transparent. We hide nothing. We pay for forensic sketches, search teams, billboards, magazine ads, flyers — all the things you'd expect from an agency which searches for missing children. We don't have a million dollars hanging around to pay anybody. That should be painfully obvious to anyone who takes a half a second to look."

"While that might be technically true of Locate My Heart, there are plenty of charities who don't run the way yours allegedly does. A lot of people use the money they raise to go on exotic vacations and get themselves fancy cars, buy their way onto television shows or go on questionable staff retreats, if you know what I mean —"

"I don't know what kind of charities you've been working with, but that's not the way we do things here. Colette has a specific vision for Locate My Heart and what we need to accomplish as an agency. Our goal is to find every single missing child ever reported to us as quickly as we possibly can."

"With all due respect Ms. —" I wait for her to finish the introduction before I move on.

"Kordes," she supplies automatically before crossing her arms and leveling a stare at me.

When I hear the exotic name, I raise an eyebrow and mutter, "Of course it is."

She gives me a startled look. "My name is Kendall Kordes, not Ted Bundy or Jeffrey Dahmer. Look, it's not my fault that I have an unusual name. My parents named me that."

"You need to see it from my perspective. I work in the cyber world where people pretend to be something they're not all the time. A lot of times people make up flowery names when they are not who they say they are, that's all I'm saying."

Kendall turns toward Tyler. "I'm sorry I wasted your time today, but I need someone who is willing to help me solve my problem, and clearly, this gentleman is not that person. I've got better things to do today than to try to soothe his ego or frayed nerves or whatever else is going on with him. There is a little boy who is on the medically-fragile side and a sick, distraught mom who isn't doing much better. I need to find her son before something even more tragic happens to him. If you don't mind, I need to beat the bushes to find someone who is willing to help us." She stares directly at me. "I'd like to say it's been a pleasure, but it really hasn't."

Kendall's sharp retort wakes me up. The frown on her face tells me I have failed in my mission to make her life easier. I've let my past color my ability to do my job. I know better than that. Usually, I do a more efficient job of compartmentalizing my life. Something about this has burrowed deep under my skin. I need to pull it together and deliver on my promise to Tristan. I told him I could be professional on this assignment.

It's about time for me to dig deep and demonstrate some of my firm resolve Uncle Sam so thoughtfully drilled into me. I reach out to shake her hand. "I apologize. I was rude. Let's try this again. Nice to meet you, Kendall Kordes. I'm Jameson Payne. I specialize in solving other people's problems. Let's get started on yours."

CHAPTER THREE

KENDALL

WHEN DID IT GET so hot in my office? I know Colette has been trying to spend less on air-conditioning, but this is ridiculous. Although he's not as tall as Tyler, Mr. Payne is an imposing presence as he stands quietly watching over my shoulder. I don't know what kind of cologne he wears, but it makes me want to forget my problems and cuddle against his chest. Wordlessly scolding myself for my wayward thoughts, I grab an index card and fan myself for a moment before I take my purse off my lap and set it on the floor beside my feet. I clear my throat and make a mental note to focus on my job.

More sharply than I intend to, I pivot around on my office chair and face my computer. I take a deep breath and jiggle my mouse to wake up my sleeping monitor. Although I know what's going to appear, I cringe when the black background slowly creeps across the surface and a grizzly skull and cross bones with blood dripping out of the eye sockets forms on the screen. An ominous countdown clock is ticking in the lower-left-hand corner. The numbers seem to be counting down faster than the speed of sound.

"Now what?" I whisper softly as I tilt my head back to look up at Mr. Payne.

He moves closer to me as he squats down and studies my screen carefully. "I can see how that would put a hitch in your workday, for sure," he answers without taking his eyes off the screen.

For several seconds, neither of us say anything. The silence is oppressive. I'm sure he can hear the sound of my racing heart. I'm not sure which is more overwhelming — the threat to my career or his presence mere inches from me. Since Quinn's death, I live in a bubble of politeness. I can interact with people in a social setting as long as they stay at a polite distance. On so many fronts, Mr. Payne is assaulting my space bubble. His very presence here makes me feel inadequate.

On a personal level, I don't let many men close to me anymore. Perhaps it is an unreasonable reaction to what happened to my son, Quinn. Still, I can't help the way I feel.

As much as Jameson annoys me, it's hard to ignore him. On a purely physical level, the man just smells good. It has been a long time since I have been struck with unadulterated lust and desire. The scent of Jameson brings back memories of long nights cuddled in front of the fireplace watching movies and feeling Lyle's arms around me. It's a beautiful fantasy, but it's not my reality. Lyle is long gone, and earlier, Jameson was questioning me as if he thought I was the world's biggest idiot. I guess I'll have to be content with living in the world of my romance novels for now.

There couldn't be a worse time for this to happen. Colette is thinking about retiring from Locate My Heart.

She wants to hand the reins over to someone who shares her passion and vision for lost children and their families. I haven't been with Locate My Heart as long as some, but my background is more varied.

Because of the way my life unfolded, I never got to go to college and get my Master's degree in social work like I planned. I've cobbled a few courses together here and there and earned an undergraduate degree in interdisciplinary studies, but I know if Colette decides to hire a Director, I'll be competing with people who are more qualified on paper. In many ways, my ability to save our network from this cyber-assault is going to be the ultimate show-and-tell of my ability to function as a Director.

When Mr. Payne reaches up and taps my thigh to get my attention, I have to stifle my squeak of surprise. I was so lost in my thoughts, I didn't notice he has been trying to ask me a question. I take a deep breath and try to calm my racing heart. "Do you think this is catastrophic?" I blurt to cover my nerves.

"I don't know enough to make that kind of determination yet. Did the same thing occur on all of your computers or only yours? Also, I wonder if this happened only to your private email, or if it's also present in the email related to your business account here?"

"I'm sorry. I don't know the answer. I didn't get that far. I only tried to open the email program. I assume it's attached to the Locate My Heart email. I don't check my personal emails on this computer. I use my cell phone," I explain as I pull my cell phone out of my purse and start to turn it on.

Mr. Payne places his hands around mine trapping the phone between them. "Please don't. I need to do that in a contained, controlled environment — in case the whole network has been compromised. I'm assuming you probably use the company Wi-Fi while you're at work to save on your data plan."

A look of horror crosses my face as I whisper, "Oh no! This crisis may extend beyond Locate My Heart."

"Why do you say that?"

"My email address from my other job is on my phone too," I explain.

"What other job?"

I slump back in my office chair. "I work a few hours a week at Parchment & Page Turners."

The puzzled look on his face speaks volumes. I quickly clarify, "It's a custom stationery and bookstore downtown. Sinead makes her own paper and specializes in indie authors."

For lack of a better term, Jameson grunts at me. "Any reason you have two jobs?"

I sit straight up on the edge of my chair and glare at him. "In case you haven't noticed, Locate My Heart is a nonprofit charity. We operate on a shoestring budget. I don't expect my boss to pay me like a Wall Street executive. I work two jobs so I can keep food on my table and have a house to put my table in. You got a problem with that?"

"With you personally? I don't think so. With agencies like Locate My Heart? Yeah, I take issue with them. Most of them are nothing but shell companies designed to make their founders rich and defraud the public and families who count on them. They give false hope and prey on people when they are going through hell. I just think it's the worst kind of manipulation, that's all. Nothing personal."

My mouth opens in shock. I've never had anyone imply the work we do here is harmful to the families involved. In fact, I have files and files of letters from parents and family members of missing children singing our praises. I don't know where this jerk comes off. He's plenty full of himself for someone who has just walked through our doors. He doesn't know anything about us or even why Colette started this agency. Who in the heck does he think he is?

I have to take a couple of deep breaths. "I don't know what you know about Locate My Heart or what you've heard about our agency, but everything you've said is patently untrue. You can read every financial report we have ever submitted. We go above and beyond the usual reporting requirements and post them out on the web for everyone to see. If you want to know why I work two jobs, all you'd have to do is read that report and see how little I'm actually paid. Perhaps you'll eat your cruel words soon. None of us here at Locate My Heart do this because we're on the take. We do it because we want to reunite families. It is as simple as that. If you have another opinion of us, perhaps we need to find another computer technician."

In a jerky, almost uncontrolled motion, I stand up and walk away from my office chair. I run to the bathroom and grab a cup of cold water. If I hadn't gotten away from him, who knows what other words would've come out of my mouth? I don't understand why he hates us with such passion. We are the victims here. Someone attacked our computer system; we didn't lash out at anyone else.

Even as that thought enters my consciousness, an unsettling idea starts to percolate in my brain. What if this cyber attacker is the family member of a victim we were not able to locate? What if this is a revenge attack? How would we even begin to figure that out?

I drink the rest of my water and splash cold water on my face. When I dry my face, I realize I rushed out of the house with mascara applied to only one eye. At this point, I can't even do anything but laugh. My disheveled appearance is indicative of how my day is going.

My heel wobbles precariously as I try to shake off my anger. I straighten my back and run my fingers through my hair. Not for the first time in my life, I wonder if pretending everything is going to be okay will magically make things turn out better. I stride back toward my desk and stand face-to-face with Jameson. "Look, we seem to have gotten off on the wrong foot here. I don't know how to fix that because I haven't done anything wrong. You're either going to believe me or you're not. I can't change that."

Jameson Payne runs his fingers through his beard as he studies me for a moment. "You're probably right about that — more right than I'd care to admit."

"Tyler Colton is a person I trust. You don't know this, but I don't trust many people. To say I trust Tyler is a big deal. Tyler says you are the best. The fate of several dozen children could be resting in those files we can't access. If they fall into the wrong hands, it could be devastating. Those files hold confidential information about family members and the places that the children were last seen. It could be catastrophic if that information was leaked to the public. It could compromise police investigations and court cases for years to come."

"What in the heck do you do with all that information?" Jameson demands.

Standing up to my full height, I step even closer and poke him in the chest. "Have you not been listening? We find children! Are you going to help me do my job or do I need to find someone else?"

"Why do you need all that confidential information?" he asks me skeptically. "Aren't you just repeating what the police are saying to the public?"

I have to swallow a growl of frustration as I sit down in my office chair and spin to face him. I gesture at my computer. "I can't even show you what we do right now. Sometimes, witnesses are more forthcoming with us because we are not officially law enforcement. They know about organizations like ours because of celebrities like John Walsh and the National Center for Missing and Exploited children. When Colette set up Locate My Heart, she had administrators from NCMEC and ChildFind come to train us. She wanted to make sure no children fell through the cracks."

"That's impressive. How do you make sure you're not just in the way?" Jameson asks, his expression softening just a little.

"We work very closely with local and national law enforcement agencies to make sure that what we do doesn't jeopardize any legal proceedings. Are we aggressive? You bet. Do we push the stories in the news media to make sure people will remember that we are looking for missing children? Absolutely. Do we apologize for that? Absolutely not. That's what we're here for. We are here to be a voice for the families when the news media is bombarded with so many other stories that it's difficult for them to choose what to feature. We are here to speak on behalf of the families when they are too upset and distraught to advocate for themselves. We are here to filter out the hate mail and the random offers from well-meaning folks and sometimes not so well-meaning people. Locate My Heart is these families' protection against the harsh reality of a world without their child."

"When you put it that way, I guess I can see the benefit a program like yours might offer a family. I'm sorry, I've just seen a very different side of all of this," Jameson concedes with an anguished look.

"It's too bad there are people like that out there, harming organizations such as ours and the families we serve. I promise you we are not all that way. The people who work at Locate My Heart are very proud of what we do. Our hearts break every time we don't find a child in time to make a difference."

Jameson takes off his baseball cap and wipes his forehead with the back of his hand. "Well, Ms. Kordes, it appears you and I probably don't agree on much. Even so, we obviously agree on the fact that every child who can be found, should be found as quickly as possible. To that end, we need to get your computer — or computers — fixed. It is entirely possible, if not probable, that your phone might be part of the problem."

I moan at his words. "I can't tell you how much I didn't want to hear you say that. My whole life is in that phone. I rarely even take paper notes anymore." I pick my phone up off the desk and hand it to him.

"I feel your pain. If I had to be without my phone, I would feel like someone removed an appendage." He smiles at me and adds, "By the way, we are going to be working really closely together over the next few days. You might as well call me Jameson."

I decide to take the olive branch his easy conversation offers and run with it. "Okay, you can call me Kendall. I hope the only thing impacted is my computer. I can't deal with having to set up a new phone right now."

Jameson raises an eyebrow at me. "Do you have anything compromising on this phone? Anything you don't want me to see?"

I snort as I ask, "I don't know. Is it considered a federal crime to cheat on Candy Crush and Draw Something? My brother likes to send me cheats he finds on the Internet — mainly because he knows I am a natural born puzzle solver and that it annoys the crap out of me when he gives me the answer before I've figured out the problem on my own. Even though we're twins, Will couldn't be more different. My brother likes to breeze through things the easiest way humanly possible, and I like to make sure I've dotted every I and crossed every T."

"It's funny that you are so different," Jameson comments as he pulls a roll of bubble wrap out of his huge duffel bag.

"What about you? Are you just like the rest of your family?" I ask, trying to expand the friendly rapport.

His face grows hard and his mouth tightens in a grim line. "It's complicated." He turns away and starts to pack up my computer. "Can you tell me which pieces of equipment are hooked up to your network?" Jameson asks abruptly.

I become a little dizzy when I process his words. "Every piece of electronic equipment in this office runs off the same network." I sink my head in my hands as I admit, "This is going to be a devastating blow." I take a deep breath to steady my nerves. "All of this is going to destroy Colette. This organization and everything in it is her baby now. How could anyone do this to her?"

Jameson lets out a slow breath as he answers, "I don't know, but I aim to find out."

CHAPTER FOUR

JAMESON

TYLER STOPS IN HIS tracks when he enters the room which just a few hours before had resembled any old dusty storage area. "You just got here yesterday. How in the world did you get up and running so fast?"

I grin at his shocked expression. "I'm used to working in odd, out-of-the-way places. These days, it doesn't take me long to turn any space into a full-blown computer lab." I went to the local salvage yard and picked up doors and sawhorses from the local hardware store and made myself a couple of computer desks. Tristan had a local computer superstore deliver a truck-load of computer equipment. So, we're in good shape. Locate My Heart had four computers and two printers hooked up to its network. Fortunately, the only phones that were potentially impacted were Kendall's and one of the college interns.

Each of their computers has one of my laptops hooked up to it running diagnostics. All of my laptops are hooked up to a larger desktop analyzing the data.

"What's the damage?" Tyler asks as he looks around in amazement. "It looks like you have all of them on electronic life-support. This can't be a positive development."

"It looks more dramatic than it likely is. First, my boss seems to have more money than God and likes to invest in expensive toys. Rather than run the computers sequentially through the diagnostics, we run them all at the same time. I wanted to protect your office and its network from any potential viruses, so Identity Bank has its own network that it runs in a secure environment separate from everything else. Essentially, I put these computers on a network inside a sandbox so we can see what's going on without risking any further infection."

"No way!" Tyler exclaims as he stops in front of a machine. "Is this one running Windows '95?"

I nod. "I feel like a jerk. Kendall tried to tell me their operation ran on a shoestring budget, but I didn't believe her. The only modern equipment they've got is the computer they purchased to run the age progression software. It's got decent specs — but the rest of the gear wouldn't even run computer games designed for toddlers. I'm amazed they're able to function."

"Colette's funny about that kind of stuff. I've had more than one conversation with her about how she could do her job more efficiently if she had better equipment. However, she insists she doesn't want the focus of her organization to be constantly on fundraising. She says she was raised to make do with what she had. If it's good enough for her. It should be good enough for her company. She actually lives what she preaches. I don't suppose you could arrange to make the older stuff inoperable so she can't use it anymore," Tyler suggests.

I spin on my rolling chair and look at him in surprise. "Come again? That seems a little cruel."

Tyler shakes his head. "You haven't heard the rest of the plan. Let's face it, your boss and one of my best friends give the phrase Secret Santa a whole new meaning. Aidan and Tristan could do some serious damage to the obsolescence in that office if they put their heads together. Aidan has done a charity event for Colette to purchase the age progression computer. I am sure he wouldn't mind pitching in again."

I put my hands up helplessly. "I don't know. I got off to a rocky start with Ms. Kordes. I basically accused her of being lower than pond scum. I'm not sure I can bounce back from that."

Tyler clutches his chest in comical surprise. "You fought with Kendall? No one fights with Kendall. She's the sweetest thing ever. She brings my officers cupcakes on their birthdays — even though my wife owns a bakery. Kendall insists that everyone should know more than one person loves them."

I cringe a bit. "I would venture to guess Ms. Kordes doesn't find me too lovable right about now. We left things at an uneasy truce, but I don't think she's my biggest fan."

Tyler's eyebrow arches. "Wow! You must've really stepped in it. Kendall is probably one of the least judgmental people I know."

"Really? That's interesting because we seem to rub each other the wrong way. She was shooting sparks from her eyes and I could practically see the steam rolling out of her ears."

Tyler grins at me. "Huh … you know I met a woman like that once. I could barely stand to be in the same room with her. Every interaction between us seemed to end in heated conflict."

"Yeah? What happened?" I kick some wires under my makeshift desk. I walk around the room and glance at each workstation to make sure everything is working properly.

"I fell in love with her and married her. I've never been so happy in my whole life."

"Whoa! Hang on. I don't think that's where I'm at with Ms. Kordes. I'm just hoping she doesn't spike my coffee with laxatives. I was beyond insulting. I questioned everything she cares about as a person and what she is passionate about at work. I don't think I could've handled it much worse."

"I don't know … sometimes sparks are good. Let's tackle one problem at a time. Can you pull yourself away to have some dinner?" Tyler asks as he gestures around the storage room.

I shrug. "I suppose I could. I'm just running diagnostics now. It's going to take some time and I suppose I don't have to babysit the machines."

"Why don't you come out to Aidan and Tara's place? He's having a little get together to celebrate Mindy's graduation. There'll be lots of great music."

"I don't know anybody except you and Logan. I've only met Aidan once or twice the last time Logan and I worked together. I don't want to intrude on family time."

"You know Tasha and Mindy too. Anyway, that's not how things work around here. Everyone's invited. If you know a member of the inner circle, you're in. The women call it the Girlfriend Posse. I suppose the guys have our version too."

I pause for a moment. "Is Kendall a member of this Girlfriend Posse, by any chance?"

Tyler shoots me a look of profound innocence. "I don't really know. The composition of that group changes every once in a while."

I adjust my baseball cap and take one last lap around the room. I look up at Tyler and ask, "This room is locked with restricted access, correct?"

Tyler nods. "Tighter than a tick."

"I guess I don't have much to lose. It'd be nice to put some decent food in my mouth. The taste of my foot is getting old."

———————◆————————

Despite my protests to the contrary, the first thing I do when I enter the large outdoor barn-like facility is search for Kendall. Eventually, I see her over in the corner. Mindy appears to be doing something with her hair. After a while, I grab a couple of sodas from a cooler and work my way over to them. Awkwardly, I hang out on the wall like a kid at school dance. I'm just close enough to overhear their conversation.

"I can't believe you invited me to your graduation party. It blows me away that you're even old enough to graduate. It seems like yesterday you came into Parchment & Page Turners looking for interesting books. I can't wrap my brain around the fact that you sing with Aidan O'Brien, that's just mind blowing. I play his CDs in my car."

Mindy giggles. "I know. It's weird, isn't it? When I met him, he was just the piano player at my mom and dad's wedding. I was so little that I called him Band-Aidan. Back then, nobody knew I would grow up to be an artist. Dad is still betting I'll be a Supreme Court justice, I think," Mindy confesses as she braids Kendall's hair into one long French braid down her back.

Mindy sighs deeply. "I probably shouldn't say anything, but I feel like I need to tell you not to focus on the distractions. You'll find the small thing you're looking for, but if you keep looking, you will find something much bigger."

Kendall turns and looks at Mindy with tears in her eyes. "Thank you so much. You can't know what that means today. I will try to keep my eyes on the prize and not get distracted by problems with technology and … other things."

Kendall starts to get up from the chair, but Mindy places her hand on Kendall's arm. "One more thing. Sometimes people who seem angry are just scared and hurt. To make progress, you have to look beyond the pain." Mindy swallows hard before she says, "Everyone's pain." Mindy looks up at the stage. "I think Tasha is looking for me. I need to go. Thanks for letting me mess with your hair, it calms my nerves. You have great hair, by the way."

Kendall pulls the end of her elaborate braid over her shoulder and looks at it. "Are you kidding me? I feel like a glamorous superstar. I should be thanking you. I'm looking forward to hearing you sing. Congratulations. I'm sure the future holds great things for you."

Mindy looks at the ground and toes some hay. "A lot of people are counting on me to make the right choices."

Kendall reaches up and gives Mindy a warm hug. "I'm sure you'll do great."

"Thanks. I gotta go. Tash is waiting for me. We need to start our set. By the way, someone's waiting to talk to you."

Kendall waves goodbye before she spins around and runs into me. I have to hold the sodas out to the side to avoid spilling on her.

"You! What are *you* doing here? Aren't you supposed to be solving my computer problem?" she accuses.

"Well, hello. Nice to see you too," I counter.

"No! Seriously! I don't think you understand the urgent nature of what we do at Locate My Heart. Every single second counts —"

"I understand. I really do — but, I can't make my diagnostic computers run any faster." I set the sodas on the table and pull my cell phone out of my pocket and show her my screen. "I have multiple alarms set on this to indicate when they finish. As soon as I am notified, I am out of here — I promise."

Kendall's expression softens. "Okay, I guess that

was a little on the witchy side. You do need to eat." She takes me by the arm and leads me over to a long buffet table at the end of the barn. "You need to try Gwendolyn and Denny's world-famous chili and cornbread. It's amazing."

As if to commemorate the moment, my stomach lets out a huge growl. I blush. "I guess I am hungry."

"That may work out in your favor. I heard a rumor that Mindy requested Hummingbird cake for her graduation. If it's anything like what my mother used to make, it's pretty rich. You'll want to save some room for it. Nobody can stop at just a couple bites — especially if Heather makes it."

I grab myself a plate and glance over at her. "That's funny. I heard a very similar compliment given to you today. I heard you make some special birthday cupcakes.

Kendall blushes. "Oh, those? They're nowhere near as fancy as Heather's. I've just learned to cherish birthdays over the years, and many times law enforcement officers don't get to be at home with their families for their birthdays, so I try to make sure they have lots of goodies. It's just a thing with me. It's not all that impressive or heroic."

"You never know. When I was serving overseas, I sometimes got care packages from people I never even knew. I can't tell you how much a few cards and some goodies and toiletries meant to me, even though I never met the people they came from. Sometimes, I would grin like a fool for a couple of months after I got one. The police officers who get birthday cupcakes from you probably feel the same way."

"I hope so. I mean — it makes me feel good to make the treats, but I hope it makes them smile too."

Kendall and I make our way down the buffet line. Although she seems to make healthier choices than I do, she isn't radical about it. She helps herself to a large serving of the chili and cornbread and a side of salad.

As we are making our way toward an empty table, the beginning strains of guitars being tuned starts to filter through the sound system. I nod toward the stage as I ask, "How do you know this gang?"

"Mindy's mom, Kiera, taught a class on interviewing clients in a social work setting for my psychology class in college. I realized I knew Kiera from my job at the bookstore. I never knew she was Mindy's mom. Mindy has been coming into the shop for a long time. Her book choices were always a big mystery to me because they were always so far above her age range, but after I met Kiera and Jeff, it all made perfect sense."

"I know what you mean. I met her while I was working on a case. I haven't interacted with her much, but she seems like the oldest soul I've ever met. She is scary smart."

"That whole group is. Have you met her cousin Gabriel? He might give your computer skills a run for your money. He's a computer genius, but he's also incredibly artistic. He runs the website for the bookstore."

Immediately my internal antennae wake up. "Exactly how well do you know this kid?"

"Very well. Gabriel Whitaker's been coming into the shop longer than I've been working there. He does the website for us in exchange for a discount on art supplies. The kid is incredible. You've probably seen his stuff on the web or maybe even on TV. He does anime. Gabriel's not even a kid anymore, he's in college on a full art scholarship — or it might even be in computer science, I don't actually know for sure. He is up at Reed College."

My eyebrows climb. "Wow, impressive."

"I think so. So, how do you know these guys? I mean, I know Tyler said he has worked with you before."

"Yeah, Aidan uses the company I work for to run his background checks. When he was having some cyber-stalking issues with one of his band members, he contacted my boss. Tristan sent me to track down the problem."

Kendall shakes her head. "Yeah, I heard about it on the news. That was some seriously screwed up family dynamics, huh?" She takes a bite of chili and cornbread before she continues. "I just found the whole thing to be completely bizarre. I work so hard to reunite families and then to have a family that should've been so close be torn apart by something as simple as hurt feelings and pride just blows me away."

I shrug. "I've seen stranger things happen. I've seen brothers and fathers and sons fight to the death over political differences. I've seen fathers kill their daughters rather than be 'shamed' by their actions. There are just some things in this world I'll never understand."

Kendall's voice grows quiet. "You and me both. There are just things that defy explanation."

Before I can probe into Kendall's abrupt change in

demeanor, my phone sends up a series of alarms. I quickly shut them off and turn to Kendall. "This is it. The diagnostics are back on your computer systems. It's time to see how deep the cyber-stalkers penetrated and what they may have gotten during the attack."

Kendall draws in a quick breath of alarm. "What happens now?"

"Well, I have to go see how widespread the attack was and I have to analyze the reports to see what the best strategy will be going forward."

"Any chance I might get my cell phone back? I feel lost without it. I'm not sure when this happened, but my phone has become like my imaginary friend in kindergarten. It's my constant shadow."

"I think that represents most of society these days. We've become mighty spoiled with our technology. I've got you taken care of either way. I'll let you know what I figure out."

As I stand up to put on my jacket, Kendall puts her hand on my forearm. "Wait. Can I please come with you? I can't stand missing pieces to a puzzle. It's difficult for me not to understand what's going on. I promise I'll stay out of the way."

"It's going to be as boring as watching paint dry. I'm sure you'll have more fun here at the party. I don't want you to miss the party for nothing."

"Mindy knows my job at Locate My Heart is the most important thing to me. Besides, I work at a small-town book and stationary store. I'm accustomed to entertaining myself in quiet environments. I want to be where I can be of the most use."

"If we don't run into any additional problems, I'll have Locate My Heart up and running soon. As long as you don't mind endless tedium and boredom, you're welcome to come see what we found."

Kendall waves goodbye to Mindy and Tasha on stage as we clear the table and head toward the front of the barn. Even as I put my hand on the small of her back and walk her out the door, I wonder if I'm making a huge strategic error.

Chapter Five

Kendall

I RE-READ A page of the rom-com novel I found so engaging yesterday. Today, it might as well be my chemistry textbook. I shift my position on one of the hard, worn, industrial chairs that line the wall of Tyler's storeroom. I can't believe how quickly Jameson made himself at home as he tries to figure out what's going on. This place looks like a set from CSI. If it weren't for the flickering florescent lights and the slight smell of dust in the air, I would swear we were in a brand-new state-of-the-art building. Okay, that's not quite true — his furniture isn't exactly cutting-edge, but it's functional. Somehow, he's even managed to score a small fridge.

Jameson whistles softly under his breath. "I'd like to know your secret. You must eat four-leaf clovers for breakfast." He waves me over to show me something on the computer screen. I hop off my chair and put my book back in my purse. With some trepidation, I stroll over, trying to appear nonchalant, even though my knees are shaking.

"Are we doomed?" I ask, revealing my stress in every syllable. As soon as the tentative words leave my mouth, I want to call them back. This isn't the image of confidence I want to project.

"Didn't you hear me about the four-leaf clover thing? I wasn't kidding."

"I guess I don't understand what you're referring to. I thought you were making fun of my lack of computer experience again."

"No, I was merely complimenting your extraordinary luck. It appears that your attackers were taking stabs in the dark and hoping that you'd fall for their bluff."

"Bluff?" I try not to sound ridiculously hopeful. "The skulls and blood seemed pretty ominous to me."

"A total bluff. The cyber terrorists didn't put any ransom ware on your computer system."

"What about my phone?" I move forward and inspect the monitors. "What are all those squiggly lines?"

"Your phone is the cleanest device here. At least you keep your anti-virus-ware up-to-date on your phone. The same can't be said for the rest of your equipment. The only computer that's in decent enough shape is the one which runs your age progression software. The rest of your equipment is vulnerable to viruses and adware. The computers the interns use are chocked full of them. They are so old that there aren't patches available to fix modern security issues. You need better computers."

I briefly sag against him in relief as I process the information. I was expecting his report to be so much worse. I'm having a hard time internalizing the good news. I half-expected him to tell me we were going to be out of commission for months and months — if not longer. I sigh heavily and absorb his warmth before I remember myself and awkwardly pull away.

"I guess it's a good thing I didn't max out my credit card at the computer superstore when I bought my god-son a gaming system for Christmas. Can you tell me what specifications I need to ask for so everything won't go obsolete so quickly? It always seems the salesmen are talking in circles when I go to places like that."

"You don't need to do that," Jameson starts to unhook all his laptops from our computers — which are as useful as paperweights right now.

"What do you mean?" I ask with alarm. "We have to have operational computers. It would've been better to have them yesterday. I can't afford to wait around to see if we get the funding — we actually need the computers to get the grant. We've already lost three days while we've been sorting things out. We can't afford to lose more. I'm aware that it's a big personal hit, but sometimes that's what you do when you work for a nonprofit, and you've got to stay on your feet. I know it might not be kosher, but I'll keep it off the books. I don't want Locate My Heart to have any blowback from this. I just want us to be up and running. Do you have a problem with that?"

"I do have a problem with your plan, but not in the way you probably think. You may not know the terms of the contract Tristan has in place with Colette. But here's the way it works — if we can't fix the computer equipment Locate My Heart has on site, Identity Bank provides new equipment as part of our usual and customary fee."

I suck in such a deep breath I almost pass out. "I thought Tyler told me there wasn't going to be a fee. We don't have any money to pay for that kind of service. We barely have money for a second-rate printing shop, and they already cut us a huge break because of what we do."

"I didn't say Tristan was actually going to charge Locate My Heart any fee. I just said the guarantee is part of Tristan's usual and customary fee. This case is pro-bono — including providing the computer equipment needed to bring you up to snuff. With all the confidential information you guys handle, you absolutely need to have top-notch computer equipment capable of handling the software you require to keep your business safe. It's as simple as that. Do you understand what I'm saying?" Jameson asks me with emphasis on his last words.

I shrug away from him. "Of course, I understand what you're saying. I'm not stupid. Unfortunately, I'm stuck between a boss who thinks we should still have rotary phones and several friends I went to high school with who are starting up cutting-edge tech firms who think the way we run things at Locate My Heart is several cards short of a full deck." I throw my hands up in the air in frustration. "Common sense says I should take everything you are offering me and throw in my life savings just for a kicker. Still, the other part of me wonders if it's going to make Colette even more anxious about working with you guys."

Jameson throws a reassuring glance in my direction.

"I don't know. Tristan's an excellent salesperson. He'll probably be able convince Colette that the whole thing was her idea to start with," he answers with a mischievous grin. "Having said that, in this case, it might be better to ask forgiveness after the fact than to ask for permission up front. Don't you think? If we can clean up all the grant data and get that turned in on time, we'd be her heroes."

Agitated, I pace around the room. It's hard to see all the wreckage around me. In Jameson's high-tech world, my little computer network might not seem like much, but it is the lifeblood of our organization and all I can think about is how much time it's going to take to put it all back together — time I don't really have.

Defeated, I return to my stool in the corner of the room and face Jameson. "Right now, that's all pie-in-the-sky thinking. I've still got hours and hours of work to do. There's a missing baby boy out there who's counting on me to make the smart decision and put politics aside. If the contract says we get new computers from Identity Bank, then so be it. Hook me up and put as much virus protection software as you can on those suckers. The next time these jerks decide to attack, they might not be kidding."

"Will do. I like someone who can see the big picture. I'm glad you're taking this approach. If you'll give me a moment, I'll be right back." He gives me a courtly bow and walks out of the room.

I'm not sure whether to follow him or stay rooted on my stool as he leaves the room. For as much as we clash when we are together, there's something inherently comforting about his presence.

I just wish I knew why he sometimes seems to hate me.

Maybe it's a military thing. My dad, Sergeant Norman Earl Kordes, was a soldier. Unpredictably, he would go to a cavernous dark place where no one could reach him — not even my persistently cheerful mother. Eventually, he just left. He told my mom he was going to go out and get some beer, and he never returned. We've searched for him for years, but we've never been successful. The police always insisted that as a grown man, he had the right to walk away from his family, even if he had a history of alcoholism and liver failure. My mom says he was never that way before he joined the service — but my mom says a lot of things she wishes were true.

I look around the store room and see the guts of the organization I'm hoping to run someday. I have to admit to myself that perhaps I'm not so different from my mother. Maybe I'm so busy trying to right all the wrongs in the world I can't see what's plainly in front of my face. My son is dead, my ex-fiancé is married and has a whole new family, my father is missing and never came back to see how his children turned out, and my mother is heartbroken.

As if all that wasn't complicated enough, I'm in the midst of epically failing the biggest on-the-job interview I could ever face. The stakes are exponentially higher than my boss being mad at me or a handsome computer expert disliking me. If I make miscalculations, the families we serve will pay the price. I guess my Mom is not the only person who has a knack for being the queen of denial.

Just as I'm about to break into tears, the storage door opens. Jameson enters as he holds the door with his very fine backside. He's pulling an oversized dolly filled with computer equipment. He has a friendly, expectant grin on his face until he sees my expression. "Hey, what's wrong? This is the good stuff. It's like Christmas — well, it is if you're a geek like me. What happened? I was just gone for a few minutes, and you look like you've seen a ghost."

I shrug as I try to put a lid on my emotions. "Between you and me, all of this has been a little overwhelming."

Abruptly, Jameson drops the handle of the dolly and walks over to me. "I know it's been a tough day, but there's nothing going on with your files that we can't fix. We'll get it all put back together, I promise."

I draw in a hitching, stuttering breath. "Thank you, I guess I just needed to hear you say that again. It won't solve everything, but it helps."

Jameson squats down beside me. "You know you didn't do anything to cause this, right?"

"I try to be careful, but you never know."

"I work with this stuff every day. Sometimes, there's no rhyme or reason to it. Hackers just randomly strike — sometimes just for the thrill of it."

Before I can stop myself, I blurt, "Why are you being so nice to me? I can't figure you out. Earlier, you were acting like I was nothing better than used chewing gum on the bottom of your shoe. Now, you're all teddy-bear-sweet. My head is spinning." After the words escape from my mouth, I hide my face in my hands and peek through my fingers as I mutter, "Sorry! I need to go take a nap or something … that was so rude."

Jameson fiddles with his baseball cap and then reaches out to gently pull my hands away from my face. "Don't worry about it. You have every right. I've been known to confuse myself. Let me start checking the files you uploaded to the cloud — that will give us some time to talk. I owe you some explanations."

"You don't have to," I insist.

"I want to. I think you're making assumptions you shouldn't be. I need to clear those up."

Jameson goes back to the dolly and starts lifting up boxes on to the counter he cleaned off earlier. "Obviously we couldn't do an even exchange for you because the technology just doesn't exist anymore. I tried to put myself in your shoes and determine what might be helpful. I got you two convertible tablets which you can use as either tablets or laptops and two desktops to leave back at your headquarters. With these new monitors, the desktop computers are easier on your eyes. They also have more storage space than you probably could use in this lifetime."

I watch in fascination as Jameson unboxes the computers quicker than anyone I have ever seen in my life. He holds one up for me to see. "I chose this one specifically for you because it will sync well with your phone and be powerful enough to work in the field."

My mouth falls open. "I don't know how to tell you this — but I don't even know how to use a Mac."

"These days, it's not a huge transition. I can spend a couple of hours showing you how it's done."

"Is that usually part of your job?" I ask impulsively.

Jameson looks over his shoulder at me and winks. "Nope. Just one of the perks."

It's been a while since a guy has rendered me utterly speechless, yet that's how I find myself as I feel my face grow hot with embarrassment. "I'm just going to go read my book while you set stuff up," I stammer awkwardly as I dig my novel out of my purse.

After several minutes, Jameson clears his throat. "I think I'm ready for you now." He flips a monitor toward me. "Can you sign into your cloud service?" Jameson holds up an external hard drive. "I'm going to download your files onto this first and make sure they're clean before we put them back on your system. If the files on your network were any indication, you likely have some run-of-the-mill adware and spyware on those files too. We might as well scrub your files before we put them on your new network. I want to perform a dry run here before I set them up at your office to make sure there are no glitches"

"New network?"

"Well, as you might've guessed, your networking protocols are about as outdated as your computer equipment. I'm going to upgrade that and introduce some file encryption technology to make your system safer and less penetrable."

I hold up my hand in a time-out symbol. "Wait! Before you do that, are any of these changes going to make it more difficult for Colette to access the information on the system? If they do, she might not be on board with this plan."

The lines at the corner of Jameson's eyes crinkle with laughter. "It doesn't take a rocket scientist to figure out that your boss is a tiny bit technology averse. So, I'll program all these changes to occur behind the scenes, so she's not even aware of them. She might have to do one more layer of sign in. I think that's probably doable — even for a technophobe like her. If you want, I can arrange for that to be biometric, so she doesn't have to type anything in."

"Okay, I just don't want it to be so complicated she doesn't feel comfortable using it."

"There might be some intricate, technical stuff going on behind the scenes, but that doesn't mean that it has to have an impossibly complicated user interface. After all, not everyone is a computer expert."

"Thanks for being so understanding about this. It's difficult working with so many people with varying levels of computer experience."

Jameson raises an eyebrow at me. "You should get extra brownie points for being so diplomatic. I'm surprised you were able to get any work done at all. I'm impressed that you thought to use an outside service to back up your files. A lot of people skip that step. In this case, it probably saved you a bunch of heartache. If that attack would've been legitimate, without those backups, you would've been lost."

"You keep surprising me. I honestly didn't expect to get a compliment from you about the way I've handled this crisis. In fact, I figured you thought I was the world's biggest idiot."

Jameson walks over to a dorm-type refrigerator he

has stuck at the base of one of his makeshift tables. He holds out a can of soda and a bottle of water in my direction with a silent questioning look. "Water is fine, thanks," I answer.

Jameson unscrews the lid, then hands the bottle to me as he pulls up a stool to sit down next to me. "For the past few days, I've been trying to figure out the best way to explain my bizarre behavior. I suppose the best way to explain it all is to just tell you as much of my story as I can."

"Okay, I appreciate that," I answer with trepidation as I study the expressions flying across his face like quicksilver.

"The other day you asked me about my family, and I dodged the question. I avoided it because there was a time in my life in which my family could've used a reputable, honest agency like Locate My Heart. Being here is a painful reminder of all I've lost."

I suck in a sharp breath of commiseration. "Oh my gosh! I'm so sorry. Why didn't Tyler say something to me? I could've asked for a different technician. I don't want this to be a painful process for you. You shouldn't have to torture yourself to do your job."

"To be honest, I was hoping I'd be able to compartmentalize a little better. It's been four and a half years since Toby went missing. I thought maybe I would have developed some calluses over my pain, so I could approach this job with the proper perspective. Apparently, I hadn't made as much progress as I hoped."

"Of course, you haven't. No one would expect you to make that type of recovery. Once you lose someone, it stays with you forever — especially when you don't have any answers. That's why places like Locate My Heart exist. Of course, we would love to have a happy, positive outcome for every family. Sadly, we know that's not possible. In the cases where we can't have an idealistic storybook ending, we can at least provide families with some answers. Some answers are better than none."

"Answers. It would be nice to have some. Deep down, I wonder if I've given up. Toby disappeared when I was serving overseas. He was a quiet kid. The kind who loved to study. He couldn't decide whether he wanted to be an archaeologist or paleontologist. His nose was never out of reference books. He'd spend hours at the library. One day, Toby told my mom he had a research paper due for school. It was the last one before spring break. He was really excited about going on vacation. He sent me a letter telling me all about the upcoming trip my family had scheduled to go fossil digging in Utah. When you're not quite thirteen years old, that's pretty much the epitome of cool."

I smile softly. "I don't know. I think it's pretty much my definition of cool now. That may say more about me than you probably want to know."

Jameson grins. "I remember reading that letter to all my buddies in the unit. Everyone there thought it sounded like a great time too. The next thing I knew, I got a call from my parents. Toby went to the library and no one saw him again."

Even though I know the direction the story was headed, I still let out a soft gasp as I absorb the news.

A pained look crosses Jameson's face. "Of course,

I was deployed in a place that I was not allowed to talk about and totally helpless to do anything. My mom was very much like the woman you're dealing with now. She almost died of a broken heart. No one was listening to my parents. They all assumed that because my brother was virtually a teenager, he must've been a dysfunctional, drug or alcohol using kid who hated his parents and his life. Nothing could be further from the truth. My little brother was the most studious, conscientious, well-adjusted child I've ever seen in my life. He would've never done that to my parents — especially with me being stationed overseas. He felt like it was his responsibility to step into my shoes when I was deployed."

"I didn't live here back then, but were you able to get much media coverage for his case?" I ask, slipping into my professional mode as naturally as I breathe.

"I was getting this information second hand from family, friends, and my distraught, overwhelmed father, but it didn't seem like we were getting very much of the right kind of coverage. My parents weren't viewed as true victims of a crime. The media treated my parents as if they'd done something to my brother to cause him to disappear or run away. Some of them were even worse. A few of them threw around bizarre innuendos. One went so far as to suggest my parents had used some of my military connections to have something done to my little brother because they were tired of being older parents."

I hold my hand over my stomach as I feel it turn over in disgust. "I'd like to say I am surprised, but sadly, I'm not. I've heard so many stories like this and had to play interference with less-than-honest news outlets.

Some of them want to produce a story more than they want to get the facts correct. I can totally see that happening. It's inexcusable that no one stepped up to do the right thing for your family."

Jameson's jaw sets and the expression in his eyes grows as hard as flint, "Oh, I wouldn't say no one stepped forward. Every form of con man and slime-ball you could imagine emerged from the woodwork to take advantage of my parent's pain and suffering. It was grotesque. There were TV producers trying to make a name for themselves, mediums and fortune tellers just hoping to get a few minutes of time in the spotlight, payday loan places hoping to score a predatory short-term loan to help fund the cost of a search. There were offers of agent representation and crazy offers from tabloid magazines for my parents to 'tell the real story' for obscene amounts of money. Apparently, they thought because my parents were educators, there must have been a dark side to the story. Because my brother disappeared in the Pacific Northwest and my parents were teachers, the tabloids seemed to want to make a connection like the Mary Kay Letourneau story where the teacher fell in love with her twelve-year-old student. The gossip rags were trying to find some disgusting motive for this when there wasn't one. "

"That's awful," I whisper under my breath.

"My mother became so ill that I was granted compassionate leave from the military, so I could come home and take care of my family. I had always planned to be a lifer in the military. But, you need to step up and take care of your family first."

I nod my head in agreement. "It's true. It's hard to set aside your dreams when reality comes crashing in." I start to dig around in my purse for my notepad and a pen. After I locate it, I take a deep breath and try to relax into my professional mode. It is often hard for me to separate my personal feelings about a case from my professional ones.

Clearing my throat nervously, I question Jameson. "Just so I understand, your brother went to the library one day, four and a half years ago, and never came home? To complicate matters, the law enforcement community misunderstood his social situation and assumed things to be true about him that were not, correct? In all this time, no one has located your brother?"

Jameson visibly flinches at my words. He scrubs a hand down his face and over his beard as he interrupts my assessment of his case, "As brutal and blunt as that assessment is, it is totally accurate."

I set my notebook and my pen down on the counter next to me. Looking him straight in the eye, I say, "I know you don't have any reason to trust me or anything my organization stands for. Still, with your permission, I would like to offer the services of Locate My Heart to you and your family. It's about time someone listened to your side of things. We need to bring your brother home — one way or another."

Jameson bows his head for a moment. He looks up at me with tears in his eyes as he whispers in a broken voice, "Maybe that's the part I'm most afraid of. If we don't have any answers, I can pretend he is okay. It's the 'one way or another' that scares the living crap out of me."

"Answers are scary, but so is the unknown. There is a chance — even if it's only remote — that there could be a positive resolution to this case. We can't afford to let fear persuade us to give up."

Jameson's Adam's apple bobs up and down as he swallows hard. "Okay, I'll need to run this by my parents first. It's not just my decision. I don't know if they're going to be willing to revisit that hellish time again."

"Let me know if you want me to explain what we do here. I'd be glad to."

Jameson stands up and heads over to the bank of computers. "You know, that might not be such a bad idea. But, before we can do that, we need to get you up and running."

An inexplicable urge washes over me. I stand up and walk behind him. I place my arms around his waist and rest my cheek on his back. I embrace him lightly. "Don't worry. I'll take care of you and your family. No one should have to endure an ounce of pain more than necessary from having a missing child. It is my job to block as much of that as possible — even for big tough military men."

CHAPTER SIX

JAMESON

The noise from the TV breaks the endless silence in my hotel room as I scan through my nightly ritual of bookmarked sites on my laptop. I lied when I told Kendall that I had given up the search for Toby. I'll likely look for him until the day I die. Every night, I visit an ever-growing list of sites dedicated to finding missing children. Some of them are aimed at what I'm specifically looking for; others are just wild chases, like sites featuring foster children and runaway teens. Even scarier, are the other sites I visit on the dark web pretending to be a person looking for a teen matching the description of my little brother. Those searches drain me of all my hope and humanity. Some days, I can summon the grit to go there — today is not one of those days.

I glance up at the clock. It's far too late to call my parents tonight. I can't help but wonder how they will react to my proposal. If they are true to form, they'll have very different responses. My mom has dealt with her pain by trying to forget anything ever happened. It's not that she's trying to be cruel, it's just that she can't handle the heartbreak. At first, my father wanted me to call in legions of soldiers to search for Toby and take care of his abductors by any means possible. As the months and years passed, even my dad became resigned to the fact that Toby is probably never going to return home. It's been painful to watch my parents turn into fragile shells of the people they once were. My parents were vibrant educators who loved their town, were actively involved in school life, community affairs, and dedicated to their church. Now, my mother barely leaves her bed and my father rants at the television or hides out in his wood shop.

Even though Kendall has graciously agreed to go with me on my visit home, I am reticent to show her this side of my life. It is so different from the family I grew up in. I'm struggling to come up with words to explain the difference. I don't want her to get the wrong impression of the type of people my parents are — or at least who they were at the time of Toby's disappearance.

I involuntarily let out an expletive as my cell phone vibrates in my pocket. When I remove it, I recognize it as Kendall's number. I pick it up with a tired sigh. I hope this isn't a second cyber-attack. "'Lo," I bark abruptly.

After a long pause, Kendall says, "Maybe I shouldn't have called — but I'm worried about you. Sharing your story takes an emotional toll. I figured I'd check in to see if there is anything I can do for you."

"I don't think so. It just is what it is. I've been dealing with all this crap on my own for a long time. To be honest, I'm not sure what having outside help is going to do for us now. I read the statistics. I know the first few hours of a case are critically important. I am aware how unlikely it will be for us to generate leads after all this time. I'm debating whether we should even involve my parents in this. Why should we open them up to a whole new round of heartbreak?"

"That's a question I can't answer for you because I don't know your family. There are cases out there where kids are found decades later. All we can do is present the offer of help. It's your family, and you guys will have to make the decision together. I won't be intrusive. I'll just present the facts as I know them and offer the help of Locate My Heart."

"Can you promise my family there won't be any charge for this service? They got burned badly the last time. I don't want them to be taken advantage of again."

"I don't either. That's exactly what I'm trying to prevent in this situation. No one deserves to be treated like that; whether your kid is missing for just a few hours or a couple of decades. You shouldn't have to run a gauntlet course of scam artists."

I let out a deep breath. "At least we agree on something. Let me sleep on it tonight and try to decide what to do. I'll call you tomorrow to see how the computer systems are working and let you know what my decision is about my parents. Then we can develop a plan of attack."

"Jameson, in case nobody has said this to you, thank you for rescuing Locate My Heart. Without your help, we might have gone dark for a while. I've been working on the grant, and I can't believe how much smoother things are going. So, thanks again. You're a real lifesaver."

I have to clear my throat a couple of times before I can answer. "Thank you for saying that. It's been a while since I've felt very heroic. Maybe we've got a few more miracles up our sleeves."

"It's hope like that that keeps me coming to work every single day. Sleep well, Jameson. Tomorrow is a new day with new hopes."

"You too," I respond reflexively as I close my laptop. "Something tells me that for the first time in I can't remember when, I might dream of something beautiful and pleasant for a change."

———•———

Before I call Kendall back, I check in with Tristan.

"Things look pretty good on this end. Fortunately, despite their lack of technology, Kendall Kordes was as on top of things as she could be."

"That's good to hear. I understand you got to play 'fairy-godfather'. That must've been fun," Tristan remarks.

"It was harder than you might imagine. Kendall didn't get as excited over free stuff as I expected she might be."

Tristan laughs out loud. "Oh, I completely understand Kendall's reluctance. Colette is wary about new technology. She's even more skeptical about people who give her things for free. Put those two together, and this job could've blown up in our face."

"So, is Kendall going to face any negative repercussions over her executive decision?"

"I don't think so. Once I explained the terms of our contract, which Colette signed, and outlined the danger of using her current equipment, she readily came on board. Of course, I have thrown in a few personalized computer lessons on the new stuff to sweeten the deal. I hope you don't mind."

"It's funny you should mention that. I was just going ask you if you care if I stuck around here a little while longer. I have a side project I need to work on with Kendall. She agreed to help me with a project I've been working on for several years."

"You mean the disappearance of your brother? I was beginning to wonder if you were ever going to ask for help with that. You know I search for people, right? It's a core value of my business."

I rub the back of my neck. *Crap! Tyler was right.* "I knew sir. I just didn't want to be presumptuous. I tried to learn from your methods though. I've been searching privately after hours on my own. Unfortunately, I haven't come up with much."

"I gather that after taking the measure of Kendall and Colette, you've decided that Locate My Heart is worthy of your trust?" Tristan asks me pointedly.

"You may be my boss, but you're a sneaky son of a —"

"Uh-huh," Tristan confirms. "Figured you'd sorted that out by now."

"There wasn't anything on this job Kinsey couldn't have handled. So, you sent me here to ensure that I'd have to work with Kendall? How long have you known about my little brother?"

"Here at Identity Bank, we are known for our rather thorough employment background checks. It's a precursor for working here. It didn't take too much digging to find that out — none at all, actually. It's all pretty much public record."

"In all these years, you never said anything to me?

What's up with that?" I demand, feeling irritated that my boss has known my secrets for years and never said anything.

"It's not like I didn't give you an opportunity to tell me. I just figured that eventually you would feel comfortable enough working at Identity Bank that you would open up and ask for help."

"So … you tried to force my hand by sending me to Oregon?"

"Not exactly — but Colette and Kendall are phenomenally great people. They do good work. Although I don't know where the case stands with your brother. Since you haven't shared any great news with us at Identity Bank, I figured there haven't been any positive developments lately. If pairing you up on a cyber-hacking was enough to get the ball rolling for you, I make no apologies."

"What if this whole search doesn't turn out to have a positive outcome? Then what will I do? I have to live the rest of my life without Toby and help my parents survive."

"With your background, I know that you know better than to prejudge the outcome of a case," Tristan cautions.

"Yeah, I do. I also know the statistics like the back of my hand. The chances of finding my brother are next to none. I know that, but I can't bring myself to break the news to my family. They are teetering on the edge of existence as it is. If the news is bad, it would literally kill them. At least if Toby is still missing, there is some hope. I've tried everything I know how to do and I haven't been able to find Toby."

"Not to sound boastful; but, you haven't tried everything. The resources of Identity Bank are deep and varied. Combined with the PR capabilities of Locate My Heart, we could breathe new life into this search. All you have to do is say the word, and every resource I have available is yours. I found my sister, but unfortunately, by the time I did, it was too late. I don't want that to happen to anyone else."

"If time was so important to you, why didn't you make me do something earlier?"

"I've worked with enough families over the years to know that imposing a search on someone who isn't ready is rarely helpful. We need a family's full cooperation before we can help. As you know, the whole thing is intrusive and painful. Unless a family is ready to take the brunt of that, I don't impose."

"Well, at least you're honest about what's involved. It's brutal beyond belief. I don't know if my parents are strong enough to handle it again."

"Having never met your parents, I don't know if they can handle it. I will tell you that finding my sister and Elliot gave my mom a whole new purpose. Sometimes resolution, even if it's painful, is required to make progress."

"I understand what you're saying. But I don't know if the chances of finding Toby are high enough to justify putting my parents through all that again," I argue.

"It won't be the same this time. Your parents have you here to protect them and the resources of Identity Bank and Locate My Heart at their disposal. We can frame this search in an entirely different way and protect them from the type of backlash they received before."

"I appreciate your offer. I'll keep it in mind. It's not that I'm ungrateful — I just don't know where they stand on all this. It's truly not my decision to make. Although my parents are suffering, they still are the ones who are going to have to make the final call."

"Understood. Just let me know what our parameters are, and we'll work within them. Good work on getting Locate My Heart up and running so quickly."

"Thanks, boss. Now I've got to go check and make sure everything is still operational and on target."

"Good luck with that. By the way, Kendall drinks tea, not coffee."

"You're downright spooky — you know that? How did you know I was headed over to her office instead of making a call?"

"Simple. If I were in your shoes, I'd want to see her body language. Good luck today, Payne. I'm happy things are working out."

• • •

A student I recognize from the background information Tristan gave me opens the door to Locate My Heart with wide-eyed astonishment as I warn, "Watch out, coming through with hot stuff here."

I don't even stop at Kendall's desk as I walk back to the little conference room where they meet with family members. I deposit large trays of hot drinks and a couple bags of baked goods in the middle of the table. When I turn around, the entire staff is crowded into the doorway trying to watch me. I shrug as I explain. "You guys work hard. I figured you could use a treat. I didn't know how everybody takes their drinks, or what they like to eat — so I brought a bunch."

Kendall sags a bit against the door frame. "It's too bad you work for us — because I'd like to give you a big ole' kiss right now. You have no idea how much I need a pick me up today."

I raise an eyebrow. "Everything going okay with the new systems?"

"Oh … Yeah, the computers are running just fine. This is operator error — or more precisely, operator fatigue. I'm trying to make up for several days work."

Bringing my head close to hers as I murmur in her ear, "How is the grant going?"

Kendall examines the hot cups of coffee and tea for a moment. "Just a moment." Kendall gently lifts the cups out of the cup holder. "I'm still trying to process the fact that you got me two different kinds of tea. I'm the only person here who drinks it. How did you even know that?" She picks up both cups.

"Just observant I guess. Unfortunately, my skills of observation couldn't tell me whether you like green tea or regular. I decided not to gamble and just got you both. There's fancy stuff to put in it … if you're into that kind of thing and a bunch of scones, bagels, danishes, and all that jazz. Knock yourself out," I ramble like a nervous preacher.

"That was incredibly generous of you. The grant went just fine, thanks to you. I had until nine o'clock this morning to turn it in, and I hit the send button at eight forty-five."

I grab myself a donut and a cup of black coffee and sit across the table from her. "Well, I guess that means my work here is done. Your equipment and files are in working order, and you got all the data you needed for your grant."

Kendall shoots me a puzzled look. "You're leaving? Just like that — like, don't let the door hit me on the butt on the way out?"

I grin and wink. "Nope. I'm not going anywhere. No one's paying me for this job. So, I'm just angling for that kiss you promised."

Kendall chokes on her tea as she lets out a startled burst of laughter. "Umm … o-kay. That's a leap of logic."

"Not so much. I'm just saying that the job is pretty much finished. So, if the only reason you're not kissing me is because I work for you, that argument doesn't hold much water anymore," I tease.

The intern who opened the door for me earlier gives me the once over as she looks at Kendall. "I don't know if I'd be turning down that offer if I were you, boss."

Kendall shoots her a look of astonishment. "Nice, Brynley. Way to make things even more awkward."

Brynley holds up her hands in a pose of innocence. "You were the one who brought up kissing. I was just telling you it's not necessarily a bad idea. I mean, Mr. Payne here doesn't do anything for me. I'm not into older guys but, you guys are probably about the same age, so whatever."

For a moment, I'm tempted to just laugh the whole situation off, but I notice Colette observing me carefully from the corner of the room.

I take off my baseball cap and roll my shoulder before setting my hat in my lap. I should probably just learn to keep a lid on my impulsive nature. It's unfortunate I didn't think about that before Kendall made her offhand comment. Who knows what's going through Kendall's supervisor's mind at this point? Sometimes I'm such a jerk, even when I'm trying to be nice. Nervously, I smile at Colette as I try to disguise my discomfort at being caught being unprofessional.

To my surprise, Colette shoots me a sly smile. "Come

now, everyone grab your food and let's go. If I'm not mistaken, Jameson and Kendall have some pressing matters they need to discuss this morning."

Brynley snorts. "I just bet they have 'pressing matters' to discuss."

Kendall looks as if she'd like to disappear under her seat. So, I address Brynley. "All teasing aside, I do have some important matters to go over with Ms. Kordes this morning."

"Whatever you say." Brynley rolls her eyes. "You guys act like my college roommates when they're trying to get rid of me. I know when I'm not wanted."

Colette walks over and puts her arm around Brynley's shoulders as she moves her out of the room. "The way Kendall has held us all together during this dreadful incident, I don't have any doubts about her ability to make smart decisions, personally or professionally. Since this isn't any of our business, let's go back to work, shall we?"

Brynley turns and looks over her shoulder at Kendall. "When the time comes, remember that my cousin does fabulous videography work at weddings. Tell him Bryn sent you."

Kendall relaxes and chuckles. "Okay, I'll remember. But really, we're just going to talk. I have no nuptial plans today ... or in the near future."

Brynley breaks away from Colette and walks over to give Kendall a brief hug. "I'm sorry if I made things weird. I'd just like to see you not be so sad. If it takes a hunk like this to make it happen, I'm rooting for you."

Kendall's eyes tear up for a moment. "Thank you for thinking of me. But this is something I need to figure out on my own."

CHAPTER SEVEN

KENDALL

I STARE IN SILENCE as I watch Jameson gather up the remaining cups and baked goods and carry them out of the conference room. I have no idea what just happened. One minute we were talking about my favorite beverage and the next minute I'm contemplating kissing a man I barely know. Well, that's not exactly true. I probably know more about Jameson than he's comfortable with. That's what happens when you have to bare your soul about loss. There's no way to avoid the inherent close bond which forms.

That simple truth is the one reason I shouldn't take advantage of the situation — even though everything about Jameson has been at the forefront of my mind since the moment I laid eyes on him. I'm sorry, the man is sexy on so many levels, it defies explanation. On one hand, he is easy-going and flirtatious with a quick, tempting grin. Yet, he moves with the smoothness of a wild cat. He reminds me of the videos of panthers and cheetahs I used to watch as a kid — smooth and fluid, yet lethal.

He is clearly more than qualified to work on computers, still I can't help but think it may not be the job for which he's ideally suited. Even though he is a self-professed computer geek, he is clearly an exceptionally well-trained soldier.

Even as my brain processes all the reasons that my compulsive suggestion was an atrocious idea, I have to come to grips with the realization that I wouldn't mind the feel of his strong arms around me. We made accidental contact the other day, and I can't stop thinking about it.

Finally, I throw up my hands in frustration. I retreat to the ladies' room in an effort to repair my tattered nerves. For reasons that escape me, I take a few extra moments to fix my hair. It is wavy this morning because of the braids Mindy put in for me. In an uncharacteristically girly move for me, I even fix my lip gloss. Whether I want to admit it or not, I've made my decision. I just hope I'm willing to live with the consequences.

I smooth the wrinkles out of my skirt as I reenter the conference room. Much to my dismay, Jameson is already sitting at the conference table booting up his laptop. My hope that I could take a few moments to settle myself and come up with some sort of strategy fly out the window as Jameson looks over the top of his computer screen and smiles at me. "Sorry —" he says at the same time as I do.

He makes a gesture with his hand. "Ladies first."

I blush. "I don't know what to tell you. Usually, I'm

more circumspect and careful with my words, but there's just something about you that makes me blurt things I don't usually say out loud. It's like you can extract the thoughts from my brain. It's bizarre."

"You know, I was thinking the same thing about you. I've told you things I haven't confessed to anyone in quite a while — if ever."

"What do you think we should do to get over this weird awkwardness?" I take a seat next to Jameson so that I can read his computer monitor.

Jameson lets his eyes linger over me in slow perusal before he answers. "It seems to me we have a couple of choices. We can completely ignore the kissing conversation ever took place. For the record, this isn't my favorite option. How about you?"

I nervously give an infinitesimal shake of my head. "I don't think I can. It's pretty much burned into my long-term memory, short-term memory, and my consciousness. That memory is not going anywhere," I confess with a self-deprecating grin.

Jameson smiles approvingly. "You're pretty unforgettable too. We probably need to table this discussion for now. As much as I'd like to take you up on your offer, this probably isn't the time or place. Still, I'd like to figure it all out — sooner rather than later. I spend a lot of time thinking about you — probably more than I should."

My brows furrow as I try to puzzle through his statement. "So, you're just going to have a go-or-no-go call on whether we kiss? Are you sure we can just plan that in advance?"

"I don't know if it's as complicated as that. I was just suggesting that we go out on an actual date that's not a family get-together or one that'll be interrupted by computer emergencies. It seems like a simple and straightforward plan to me."

I try to hide my face in my hands. "I don't know what it is about me. I complicate everything beyond belief. A date sounds fun. When do you suggest we fit it into our otherwise cramped schedule?" I ask, as I pull out my cell phone and bring up my calendar.

Jameson tries unsuccessfully to hide his grin at my industriousness. "Look, I hadn't gotten that far yet. I figured we needed to solve a few things first. I had some ideas about your missing infant case. As long as I'm going to be here, you might as well have the resources of Identity Bank at your disposal."

"I don't want to put Tristan out any more than necessary. He's already done way more than enough for Locate My Heart. To ask for anything more seems greedy."

"Funny thing I'm discovering about my boss; he has a different definition than the rest of us about what's overly generous. So, for the sake of Asher, I think we should take him up on it."

"That's true. What more do you think Identity Bank can bring to the table?" I ask.

"Well, Tristan is a software designer, and he has the ability to see a problem from a large-scale perspective. He sees the interrelationships between things, people, and events the rest of us might miss."

"I've only met him once, but he does seem to view

things a little differently."

"So, we can take advantage of that. We're going to put as many investigators on the ground as we can. Something about this case struck us all as very odd. This abduction doesn't seem random. If it's not the usual family suspects, it's someone in their circle of extended family or friends. I can almost bet on it. With Tristan's network of seasoned interrogators and investigators, I'm sure we'll eventually run into somebody who knows something."

I sigh. "These days the interrogators are likely to run into members of the media more than anyone else. After the piece that ran on Crime TV, Bethany told me the tabloids are dogging her whole family. Edwin can't even enter the courthouse without having accusations yelled at him."

"That's so awful. They are in enough pain without having to deal with all that garbage."

"I know. I wish I could do more for them. I've turned this problem over in my head so many times it haunts me in my sleep. They're just really aren't too many other ways to go with this scenario. It's Colette's call, but if it were my call to make, I would say bring in Tristan and all of his big guns. We need to find Asher before something terrible happens to him. He is medically fragile, and I am worried sick about him."

"What if I told you it's your decision?" Jameson takes a long drink of his coffee and a bite of his donut.

Startled, I send him a questioning glance. "What do you mean? This isn't my decision. Resource allocation is Colette's baby."

Jameson shrugs. "Have you checked your messages? She sent me a message and told me you were in charge. She told me to deal with you."

My mouth gapes open in shock. "Why?"

He digs out his phone and shows me the message. "I guess her sister is in the hospital."

"Are you sure we're not reading too much into her message? I'm not officially anything except her executive assistant."

"Colette expressly says she wants you to act as the director. I think she sees you as the future of Locate My Heart. She's willing to give you a chance to run with it and see where you take it. Are you up to the challenge?"

"It might take a while for my brain to catch up with my racing heart, but yeah … I'm ready. We've got kids big and little to find."

"It's odd you bring that up because that's the other thing I wanted to talk to you about. After we get things set up with Tristan, can you come down to my parents' house with me this weekend? I think we owe it to Toby to widen the search. I can't leave chances on the table. If there are things left to do, we need to do them. I'll have to bring my parents onboard one way or another. You are so compassionate with families and passionate about finding kids. Maybe your enthusiasm will rub off. I hope you'll understand what my parents have gone through and won't judge them too harshly. They're not the people they were when Toby was young."

I reach out and grab Jameson's hand. "I can't promise you anything about the outcome of your brother's case, but I can promise you that I'm not going to judge a single solitary thing about the impact of your parent's loss on their lives. When it comes to things like this, you deal with it best you can and pray the rest resolves itself. Sometimes, the process goes smoother than others."

"I hope you're right. Because honestly, some days I just don't understand."

I squeeze Jameson's hand as I try to shield my own emotions. "If there's one thing I've learned throughout everything I've experienced in my life, it's that love and loss never makes sense one hundred percent of the time. It just can't — and that's okay."

As I wait for Jamison to respond, his eyes grow intensely dark as he reaches up and waves his fingers through my hair. He cups my cheek with his other hand as he murmurs, "Speaking of not making sense… I know better than to blur the lines like this, but —" He leans in and gently kisses me with featherlight kisses as he strokes my cheeks with his thumbs. I clutch his shoulders and melt into him.

I break away to catch my breath and rest my cheek against his chest. I feel his heart pound. "Wow!" I stammer. "Spontaneous is hard for me. But I kind of like it."

Jameson pulls me close for another kiss. When he finishes and brushes my hair back over my shoulder he says, "I'm becoming quite a fan myself."

⸺•⸺

My stomach growls audibly as I smell the food sitting neatly in foil containers in the back seat of Jameson's rental car. "Are you sure I shouldn't have baked something?" I ask as I place a hand over my stomach. "It just feels as if I am letting down generations of ingrained manners. This doesn't seem like a grand enough meal for your homecoming."

"Relax. My homecoming isn't really a big a deal. Besides, my parents love food from the deli. My dad is all about the ribs, and my mom swears this rotisserie chicken is the best recipe she's had anywhere."

"Who's the macaroni and cheese for?" I tease.

Jameson rubs his stomach. "Give a guy a break. You're not the only one who's hungry here. A little comfort food never hurt anybody. I'm bummed that they were out of ambrosia though," he adds.

"You should have said something. We could've bought the ingredients, and I could've made it at your mom's house. It's a simple recipe."

"Kendall, I want you to be prepared for what you might see today. I haven't been back in a couple years, but the last time I was here, my parents weren't functioning well. They had pretty much given up on their lives. We may or may not even find clean dishes in the house. It may be one of the most difficult environments in which you've ever interviewed the parents of a missing child."

"Somehow, I doubt that. I've been to some pretty awful places. It doesn't even matter if it is the worst because that's where your parents are at. We have to meet them there. With any luck, we'll be able to help them crawl out of the world they've had to create for themselves."

Jameson swallows hard. "I didn't think you'd

understand. I was wrong about you — again. Someday, I'm going to have to stop underestimating you. Remind me when all this is over to let you know how truly extraordinary I think you are."

I blush all the way up to the roots of my hair. "I don't know if I have been all that extraordinary. I'm just trying to cope with life the best I can and help as many other people along the way as I can. I'm not sure if that even qualifies as extraordinary. Necessary? Yes. Extraordinary? I hope not."

"I think we're going to have to agree to disagree on your self-assessment. If you can reach my parents and help them through their pain, I would love you for several lifetimes."

"I make no promises. But I'll do the best I can. I'd love to see your family whole again."

My heart breaks for Jameson as he takes stock of his parent's current circumstances. I understand how Jameson could see it all as a badge of shame. Yet, that's not what I see when I look around the cramped, stifling home. I see a tiny woman and a once stoic, strong man trying to cope in a sea of hidden grief. It's as if their lives are divided into a before and after of perfect and hell.

I try not to let my stress show as I carry the plastic picnic ware out toward the back patio. "Those are pretty impressive sunflower plants. Mine never seem to do very well."

Mrs. Payne examines me for a moment before she

says, "I bet you're one of those who tried to plant your sunflowers beside a cute white fence or trellis, right?"

"I did! How did you know?"

"Honey, that's what I did at first too," she says with a knowing look. "I tried to constrain the warmth and power of my sunflowers and will them to my wishes. After I set them free, they did much better."

I draw in a quick, sharp breath. This may be the opening I need. "That sounds like a philosophy that could apply to lots of things," I reply carefully.

"We're not talking about sunflowers anymore, are we?" Mrs. Payne responds.

"Perhaps not. Did Jameson tell you how he met me?"

"I imagine it had something to do with computers, if I know my son."

"You know Jameson well. Your son saved the organization I work for from a malware attack. He's very talented."

"I always knew that about him. Where do you work, Honey?" she asks as she starts to unpack the deli food we purchased.

"Well, my organization Locate My Heart helps search for missing children. We are a resource for families."

A myriad of emotions cross Mrs. Payne's face. "Did Jameson tell you about his brother?"

"He did," I confirm. "I'm sorry for all you've been through. I'd like to think Locate My Heart has learned some lessons from cases like yours."

"Jameson must trust you a lot. He doesn't allow other people to be the keeper of his pain. If he told you the story, there must be a reason."

"There is. I would like to offer the assistance of Locate My Heart to your family."

"I would be quite interested, but my husband is not likely to be. We got burned the last time. I'm not sure Wesley is going to trust anyone."

"I can understand that. Jameson told me the appalling details. You shouldn't have been subjected to anything like that. That's where an agency like Locate My Heart comes in. We can help screen out the public responses and filter them down to the most helpful. At this point, Toby has been missing long enough that it is going to take the involvement of the public to generate tips."

"That sounds helpful, but we've been fooled before. When Toby first vanished, we had offers coming in from everywhere. Sadly, we were not very good at figuring out which opportunities were legitimate. We got taken to the cleaners, for lack of a better term."

"The services of Locate My Heart are completely free to families of missing children. We have corporate sponsors and grants to fund our work. We never charge the families a single dime."

"That's nice to know. But … what do you think can be done after all these years; it seems as if Toby has been missing forever. I am afraid to even think about it. By now I've given up hope. I don't know whether to hope he's dead or alive. If he's alive, I'm afraid that something god-awful is happening to him. If he's dead, don't you think I would know that as a mother?" Mrs. Payne bursts into tears.

Handing her a napkin, I answer her question as honestly as I can. "I've been doing this long enough to know that no two searches are ever the same. Some people have a strong sense of intuition about what happened to their child; others don't get that feeling at all. It has nothing to do with how much you love and miss your child. It's just one of those things."

"So, you don't think I am a terrible person for losing my child?"

"No, of course not. It is not your fault." Gathering my strength, I reach up and touch the memorial tattoo on the back of my neck. "My situation is not the same as yours, but my son, Quinn died."

"Oh, you poor thing. You're far too young to lose a child. What happened?"

"When my son was fifteen weeks old, he died of SIDS."

"One of my girlfriends lost her daughter to crib death. It's a terrible thing. Nearly three decades later, she is still mourning the loss."

"I totally understand that feeling. I don't know if I will ever stop missing my son. I don't usually share this part of my story with my clients, but I thought it would be helpful for you to understand where I'm coming from. I know all about second-guessing yourself and wondering if you should've known something earlier." I grab a napkin to wipe my tears away.

"I've tried to describe that feeling to my husband,

but he simply doesn't understand."

"I think it's hard for men. Lyle and I were engaged when it happened, but the stress was too much for our relationship. Quinn's death still affects me, even today. Every night, I relive that one day over and over as if it's Groundhog Day, like in that movie. No matter how hard I try, I can't escape the nightmare of his death. I can only move forward. That's why I'm so dedicated to my job at Locate My Heart. I was not able to do anything about my situation, but I can help other families have successful reunifications."

"What if it's too late to be reunited? What am I going to do if, God forbid, my son is dead? I live on the hope that Toby is just somehow unable to get to us. The more time that passes, the less hopeful I am."

"I can understand that. How long has it been since anyone actively searched for your son, Mrs. Payne?" I ask.

She walks around the table and places her hand on my shoulder. "Honey, I think two women who have been through what we've been through should be on a first name basis. My name is Bonnie. My husband, over there is Wesley. We don't stand much on formality here."

"Bonnie, I'm pleased to meet you, although I'm sorry for the circumstances. Jameson is a very nice man. You've done well raising him," I add awkwardly.

Bonnie's eyebrows fly up in surprise. "You have no reason to be so polite with me. I know what my son's reaction to you likely was — it probably wasn't all that nice. If I know my son, he was probably more than a little rude to you. In fact, he probably hated you on sight. He doesn't suffer fools lightly. Not that you're a fool, of course. But when we were involved with the search groups initially, we encountered mostly idiots and con artists and very few people who knew what they were doing. I wouldn't put it past Jameson to lump you in with all the riffraff who tried to help us the first time."

I can't help myself — I laugh out loud at Bonnie's startlingly accurate assessment.

I blush. "Okay, you busted me. Things were a little rough in the beginning, but they're better now. I think Jameson trusts where I'm coming from, or he would've never brought me to your home today."

"That's true enough. Jameson is very selective about who he shares our story with now. I'm still a little nervous about all of this. Honestly, I don't know what the menfolk have been doing about this and I am afraid to ask. Wesley's been so closed down over it all. He can't even stand to teach anymore. It's like all the students he saw in his classroom were mini versions of Toby. So, he had to retire. It was the most heartbreaking thing. Wesley was an amazing teacher, and one day changed his whole future."

I reach up and place my hand over hers on my shoulder. "I'm sorry. That must've been so difficult; to have everything in your life unravel at once."

"That was only part of it. I had to retire too because of my health issues. Losing Toby literally broke my heart and everything else in my life. Now, I just exist day to day. I pray day in and day out for Toby to come home I don't know how to restart my life without my son. How does a person just lose their child? I was a competent adult who was in charge of dozens of children every day. I'll never understand what went wrong. He was going to a safe place. How was I supposed to know that the public library was a dangerous place? Toby had been going to the library by himself since he was about eight. Does that make me a terrible parent?"

"No! It doesn't make you an awful parent. It makes you the victim of terrible circumstances. There is a difference."

"It doesn't feel like there's much of a distinction. I let Toby down in every way possible."

"I understand why you feel that way, but we can't go back and rewrite the past. We can only reconstruct what we know and try to fill in the blanks. Maybe there was a clue that was overlooked because the police were looking in the wrong direction. We'll try to shine a different light on the case and see if we can generate some tips. How do you think Wesley will react to reopening Toby's case?"

"I don't know. As long as Jameson believes in what you plan to do, Wesley will probably come on board. He is as desperate to find our son as I am. If you offer an honest ray of hope, I think Wesley will jump all over it. He misses our boy as much as Jameson and I do."

I stand up, turn around, and embrace Bonnie. "Okay, let's go talk to him and develop a plan."

Bonnie sobs against my neck for a moment. "Thank you for giving me back my hope. This is the first time in years I've been able to take a deep breath."

CHAPTER EIGHT

JAMESON

"Does Tristan always put you up like this when you travel?" Kendall asks as she shifts the laptop on the desk to remove the glare from the window.

"This is a downgrade from what he typically provides. I had to convince him that regular corporate extended-stay accommodations are fine for me. It's an upgrade from military installations in the middle of the desert. I think sometimes Tristan forgets how spoiled he has become."

Kendall twists her long hair off her neck and sticks a pencil through it. "I imagine you'd become accustomed to luxury a little at a time and you'd forget how hard it once was."

I shrug. "I suppose so, but that's just not my experience."

Kendall smirks at me. "Says the man of a million gadgets."

"*Touché.*" I spin my baseball hat around in my hands.

"Even with my fancy gadgets and your media appearances, it's been weeks and we're not making any progress on my brother's case. Maybe I set my parents up for failure again? While you were persuading my mom, I had to do a hard sell to get my dad to even consider trying again with Locate My Heart. Now, I wonder if I sent him on a wild goose chase."

Kendall flinches and rolls the desk chair back toward the window. Her mouth grows tight, and she averts her gaze from me. I watch as she takes a deep breath before turning back. The look of disappointment on her face is heart breaking. "I never promised you this was going to be easy. Toby's case is ice cold. We don't even know if he is still in the area. He could be halfway across United States or in another country. We just don't know. We can only guess what he looks like now based on the computer-generated age progression software. I have one of my best friends who is a sketch artist working on it to refine it based on what you looked like at seventeen. We are trying to overcome the perception that Toby's disappearance was voluntary or that your parents had something to do with it. In short, we're climbing a very steep mountain."

"If you thought this was so hopeless, why did you encourage me to start down this path?"

"Because doing nothing guarantees no results. Your brother deserves a chance even if it's slim. Maybe somebody, somewhere knows something. We have to turn over every stone. It only takes one good tip."

"If there were clues just hanging around, don't you think the private investigators my dad hired would've uncovered them?"

Kendall rubs her wrists, stretches out her thumb and flexes her fingers. She opens her mouth to speak and then closes it for a second. "It's difficult to reconstruct someone else's work years later. I have no way to determine how competent your investigators were."

"I should hope they were competent. You don't even want to know how much money my dad paid for those people."

Kendall sighs. "I wish I had better news for you, but the investigators homed in on your military background and your dad as potential suspects and didn't look much further. I found some handwritten notes in the file and I recognized some names I work with from local stations. Apparently, the investigators weren't shy about sharing their suspicions with the media either."

"I suspected as much, but to have it confirmed is freakin' unbelievable. They're lucky I was not stateside when all this happened, or things could've gotten much uglier."

Kendall presses her lips together in a grim line. "Let me guess? I bet you were making similar statements at the time. It's not as if I don't understand your frustration. Even so, it may explain why they focused in on you."

"I never understood that theory. I wasn't even in country when my brother went missing. What would I have to gain from his disappearance? I was out of the house and earning my own money."

"The thing I have learned in this line of work is that you can't stop what people assume about you. The story takes on a life of its own."

"So, basically what you're telling me is my dad was taking second and third mortgages out on the house to be able to afford an investigation on himself? That's the definition of insanity."

Kendall looks at me shrewdly. "Jameson, you are smart enough to have gone through these files yourself. What were you hoping I would glean from them that you didn't?"

"I've been through those reports with a fine-tooth comb. It's one of the reasons I was so skeptical of taking the job at Locate My Heart. We trusted these guys and told them about our private lives so they could find my brother. They took our information and betrayed us in the deepest ways. I don't care how they talk about me, but the fact that they victimized my parents, not once but twice, is maddening. I was hoping that maybe I was reading things into the situation that weren't there."

"Even though I wish I could argue with your reading of the case, I can't. The private investigators strongly suspected your parents and didn't look any further. I question their ethical standards and their methods. I was not able to glean much else from their work with one small exception — their report did alert me to your brother's social interactions prior to his disappearance. It opens up another door of potential leads."

"Really? I wasn't aware my brother had much of a life outside of books and watching geeky scientific documentaries on television. He was quiet and shy. He didn't make friends easily."

"That might be what it looked like in the real world,

but in Toby's corner of the universe, he was a rock star."

"My brother? How was Toby a rock star,?"

"He had a thing for role-playing games."

"I'm aware. As educators, my parents limited his access. I don't know how involved he could've been, given those restrictions."

"Could explain why he chose to spend so much time at the public library. Instant Internet access — no questions asked."

"Even back then?"

Kendall giggles. "This might be a news flash, but we're getting old. At least some libraries started offering Internet access about twenty years ago. Since your brother hasn't even been gone half that long, I suspect he had no difficulty."

I scrub my hand down my face in frustration. "I can't believe I was so blind to that possibility. I just figured that mom and dad had Toby on such a tight leash, he couldn't be involved in all that stuff."

"Never underestimate a teenager's ability to work around the rules if they have enough motivation."

I know Kendall is teasing, but something about her comment rubs me the wrong way. "Are you saying this is even remotely Toby's fault? That's not fair. You didn't even know him."

"No! It's not a comment on Toby or his character. It's just an observation about life in general. It doesn't matter what Toby did or didn't do; nobody deserves to be abducted."

"Abduction? Is that the official position of Locate

My Heart? Has your investigation turned up something new that definitively supports an abduction theory?"

"Not necessarily I'm just thinking out loud here. I haven't been in charge of this case long enough to make any official statements regarding what happened. I don't think any of us know the full truth. It just seems more likely than not. As near as I can tell, no one reported seeing anything unusual."

"Well, an abduction in broad daylight might be considered unusual."

"It would be — but what if he went somewhere voluntarily expecting one thing, but got another? There might not have even been an unusual scene to witness."

My shoulders slump as her words sink in. "I don't even want to consider it. Yet, it does fit with Toby's personality. He was always concerned about other people. Maybe that got him into trouble that he couldn't get out of." I twist my back around and flex my shoulders. "Every night I kick myself that I didn't spend more time with my kid brother teaching him hand-to-hand combat skills to get out of any situation, anywhere, anytime anyhow."

Kendall slowly gets up from the desk and walks over to the bed where I'm propped against the headboard. She crawls up against my side and puts her head on my shoulder. It's an odd sort of embrace.

"Jameson, you can't do that to yourself. We all go back and think of things that we would've done differently, but you didn't know this was going to happen. There's no point."

"What do you know about any of this? Is this all

clinical psychobabble to you? You don't know what it's like to love someone and have them vanish without a trace."

Kendall draws in a quick breath. "I do know."

"Know what?" I demand.

"I know what it's like to love someone and in a blink of time have them gone. I am intimately familiar with that pain — more than you can even imagine."

"So, I was right. You're doing all this for a reason."

Tears fill her eyes and she looks away.

After a few moments she meets my gaze. "Look, I know you're worried about your brother, but there's no excuse for you to be a jerk. I don't even know why I'm telling you this."

"Tell me what? You haven't said a thing that makes any of this makes sense."

I'm not sure why I feel the need to press this point. It's almost as if all the anger I've been tamping down and ignoring over the years is suddenly erupting into its own multi-headed monster. The pain, confusion, and anger on Kendall's face are stark. Yet, I can't seem to stop my vitriolic words.

"I don't have to tell you anything. It's not part of my job. Up until just now, I liked you, so I'll share my pain with you — maybe it will help you understand why all this matters to me."

"I suppose you have some big, long, elaborate sob story to tell me about how this has been your lifelong mission — if so, just save it. My parents and I have heard every single version of that story. Most of them didn't turn out to be true."

Kendall stands up and goes back toward the window. In a voice, so quiet I have to strain to hear it, she answers, "You can check the death records. I have nothing to hide."

"Death records?" I confirm, hoping I misheard.

Kendall whirls around on me and pins me with a direct gaze flashing with rage.

"Yes, death records. I once had a son, now I don't."

Her words hit me hard. I don't know what I was expecting her to say — but that wasn't it. "A son?" I stammer.

Kendall lets out a strangled sob. "Crap! We're not supposed to be talking about this. We're working on finding your brother. This is not about my story."

"I'm sorry, I made it about you. I was out of line. I'd like to know what happened, but you're right. It's none of my business."

"It's not as if it is a huge secret or anything. I knew it would have to come up between us sooner or later."

I move over to the little love-seat and pat the space beside me. "I guess this is probably as good a time as any since I've already stepped in it."

Kendall nods stiffly. "You're right. There is no right time for this conversation." She takes a seat next to me, but this time, she is not curled up against my side. Sitting as far away from me as she can, she perches on the edge. I guess I can't blame her. It's what I deserve for being a colossal jerk.

She sighs and draws in a couple of slow breaths as

if she's trying to gather herself. "At one point in my life, I had my definition of perfect. I was engaged to a man I thought would love me forever, and I had a beautiful baby boy named Quinn. Motherhood was everything that I thought it would be and more. I was blissfully happy."

Kendall reaches up and massages the tattoo on the back of her neck.

"When he was almost four months old, Quinn was feeling a little under the weather, so I went to the drugstore to pick up some fever reducer, some decongestant, and diapers. I remember feeling worried about his cold, but relieved that I didn't have to cart him into the store with me because he'd been crying so much. It was like a little moment of freedom."

I want to kick myself for causing her to relive all of this again. Why do I always have to push so hard?

Kendall swipes at the tears on her cheeks. "I can't believe I was ever mad at Quinn for crying. I've missed the sound of his cry every day since."

"I wish there was something I could say —"

"I know. Everyone does. There's nothing that can be said or done. When I went to the store, I was a happy fiancée and an overtired mother. I returned home to a houseful of police officers, EMTs, and Lyle's family. Quinn was gone."

"What happened?"

"My fiancé, Lyle volunteered to stay home with Quinn. It didn't happen very often because I was breastfeeding and didn't want to be far away. Lyle could tell that I was getting a raging case of cabin fever, so he convinced me that a quick trip to the store would give me a chance to catch my breath. He reminded me that parenting is supposed to be about being partners. He told me to tag him in. We treated it like a big joke because Lyle was such a fan of wrestling. Lyle said Quinn had one of those epically explosive poopy diapers, so he gave him a quick sponge bath and put him in his Star Wars jammies and laid him down for a nap."

Kendall blows her nose and clears her throat.

"Lyle was studying to take a real estate exam for his new job. After a while, it occurred to him he had not heard Quinn cough in a while. Quinn had been sick for nearly three weeks and developed a distinct persistent cough. We had taken him to the doctor a couple of times, and although the doctor was polite enough, he basically told us to stop worrying over a childhood cold. I felt silly being a stereotypical new mom calling the doctor for routine stuff."

"Sometimes, it would be handy if children came with operational manuals."

Kendall smiles wanly at me. "It would've been nice. In this case, I don't know if it would've helped. When Lyle went to check on Quinn, he wasn't breathing. Lyle started CPR but wasn't able to revive him."

"Do they think he died as a result of his cold?"

Kendall shakes her head. "I don't know that anyone was able to entirely rule it out, but the death certificate lists SIDS as Quinn's cause of death."

"I'm surprised you don't blame your ex."

"Sometimes I do. When Lyle and I got engaged, we

had big plans — but life got in the way. We thought we would get married and always be together. I unexpectedly got pregnant with Quinn and — well you know what happened with that. After he died, all the love between us died too. My dreams of a happy life just vanished."

Kendall's sadness permeates the room. I war with myself about whether to intervene and comfort her. Even though it's difficult for me to watch her relive the memories, I need to hear it. I take a seat on one of the antique chairs in the room and try to will her some strength and peace as I listen to her continue her anguishing tale.

Kendall starts to pace the room as she continues to explain, "After Quinn died and it became clear my wedding was off, I threw myself into school. I tried to make sense of what happened to my perfect life. One of my college classes required me to interview people in a social work setting. My advisor suggested Locate My Heart. After I met Colette, I knew I had found my calling. If I couldn't do anything for my own child, I could at least try to reunite families who could still be saved."

I shake my head at Kendall. "You are far more forgiving than me. If I were you, I'd still be furious at Lyle for ditching me."

She turns back toward me with a smirk. "Oh, make no mistake. I built up a hefty case of rage against my ex-fiancé. Mostly I was just sad and disappointed that we couldn't hold it together. I think we both let the grief and despair kill everything that was healthy in our relationship. In the long term it worked out. I'm in a much better place now than I was when I was with Lyle.

I thought I loved him, but he never understood who I really was. Lyle wanted someone who could stand silently by his side, look pretty, and be always gracious while he sold upscale homes. I tried to be that person for him, but it was never going to be enough for me. Losing Quinn just made me realize that more quickly than I might have otherwise."

Unable to hold back any longer, I put my arms around Kendall and pull her close. She weeps against my shoulder, but then shrugs away.

Kendall wipes her face with a tissue. "This never gets any easier. I thought as time went on, the pain would go away. But it still lingers."

"Like you once told me, 'You don't just get over something like that.'"

"You wanted to know if I knew anything about losing someone or if I was just making up all of my platitudes I give to grieving families. There's your answer. I know more about the suffering of losing a child than any mother should know," Kendall says as she abruptly gets up from the love seat and walks over toward the window.

I walk over and try to place a comforting arm around her shoulder. Kendall ducks away from my arm, resisting any contact as she frowns deeply. "I have been dealing with this by myself for many years. I don't want anything from you right now."

CHAPTER NINE

KENDALL

I JUMP A LITTLE when I hear a knock on my door frame. Honestly, I'm not quite used to having my own office. The privacy is disconcerting. When I look up, Jameson is holding a cup of my favorite tea in one hand. He is clutching a red rose bud in the other hand as he knocks on my door frame with his knuckles.

"Can I help you?" I try to cover my surprise at his presence.

"Am I still in the dog-house for being a moron the other day?" he asks as he offers the tea and rose stem with baby's breath and pretty ribbon. "I'm so sorry. Sometimes my mouth gets ahead of my brain."

I smile as I set them on my desk. I open my desk drawer and remove a packet of sugar and pour it in. I stir the tea with the slim, brown stirring stick and gratefully take a sip of the fragrant cinnamon tea. "This is perfect, thank you. You weren't the only one with regrets from that day. I was snippier than I needed to be. You were only trying to comfort me."

"I should have never pushed you so hard," he counters as he steps closer to kiss me. When he sees a picture of an unfamiliar child on my screen he kisses me lightly, hugs me quickly and backs away. "You must be in the middle of something," he says as he walks out of my office.

"I am. We got a new case. This one has an AMBER Alert. I'm trying to get our media packages set up as quickly as I can. I'm almost done. I just wish I had some help to disseminate them. Unfortunately, Brynley has class today."

I watch through the doorway of my office as Jameson checks the time on his phone. He walks over to the station the interns use and takes his laptop out of his bag and sets it on the desk. He glances over at me. "What do you need?"

"For some reason, I'm having trouble resizing the image for the poster. I do this all the time, but this one is strange."

"I can do that one for you. Shoot it to me via email. Do you need it in 72 dpi?"

"I was trying to do two versions — one for print and one for electronic. Can you do that?"

"Easy-peasy. When I'm done, I'll put it up on Tristan's company bulletin board with Identity Bank. His company has huge reach."

"Thanks, I appreciate that. I think Tristan already highlights AMBER Alerts on Identity Bank's website though."

"Did you know he also has a separate

announcement system where he releases information about new video games and software products? I can pop it up there, so it scrolls through that announcement system too."

"I didn't realize he had a separate platform. That would be awesome! Thank you."

I take a moment to study Jameson as I wait for the picture to load into my email program. Today he is wearing a button-down with the sleeves rolled up exposing his tattoos. His beard is trimmed and his head freshly shaved. He looks like a coiled-warrior. His tense body language reminds me that he came to see me. "Was there a reason you stopped by, other than to bail me out of my computer woes?"

Jameson appears startled by my question for a moment. "Yeah, there is. This isn't the only pressing case you've got. I guess you didn't get the message from Tyler? He wants us in a meeting in about forty-five minutes."

"I didn't get anything from Ty. Then again, I've been focused on this. Do you know what this is about?"

"I'm not sure. I thought maybe you knew. It's probably about Asher Livingston, don't you think? It's the only case we're all working on together."

My heart drops to my toes. I glance over at Jameson to gauge his reaction to the news. "I have a really bad feeling about this," I blurt.

Jameson looks up from his computer with a startled expression. "Why?"

"Think about it ... if he had good news, Tyler would just call. So, they must have found something dreadful."

Jameson's shoulders slump. "The time delay could be so he can arrange a formal press conference. I never thought about that. I hope we're wrong. I want Asher's family to have a sense of peace my family hasn't reached yet."

"I could be totally off base. But, it just seems weird Ty didn't call one of us."

Jameson gestures toward his computer screen as he asks, "What's the story behind this one?"

"Imogene Faith Decker was abducted from her babysitter's house by her birth father who lost custody because of abuse. He was caught on surveillance camera, and we have a description of the car and license plate. You could tell Imogene wasn't sure she was supposed to go with him. She is considered endangered because she is a Type I diabetic and medically fragile."

"Does that explain why she looks like she's about half her age?"

"I don't know much about her personal history other than she spent a lot of time in the hospital as an infant. She was one sick child. We need to get Imogene back where she belongs."

"Okay, here is your poster. Let's get this out into the world so we can find this little girl and put one family back together."

A scrolling message travels across my desktop, reminding me of the time. "I guess it's time for me to officially call it a day. I need to put up the closed-sign."

Usually, I have to use a special wand to reach the

open and closed sign over the door, but Jameson simply reaches up and flips it closed for me. He puts on his sports jacket and takes a moment to brush the hair out of my face before he smiles. "We both know this sign means absolutely nothing. I know you are on the job 24/7."

Trying not to be distracted by Jameson's closeness, I shrug. "It's hard not to be. Missing kids don't keep office hours."

"It's hard for you to find balance in your life that way, though," Jameson remarks as he pulls my hair off my neck and massages out the knots.

"I'm trying. I gave up my job at Parchment & Page Turners. I couldn't juggle the promotion here and my hours there. I felt like I was giving less than half of myself to both and it just wasn't fair."

"It's a smart move. You said it yourself; you got a promotion here. So, you're making progress," Jameson argues as he tucks me back against his chest and rubs his hands down my biceps and forearms, working the tension out of my muscles. "You'll be able to focus more on missing kids. It is a positive thing that your attention won't be divided."

I sigh as Jameson kisses my neck. "I hope it will be, eventually. Right now, I'm just feeling completely overwhelmed by my responsibilities. I hope my first case isn't a fatality. Tyler's not known for playing games — especially with the press. So, I'll rest easier when I learn more about what's going on."

I lean against him and rest my forehead against his as he leans down. I take a few moments to bask in his warmth and strength. Reluctantly I leave the comfort of Jameson's arms and return to my desk. I feel a little better now. Things have been different between us since our conversation about Quinn.

After a couple of minutes, my email box lights up with a series of messages all from Jameson. Not only has he resized the images for me, but he's also already inserted them into the poster templates we use at Locate My Heart to augment the AMBER Alert already issued by the authorities. Just like that, the media package is ready to go out. I mouth a silent 'thank you' to Jameson as I smile and press send.

I grab my purse from the bookshelf by my desk and shut off the computer system before I walk over to the intern station where Jameson is sitting. "Well, I guess it's time to figure out what awaits us and more importantly whether there's still hope for Asher."

———•———

My heart is racing as we enter the Sheriff's Office. Every scenario playing out in my head is more horrible than the last. By the time we are escorted to Tyler's office, my knees are shaking so violently I can barely stand. Jameson notices my difficulty and reaches out to steady me. "Take a deep breath. We don't know anything yet," he murmurs against my temple.

I draw a quick sharp breath. "I know. I'm trying to remember that, but my brain simply won't shut off."

"You can't get ahead of the facts. It won't help anything."

"I know that too. Unfortunately, sometimes I'm not

all that logical. I like to lead with my heart."

"I've noticed," Jameson responds with a grin. "What if this isn't about Asher at all? What if it's about Toby?"

I stop so abruptly that Jameson runs into the back of me. "Does Ty even know about our search for your brother?"

"I was helping Tyler's sister-in-law, Madison, with a hard drive failure, and I mentioned our search to him."

"What did he say?"

"He thinks it's a great idea to bring you guys on board. It's not exactly his jurisdiction since my parents live in a different county, but he says he'll do whatever he can to help us."

Before I can say anything else, Tyler's door swings wide open. "Sorry about that, I was tied up on a multi-jurisdictional conference call. Come on in."

Jameson and I shuffle in and sit on the old vinyl chairs in front of Ty's desk. He offers us some cookies. "Go ahead, Heather is trying a new line of recipes for her bakery and wants feedback from as many people as possible. If I eat any more of these, they're going to have to order me new uniforms."

Jameson grins. "All in the name of science — I'll be a willing guinea pig." He reaches across me and scoops up about eight cookies.

Tyler gives me a pointed look. I shake my head as I admit, "I am too nervous to eat. I want to know what's happening. Maybe after we get it all sorted out, my stomach will settle down."

Tyler's eyebrows raise in surprise at my distress. "Geez, Kendall. I think I might've left you with the wrong impression. I didn't bring you here to give you bad news. In fact, it appears I may have some positive news. It's not a completely done deal yet, because we have to confirm his DNA, but it looks like we are on the trail to find Asher Livingston."

"Really? Why didn't you call me to tell me that? That's what you would usually do," I insist.

"If it was just my agency, I'd probably do just that — but there are lots of law enforcement agencies involved in this one. It's complicated."

"What do you mean?" Jameson presses.

"Well, the story gets pretty convoluted — which is why I called just the two of you. At this point, we are not prepared for this story to receive wider dissemination. We're still confirming lots of details. It's still early in the investigation, and all of these developments may or may not pan out. I'm including the two of you as representatives of Identity Bank and Locate My Heart because you are liaisons with the family and the media. For the moment, this briefing is private and confidential until I get clearance from the other law enforcement agencies involved to release the information to the public."

"Of course," I agree, curious about what could be so top-secret.

"Enough beating around the bush. What do you know?" Jameson demands as he looks at Tyler intently.

"If we can confirm this with DNA evidence, it would appear that Asher Livingston's life might have been saved by an alert women's ministry pastor at a church in Arizona."

"What do you mean?" I ask.

"Pastor Alvarez sensed something was not right in her congregation. One of her parishioners, Naomi Fitzgerald, was set to adopt a little boy. Unfortunately, that child died as a result of an umbilical cord accident during birth. Ms. Fitzgerald was understandably distraught and asked for prayers from her women's group at church. Pastor Martina Alvarez became concerned when Ms. Fitzgerald's aunt, Latrice Rann, showed up with a new baby boy, complete with all new baby gear. When Pastor Alvarez saw the postings on Locate My Heart, she knew something was dreadfully wrong. She felt compelled to alert authorities and get the ball rolling."

"Why would Latrice Rann take Asher in Oregon if she's from Arizona?" I ask, hanging on every word.

"That one detail was how we identified this a solid lead and not just someone seeking their fifteen minutes of fame. Ms. Rann works as part of the janitorial staff at the strip mall where Asher Livingston was taken."

"What are they waiting for? Why hasn't she been arrested? It seems simple enough to me. Asher Livingston doesn't belong to Latrice Rann."

Tyler pops a cookie in his mouth before he answers, "I'm inclined to agree with you, but that's not how it works when you have multiple agencies and states involved. The good news is that Asher is in the custody of law enforcement officials and we are in the process of confirming his DNA so he can be reunited with his parents."

"I may be reading a bit between the lines, but is there something else going on?" I ask as Tyler pauses awkwardly.

"It's hard to know, but the local authorities in Arizona are being awfully closed-mouth about Naomi Fitzgerald," Tyler answers with a sigh. "Between you and me, I have a good gut feeling about Naomi. I spoke to her for several minutes. She is mortified by the stunt her aunt pulled. Her whole world has gone crazy. This poor couple was getting ready to adopt a handsome baby boy and then had to go through losing it to stillbirth, only to be caught up in a kidnapping drama. She doesn't know how to explain Latrice's actions. Naomi was as surprised as anyone else. I firmly believe she had no idea that her aunt was planning to 'fix' her problem like this. Naomi was completely horrified and disgusted by the actions of her aunt. I don't think she colluded with Latrice Rann at all. But, I'm only one sheriff on this whole case. My opinion carries next to no weight."

"I guess I am a little confused. I don't understand why we're not popping open the bubbly here. This is good news, right? Asher is safe and being checked out at the hospital, correct?"

Tyler nods.

I look over at Jameson for confirmation. "What am I missing?"

Jameson shrugs. "They're probably just waiting for DNA confirmation. Something about this case must strike one of the investigators as odd."

Jameson's words ring true to me. Suddenly, it all makes sense.

"I think I get it now. I bet the authorities can't quite bring themselves to believe the abduction of Asher was as random as it was, and they want to take a closer look at Bethany. If you add the complicating factor of the stillbirth and the adoption into the kidnapping, it just becomes exponentially more complex, and your list of potential 'suspects' grows ever wider. The sad part is, most of the people caught up in the net have nothing to do with Asher's kidnapping. They just happen to be tangentially related."

Tyler takes a long sip of his coffee. "I might quibble with a couple of details here and there. However, the basic premise of your argument is correct. We try to go into each case with no preconceptions, but in reality, that's not how it works. We all have our biases which carry over from past cases. In this case, there are so many complex issues weaved together that each investigator has to overcome their own biases to come up with a theory of the case that makes sense. I think the complex nature of the case makes it harder to see the big picture."

"I understand that. I have a couple of questions. First, now what? What's next? How involved are the Livingston family in the new developments? What do they know and who is keeping them informed?"

"As you might expect, as soon as the Livingstons got wind of the fact that Asher had been found, they made a bee-line to Arizona to reunite with him. They didn't wait to be invited by the local authorities. Fortunately, the local field agent with the FBI is handling the coordination of law enforcement agencies. It'll eventually be worked out on their end. I don't expect there to be an issue with the DNA match. It's a matter of straightening out the paperwork and getting Asher released to the Livingstons, and arrangements need to be made for him to travel safely back home. I understand that he's slightly dehydrated"

I nod. "I don't blame the Livingstons. I would've done the same thing if I were in their shoes. I'm worried about Bethany though. She was sheltered from the media attention the first go around because she was having medical issues. Is she prepared for the onslaught of media attention now?"

Tyler twirls a pen between his fingers. "That's a good question. I don't know. I'll ask."

"We could put some reinforcements in place through Identity Bank to help protect the family if you think that'd be helpful. A news story about a cute baby being rescued is going to have lots of legs. Bethany is going to need some reinforcements — even if she thinks she's prepared. There's nothing America likes more than a good feel good story with a happy ending." Jameson remarks.

Tyler looks thoughtful for a moment. "I've spent some time with both Phyllis and Bethany. I'm not sure sending a random person is going to be helpful at this point. It will be an emotional few days. I think they would be better off with people they know. I'm inclined to send the two of you. Phyllis was singing your praises up and down and sideways."

"Mine?" I ask with surprise. "I wonder why? I haven't had many interactions with Phyllis. I have answered a few preliminary questions for her and spoken with Bethany a couple of times. Beyond reassuring her that everything possible was being done in the search, I couldn't do much because I didn't have any additional information."

Jameson reaches out and massages the back of my neck. "I think you discount how well you listen and empathize with people. Even when I was incredibly rude to you, you still went out of your way to hear both what I was saying and what I wasn't. That is incredibly soothing — especially for those of us who are in extreme pain."

Tyler nods. "Jameson is right. The Livingstons are going to be on edge however this goes. They could use your calming influence."

"But I'm not calm!" I protest. "I just got a huge promotion thrown at me. I have so much to do, and we just got a brand-new case. I don't know that this is the best time for me to up and disappear."

"Weren't you just telling me this morning that you got an update from Colette?" Jameson asks in his quiet, rumbly voice.

"Yes, she called to say her sister is doing well after surgery and that she's around if I need her for anything."

Tyler claps his hands together. "There you go. Call her up and figure out the best strategy. I really don't want to leave the Livingstons to fly solo on this one. They are the type of family that the media loves to pick on. I truly believe they are innocent victims in this. They've been through enough. Let's protect them if we can, okay?"

I slump back in my chair. "You're right, of course. We don't need to make this any more challenging. They deserve a happy reunion." I turn to Jameson. "I know you don't like to take advantage of Aidan, but his private jet might not be a bad idea for the trip home. It might save the family from prying eyes."

Jameson strokes his beard as he grins at me. "Already ahead of you. I sent Aidan a heads up to see if his plane was available. It's on standby if we need it."

I blow my bangs out of my face as I mutter to myself, "I hope Colette was serious about wanting to come back to the office because it sounds like I'm going to Arizona."

CHAPTER TEN

JAMESON

I throw the duffel bags on the hotel bed. "I didn't expect it to be raining in Arizona," I comment as I check my phone. After I check the message from Isaac, I glance up from my phone and give a fist pump. "I guess Ricky Foster doesn't like the feeling of being chased," I smirk. "As soon as his story started getting national attention and making all the major news outlets, he left Imogene on the playground at a fast food place."

Kendall looks up from the hotel guide she's studying and grins broadly. "I love it when cases wrap themselves up quickly."

"Imogene is no dummy. She helped herself. A customer was using a glucometer and Imogene asked to borrow it. She said she wasn't sure if her dad had left, so she was afraid to come right out and tell anyone she needed help. It turned out that Rhonda Schillings is a grandmother of six and she saw the AMBER alert on television. She knew Imogene was in danger and called the authorities right away."

"Did Tristan say anything about what happened to the dad?"

"Well, Ricky is having a bad sort of day. He ran out of gas. It's an awkward thing to do when there is a nationwide BOLO on your car and law enforcement agencies, and news copters from across the nation are looking for you. I can tell you he looked funny running through the streets in sweats that were two sizes too big. He may or may not have lost his sweats and exposed a big ole' fecal stain on the back of his shorts. Tristan attached a video if you'd like to see," I offer with a chuckle.

Kendall wrinkles her nose at me, "No thank you. That's a sight I'd rather avoid this morning. I need to focus my sights on how to help Bethany and Phyllis cope with the onslaught of media attention today. Based on my research, I believe the DNA tests may come back today. I'm surprised something hasn't leaked from the labs already. Usually, that's how it works. It's not uncommon for the media to have the test results before family members are told. I hope that doesn't happen in this case, but it could."

I grimace as memories wash over me. "I remember trying to sort out real leads from false leads. I was half a world away, trying to calm my parents down while I sorted out fact from fiction. It was the most frustrating thing I've ever been through. It still is."

"Speaking of social media, one of the tabloid outlets is reporting they have inside sources that are tracking a huge development in the Livingston case. A 'family friend' has confirmed that the Livingstons are assisting the FBI to properly identify a child who has been found."

"And so it begins —" I take off my baseball hat and wipe the sweat off my head. "Do you think we've made it here in time to make a difference?"

"It depends on how you define making a difference. I interpret it as trying to limit the pain inflicted on the family."

"I hear you. We need to make sure that Asher is safe — assuming that it is Asher, we need to shield the Livingston family, and we need to protect the investigation from compromise."

"That's a nice to-do-list, but I'm not sure all that falls on our shoulders. I think we're just here for Bethany, her husband, and her parents. In my opinion, law enforcement needs to take care of the rest of it."

I scowl at Kendall. "I assumed you were not so trusting of the boys in blue after what you've been through with Quinn."

Kendall flinches as if I've punched her. "I never said that. It … uh … I don't even know if I can explain. They had to do what they had to do. I wasn't there when it happened. I don't know what Lyle did or didn't do for sure. I knew his character and his heart. I knew I was in love with him. I knew he was gentle and caring with kids. I was sure he loved Quinn and looked forward to him being born. I was aware Lyle tended to get distracted easily by video games, television shows, books, homework, and talking on the phone. I was confident he would never, ever hurt our son. What I didn't know was what happened while I was at the grocery store. The police had a job to do."

"You're pretty forgiving. I still get a knot in my tail if anyone starts questioning me about my personal life."

Kendall quirks her eyebrow. "I've noticed. I don't

know if I'm so forgiving. I spend a fair amount of time beating myself up over my decision to go to the store for medicine I wasn't sure was going to help Quinn feel better in the first place. Maybe if I'd stayed home, things would've turned out differently. Even thinking that kind of stuff is unfair to Lyle because it makes it sound like there was something he did to cause Quinn's death. According to the coroner, that's not what happened either. So I'm stuck in this vicious circle of logical response and extreme self-blame. It's not a pretty place to be, trust me."

I walk over to Kendall and pull her into a tight embrace as I kiss her forehead. "I'm sorry. I didn't mean to bring everything up again and pull you off your game. You're right. We are here for Bethany. If this baby turns out not to be Asher, she's going to be devastated, and we need to be prepared for that scenario too."

Kendall swallows hard, gives me a tight squeeze, and nods against my chest. She backs up and dabs at her eyes with a Kleenex she pulls from her pocket. She shakes the tension out of her arms, goes over to the desk beside the bed, and studies her file briefly. "Agent Jason Foxwell has them down at his office. When he's finished with them, he'll meet us in their suite. I had the hotel move their belongings to a more private one. It's the one that they use for celebrities when they come here to play golf."

"Wow, you move fast! When did you do this?"

"At the same time I made our reservation. I knew we were going to need better privacy arrangements whether this baby turns out to be Asher or not. This family doesn't need to deal with the glare of cameras and the constant barrage of questions as reporters are fighting to be the first with exclusive interview footage. There will be time for that later."

"Speaking of time, do we have time for some coffee? I'm dragging today."

"I guess it doesn't make a difference whether we wait up here or down at the coffee shop. Agent Foxwell is supposed to let me know when he's on his way."

Kendall's phone buzzes, and she holds up her finger. "Hold that thought."

Her brows furrow as she reads the text message. She bites her bottom lip and looks down at her gauzy skirt. "Okay, this is weird. We need to wear jeans, and I'm supposed to wear one of your sweatshirts. Did you bring one?"

I shrug. "Yeah, I brought my Blazer hoodie to wear on the plane. Why?"

"I don't know. We're supposed to meet a nurse named MacKenzie by the loading dock at the hospital. The media has the hospital surrounded. Foxwell has been seen with the family, so he wants to throw the media off. He doesn't want this to turn into a scene like they had in Ohio when the women who were held hostage for several years were rescued. Foxwell says to take the bus."

I look up the bus schedule on my phone. "It looks like a straight shot from our hotel." I grimace as I look at the time. "If you're a quick-change artist, I think we can catch the next bus."

"Hey, I wasn't a band geek for nothing. I can change my clothes on a school bus with someone sitting beside me," Kendall says as she strips her shirt off and shimmies out of her skirt and starts to dig through her suitcase. She seems completely unaware of the fact that she's standing there in pale pink underwear and a sexy-as-all-get-out lacy bra. "I don't know what I'm dressing for, so I'm going to put on a tank top just in case." She slips a bright red tank top over her head and pulls on well-worn jeans with a patch on the butt.

She takes her ID and a couple of credit cards out of her purse and puts them in her phone case. She stuffs her phone in her pocket. "I'm good to go. I'm not sure what we're doing, but I guess I'm up to it. I agreed to help any way I can, and this is where they need us."

———◆———

After I help Kendall down the bus steps, I grasp her hand and walk down the sidewalk with her as if we're high school students. She looks a bit like a cheerleader, with her hair up in a ponytail threaded through one of my baseball caps. Her body is dwarfed by my favorite Portland Trail Blazers sweatshirt. Suddenly she stops in the middle of the sidewalk and gives a full body shudder. "I feel like my eyeballs need a shower. You realize I can't unsee that. That guy was practically giving the poor girl a tonsillectomy with his tongue right in front of everyone. I swear the kid couldn't have been more than thirteen."

"It was pretty awkward. When I was that kid's age, I was still too scared to talk to girls. It would've never occurred to me to kiss one like that. I don't even want to consider where he learned his kissing skills."

"Good idea. Let's not think about it — it's way too disturbing."

As we round the corner to the hospital, I realize the reason for the cloak and dagger routine. The parking lot is filled with media trucks and reporters milling around. "Somebody somewhere said something to someone. I wonder how much damage control we're going to have to do. The media coverage have already been crazy. Any leaks will compound things."

Kendall looks a little green. "From the looks of things, I'd say we're in crisis mode. So much for an orderly response to all of this. I expected a missing baby to be a big story, but the interest in baby Asher is more than I guessed. When the media discovers we found him, every word from anyone involved is going to go viral."

Staying out of the line of sight of the reporters, I spot the entrance by the loading dock. I squeeze Kendall's hand and motion with my head to show her where to go. We duck behind a couple of cars and a large truck to avoid being seen by any reporters. Just as I am about to knock on the door, it opens, and we are whisked inside by a breathless nurse.

"Hey, I'm MacKenzie. You guys got here fast! When the agent told me you were coming by bus, I thought it would take a while. It's a good thing you're here. The nurses are having a heckuva time trying to keep people away from our floor. We have lots of patients, and we are trying to be fair to everyone, but all these people who are trying to break into our hospital are way more than our usual security can handle. We're just a small regional hospital."

"It's nice to meet you, MacKenzie. I have to admit that this case is moving faster than we can keep up. Why exactly are we here?" Kendall asks as she intently studies the perky young nurse.

I step forward and introduce myself. "I'm Jameson. I take care of all the computer stuff."

The nurse's eyes widen as she takes another look at me. "Oh! I thought for sure you were law enforcement. You just have that sort of bearing."

"That's not the first time I've heard that. Don't worry about it. So, why are we here?"

MacKenzie ushers us to a private alcove and says quietly, "First things first — can I see some identification please?"

Kendall hands over her driver's license and I use my military ID.

"Thank you. I just want to be cautious given the circumstances around this case. Thank you for your service Sergeant Payne."

"We appreciate your diligence. Anything to keep Asher safe is a good thing. We're all playing on the same team here. We just haven't been given the playbook," I quip.

"You've heard of drug smuggling? You two are about to become baby smugglers."

"We are?" Kendall's eyes sparkle with excitement.

MacKenzie motions for us to follow her. We enter a quiet room where Asher is laying in the middle of a crib with metal bars. He looks like a caged animal at the zoo. MacKenzie closes the door behind her. "This little guy is ready to see his mom and dad. Naturally, we can't walk him out the front door without causing a huge disruption to everyone. There is a lime green car waiting for you behind the post office, next to the delivery vehicles. The keys are in the ignition. It belongs to our chaplain. There is an infant seat in the back."

MacKenzie unwraps a new front carrier and hands it to Kendall "You might find this helpful."

Kendall whips off my sweatshirt and puts the front carrier on with ease. I can't imagine how difficult it is for her to do. She probably hasn't worn one since Quinn's death. Kendall walks over to the crib as tears stream down her face. "You ready to go for a walk, buddy?" Kendall asks in a soft singsong voice. She tucks him into the front carrier and then pulls my sweatshirt over her head.

MacKenzie studies the situation for a moment. She takes a pair of scissors from her pocket and carefully reaches up under the sweat shirt with her other hand to protect Asher as she asks, "Do you mind? I would just feel better if he had a little more airflow."

"I understand," I say grimly. "I can always get another sweat shirt. Li'l dude needs to breathe."

"Okay, let me let the administrator know we're ready for him to make his announcement to distract the media."

"Statement?" Kendall asks with alarm in her voice.

MacKenzie winks at Kendall. "Don't worry about it. Mr. Gutenberg is simply going to make a statement which says we have nothing to say about the matter. Having worked for the man, I can tell you that might take a while. He has a unique talent of making simple things complicated and complicated things even more complicated. By the time the media sorts out what he's actually saying, you guys will have made a clean escape."

Kendall glances over at me as she gently rocks back and forth to soothe Asher. She's not saying anything, but her eyes are speaking volumes. She looks terrified but determined to carry out our clandestine mission.

MacKenzie comes back in the room and gives us the thumbs up sign.

"Oh wait!" she says, stopping us mid-stride. She digs a few pacifiers out of her pocket and sticks them in the pocket of Kendall's sweat shirt. "Here are some spares. Trust me, with this little one you don't want to be without these. He's a much happier camper with them around."

MacKenzie escorts us out the back door. She whispers, "Good luck!" as we edge our way down the stairs. I noticed the post office when we got off the bus. There is one corner of exposure to the reporters in the parking lot. I hope the diversion works. I slide my arm around Kendall's waist and hope we look like a couple on an afternoon stroll as we head toward the sidewalk. I remember why I leave the fieldwork to Tristan and Isaac. This is incredibly stressful. I feel like everyone in the whole town must be watching us. I haven't felt this way since I was serving in the sandbox.

By the time we reach the car and get Asher situated in his infant seat, we are both a little breathless. "Who knew I would need a degree in engineering to buckle a baby into a car seat?" I ask as I pull out of the parking lot.

Kendall chuckles as she shrugs out of the sweatshirt and front carrier. "I'm definitely out of practice, but it gets easier when you do it all the time. It's always more challenging with a brand-new seat."

I reach out and interlace my fingers with Kendall's as I ask, "Do you think Bethany and Edwin have any idea that we are bringing Asher to them?"

Kendall draws in a quick breath. "Oh … I don't know. If they don't, that's going to be a huge shock. I'm glad they get to do it in private, without a million cameras, cell phones, and reporters around. This is not a time when they need to worry about censoring their reactions because someone else is watching."

"That was one of the reasons that my parents were reluctant to restart the search for Toby. They remember the intense, claustrophobic feeling of always having someone scrutinize every reaction and decision they made."

"I hate it when people you don't know feel like they

have a right to judge what it's like to be in your shoes." Glancing over her shoulder at Asher, Kendall says, "Even though the outcome in this case is as happy as they come, I know for sure I'm going to need some Kleenex."

"I might need some too. I hope someday my mom gets a surprise like this. Although it's going to look a little different. Toby is almost an adult now. It's hard for me to envision that in my head. In my mind, he's still a quirky kid who likes Percy Jackson and Harry Potter."

Kendall's eyes tear up. "I hope Bonnie gets her happy ending too. We're doing pretty well. So far, two out of three. Let's hope our lucky streak continues."

"I think Toby is going to need a little more than luck. He's going to need divine intervention and who knows what else."

"Stranger things have been known to happen."

By force of habit, I scan the hotel parking lot as I pull into the private parking area. It is the middle of the day, and everyone appears to be gone. "It might be extreme, but with the number of reporters just up the street at the hospital, I think we should use the same protocol we used to get him to the car. Can you get the carrier and sweat shirt on from where you're sitting?"

Kendall nods. "That should be easy enough, getting the baby from the car seat into the carrier might be a little trickier."

"I think I can do that. I used to be the quarterback in high school; Asher's not much bigger than a football."

"Do you guys come standard with an identical playbook or something? Lyle used to say the same thing about Quinn."

"What? It's true," I protest as I hold my hands up in front of me as if I'm measuring Asher. "I can't guarantee people walking by won't think we're up to some kinky shenanigans in here but I think it's doable."

Kendall wiggles around in the front seat as she struggles to buckle the last buckle. "Definitely should've left this on. But I think I've got it now."

I examine the situation a little closer and make a decision. "I'm going to have to do this from outside the car. I don't want to take the risk of dropping him. I'll just bring Asher around to you. There's no one in the parking lot. Besides, we're in the VIP section; there aren't very many other hotel guests who have access to this space."

"Good point. No need to play Twister if we don't have to," Kendall replies as she exhales roughly.

I lift Asher from his car seat and have to adjust my grip as he stretches and yawns. I stride over to Kendall's side of the car and help her place him in the carrier. As soon as he is buckled in, she puts my sweat shirt on and we stroll hand-in-hand into the hotel as if something monumental isn't about to happen.

The doors of the elevator close and Asher lets out an audible sigh. Kendall gently rocks from one foot to the other to soothe him. "Are you ready to make someone's fervent prayers come true?" Kendall removes her phone from her pocket and sends a text message.

I've been involved in countless military operations, but I don't think any of them have been quite as nerve-racking as this one. My heart is racing, and my hands are trembling from adrenaline. I have to steady my breathing as we wait for the private elevator to go up to our floor.

We barely make it to Bethany and Edwin's room before the door swings open. "Please tell me you brought the test results with you?" Bethany asks. When she sees us, she breaks into tears. She staggers back to the elegant desk and grabs a tissue. She sinks down into the leather chair and watches us with hopeful eyes.

We step inside the door and wait for it to close. Once inside the door, I recognize Asher's whole family from their media appearances. Agent Foxwell is standing in the corner looking stoic. His expression gives nothing away. I don't think the same can be said for mine as I try to hide my grin as I help Kendall remove my sweatshirt before she turns around. "We brought you something much better."

"Oh my Gosh! Is that really Asher?" Edwin asks, when he can't process what he sees.

I can't help but grin. "Yeah, buddy, it is. With a 99.93 degree of certainty."

Edwin looks over at me as he takes Asher out of the front carrier. "I'm sure at some point I'm going to care about the details of how this happened, but right now I just want to hold my son."

"Is he okay?" Bethany whispers from a leather chair sitting by the desk. She seems frozen in shock.

Kendall kneels beside Bethany as she explains, "He's good. The doctor said he was a little dehydrated and exhausted, but he is healthy."

Edwin brings Asher over to his wife. "Look, he's hungry. He's doing that funny little thing with his face."

Bethany reaches out and strokes her son's cheek as tears flow down her face. She takes a deep breath as she picks Asher up and clutches him to her chest. She studies his face as if she can't quite believe he's real. When he lets out a distressed wail, she says, "There must've been a reason the breast pump failed this morning. I'm going to go lay down and feed this guy. It seems like I've been waiting months to do this. I honestly thought I might not ever get the chance to hold him again."

"Bethany, do you need me to do anything?" Phyllis asks.

Bethany shakes her head as she cuddles Asher's face to her cheek. "No, I'm fine. Everything is finally right in my world." She turns toward us. "Thank you so much. There are not enough words."

My face grows hot. "Just glad I could help."

"Bethany is right. We can't thank you enough," Edwin replies. He turns to his wife. "Are you sure you don't want Mom to grab you something to eat?".

"You're right. I was too nervous to eat. Can you pick me up a sandwich or something?"

"Why don't I go pick up something from the deli for everyone? That way you all can enjoy some family time."

When Agent Foxwell makes a remark, I jump in surprise because in all the drama of the family reunion, I forgot he was there. "I think that's a good idea. No one knows that Payne is working with us. Another agent gave me a heads up about increased media presence at the hospital and near our hotel."

Bethany's father-in-law stands up and grabs his cane. "All right if I go? Nobody knows me either. I'm tired of being cooped up in this hotel."

Agent Foxwell nods. "Don't see the harm. For the record, I'd like a Rueben and ranch with my fries. Coke or Pepsi works. I'm not choosy."

Kendall looks up at me. "I'll take whatever."

"One turkey with avocado on sourdough it is. Would you like your tea hot or cold?"

"Iced tea please, sweet if they have it."

"Any idea what Bethany might like?" I ask, nodding

toward the bedroom.

Everyone in the room except Kendall answers, "French Dip."

I laugh out loud. "Guess that's clear enough. Phyllis?"

"Chicken salad, please."

"Edwin, that leaves you."

"I don't care. At this point, it could be peanut butter and jelly, and I wouldn't taste it. I've got other stuff on my mind. Just pick me up the special or whatever you think looks good," he answers looking distraught.

"You okay, buddy?" I ask as I watch him take a deep breath and wipe his eyes.

"No, I'm not okay. I don't know if I'm ever going to be okay again. My wife went into the bathroom to change a dirty diaper, and someone stole my son. I know how close we came to never being able to have a day like this. How do I ever trust anyone again? Even though Asher isn't old enough to remember what happened, I'll never forget as long as I live. This will affect everything in his life. I'll be too scared to let him go to daycare, start his first day at kindergarten, ride his bike in the neighborhood with his friends, go to his eighth-grade dance, go on his first date at the movies or his senior prom."

"Honestly, I'm the wrong person to ask how you go about rebuilding normal. My brother disappeared more than four years ago and has not been found yet. I haven't found a state of being that resembles normal yet. Maybe other people are better at it than I am, but I don't pretend very well. I am who I am."

"So, is that why you're helping out Locate My Heart?" Edwin asks.

"Actually, that's why I almost *didn't* help Locate My Heart. When my brother went missing, a lot of people took advantage of my parents, and I was distrustful of organizations like Locate My Heart."

"You were a bit snippy, but you had your reasons," Kendall argues.

"Kendall is way too polite. I was incredibly rude to her and her supervisor. I questioned everything she stood for and called her a thief before I even understood who she was or what she was about. It's amazing she still talks to me."

"Are we gonna stand here and gab all day or are we going to go get some food?" Edwin Senior asks.

"I guess we're going to go."

"Hey, pick my wife up something with some chocolate. By the time this is all said and done, she'll probably want some."

Edwin senior claps me on the shoulder as I hold the door open for him. "I taught that boy right, didn't I? Treat your wife well, and all will be right in your world."

"Words to live by Mr. Livingston," I answer as I wink at Kendall.

As soon as Mr. Livingston gets in my rental car, he turns to me and demands, "Tell me what's going on in the case — not some politically correct answer. One military man to another, what's the real SIT-REP?"

Something about his bearing makes me sit up straighter in my chair. "Sir, Kendall and I are here to help you deal with the onslaught of media that will focused in your direction. I don't have any information on the case you don't already have."

"You think my family needs protection from a couple of newspaper reporters?" Edwin Senior asks incredulously.

"I don't think you quite understand sir. The media business has changed a lot in the last few years. You're going to be bombarded from all different directions. People are going to say things that are radically untrue about you all over social media, and you won't be able to escape the accusations."

"Why would they say anything about us? We were the victims."

"In this day and age, truth doesn't seem to matter. Rumors spread like wildfire."

"How in the world can I protect my family from all of this? They have been through enough pain," Edwin puts his head back and sighs.

"You let people like Kendall do their jobs," I reply.

"You trust her?"

"I do," I respond candidly. "I'm still living the hell you were up until about a half an hour ago. I think if there's anyone on the planet who can help me find my brother and my way out of that hell, it's Kendall."

Chapter Eleven

Kendall

I hold my breath as I watch Bethany's hands tremble. She swallows hard and starts her statement. Even though she's nervous, her voice is clear and strong.

"I just want to thank everyone across the nation for helping us find our son. Because of your efforts, he is doing well. Asher is a born fighter, and he has shown he has more grit and determination to stay alive than anyone I have ever met. I want to thank the person who stepped forward and did the right thing, even though she knew it might hurt people she cared about. You made it possible for my family to be whole again. There aren't enough words of gratitude."

Bethany takes a deep breath before she clears her throat. She grabs Edwin's hand and smiles.

Looking directly at the television cameras in the back of the room she says, "To the person who took my child: I know you were trying to make a horrible situation better — but tearing my family apart was not the solution. I consider the other party involved in this to be an innocent bystander. She couldn't predict the actions of another and never dreamed someone would go to those lengths to help her. She doesn't condone the actions that were taken in her name."

"Do you plan to sue anyone?" A reporter shouts.

Bethany seems nonplussed by the question. "I'm still in the process of recovering from the emotional trauma of this event and re-bonding with my son. I haven't been able to make any plans beyond day-to-day living, let alone decide any comprehensive legal strategy. If you're asking whether I'm going to sue someone because their family member did something unhinged, the question is no. It wasn't her fault."

"Why were you in that store? Did you know any of the people involved?" another reporter presses.

"No. My son was born prematurely and spent some time in the NICU. He became very attached to a particular kind of Binkie. The kind they only have at the NICU. Well, the NICU… and this one children's outlet store. Asher has been struggling with reflux and other issues which make him cry a lot. I was at my wit's end. So we went to the store in search of these crazy Binkies. By the time I went into the restroom to change his diaper, I was feeling pretty cranky myself. My mother-in-law thought I was upset with her for hovering too much. She left me alone to collect my thoughts. The next thing I know, I was on the bathroom floor, and my child was gone. There was blood everywhere, and I was so dizzy I could barely stand up. I screamed at the top of my lungs for help. I never saw the person who took my child until I saw her picture on the news."

"Is it true Latrice Rann confessed?" A reporter shouts from the back of the room.

"I see the same news reports as you. I don't have any inside information." Bethany sighs. "Sometimes I wish I knew everything, but there are other times when what little I know is scary enough."

Bethany's breathing grows shallow, and I see a line of sweat on her upper lip. I lean forward and speak in my microphone. "Law enforcement officials have asked Ms. Livingston to refrain from commenting on an open investigation. There are many law enforcement agencies involved — both state and federal. As you might guess, investigations this complex can be a bit unwieldy and information can come out in fits and spurts. The Livingstons do not want to do anything to impede the investigation. I'm sure you understand. I know that the public is curious to know what happened to Asher. The drive to know all the answers immediately is natural. However, divulging any more information may put any future court proceedings at risk. Just know that Asher is an adorable, sweet and active baby. This family is grateful for the tips and messages of support that they have received from the public. Without your help, this case could have ended quite differently. That's it for today's press conference. If there are any significant developments in the case, we may be back to address additional questions. Thank you for your time today."

"Who are you?" A guy asks as he holds up an iPad

to film me.

"Kendall Kordes. I work for Locate My Heart."

"Why do you work in such a difficult field?" he pushes.

"Because every heart deserves to be whole and your heart can never be whole if you're missing part of your family."

Agent Foxwell steps up to the mic, and I stand up and back away. "I would like to thank the Livingstons for their cooperation and thank them for their patience. Additionally, I would like to acknowledge the contributions of Locate My Heart for helping us achieve a positive outcome in this case. It was through their outreach efforts and their presence on the Internet that our tipster was able to put together the puzzle pieces she needed to understand there was a problem. Without the efforts of Locate My Heart, this case would not have proceeded as smoothly."

Bethany leans toward her microphone. "Yes, I would like to thank Kendall Kordes and her team. They were a voice of sanity in a world that was insane. I'm so thankful they were there to help me make sense of a process I couldn't even begin to understand before I had to go through it."

"Have there been any arrests in this case? What is taking so long? If you found the child, why haven't you arrested the person who snatched him?"

Agent Foxwell steps up to the podium and straightens his tie before he answers. "As you well know, collecting evidence and sorting through it is a painstaking process. This is especially true when crime scenes cross state lines and multiple jurisdictions. We want to make sure that all chain of custody issues are handled properly, and that nothing gets missed in the process."

He pauses and looks over at the family for a long moment. "Though the outcome was positive in this case, make no mistake. This was a serious crime. Not only was Asher kidnapped, he was put in grave danger and his mother was assaulted. Don't confuse careful police work for inaction. We are not filming some action field crime show here, we are doing real get-your-hands-dirty-and-turn-on-your-brain police work. That means crimes are not solved in an hour with time for popcorn and a soda."

A titter of laughter goes through the audience.

"If there are developments in this case, the public will be updated when it is warranted. Our primary responsibility is to make sure victims are safe and that the criminals responsible for the crimes are prosecuted appropriately."

"We've heard from other sources that Latrice Rann has already confessed. Can you at least confirm that for us?" an investigative reporter I recognize from the local news asks insistently.

"At this point, this is an active case. We are dealing with multiple leads. It's going to take some time to sort through them all. The agencies involved don't comment on ongoing investigations —— to do so would be irresponsible. I would like to thank all of you for coming today. The Livingstons have been very forthcoming with you about their experiences throughout this process. I ask that you allow them to return to their private lives as average Oregonians. They have some healing to do and they need time and space in which to do it. For the sake of Asher, let us all respect their privacy."

Most of the members of the audience put away their notebooks and pens, computers and tablets, and I breathe a sigh of relief. Maybe, just maybe this won't turn into a feeding frenzy after all.

"What are you doing working this hard on a Saturday? I thought with all the wins in your column, you'd be taking it a bit slower." Jameson rubs my shoulders as he peeks at what I'm reading on the computer. He chuckles softly. "Careful now, you're starting to be as paranoid as me."

"I'm not being paranoid; I'm just monitoring the temperature of the social media feedback to see if we need to adjust our approach."

"Do you see anything to worry about?"

"I don't think so. Comments seem to be supportive of the Livingstons and news coverage appears unusually accurate."

"Funny, I don't remember that happening much. I'm glad it's working out for the Livingston's. They seem like a really nice family. Unfortunately, sometimes being a nice family isn't enough."

I close the browser on my computer and shut it down. I lower the blind on the little window in my office and shut the door. Jameson is propped up against the wall and is quietly observing me.

I walk over to him and unbutton the top button of his shirt. I take a deep breath before I softly kiss the top of his sternum. I can feel his pulse racing. "I'm sorry," I whisper.

"Sorry for what?" he asks in a rough voice.

"I'm sorry we haven't found Toby yet. Your family deserves a press conference to vindicate them just like the Livingstons. It's hard for me to be happy for one family when I haven't been able to solve the mystery on another — especially when you mean so much to me."

Jameson puts his hands on my shoulders and pushes me away as he searches my face. "Are you doing less for my family than you would for any other family?"

"No! Of course not. I lay awake at night trying to figure out new approaches, and new places to search or to post about the search. I wrack my brain over where to ask for new leads. I've exhausted all my lists of people to share and to retweet and to ask for posters to be put up in their local communities. I've tried reaching out to online communities made up of kids who would be your brother's age. I don't know what else to do. It broke my heart to have a press conference for the Livingston's while knowing your brother is still missing."

"Kendall, I can't expect more than that. In fact, you've probably done more for my parents than anyone has done since the day my brother went missing. You treated them with dignity and respect and listened to what they had to say. You didn't gloss over their pain or take advantage of their vulnerabilities. You didn't promise them the moon, and you didn't dash their hopes. I don't know what more we can ask of you."

"If you say so, but I would still feel better if we could give your family some definitive answers — you deserve that."

"I learned a long time ago we don't always get what we deserve in life."

"I know that lesson far too well."

Jameson pulls me in for a deep lingering kiss. "I'm going to assume you're off the clock now. You have been working way too hard trying to balance media requests and all the new inquiries about Locate My Heart since the story went national. I think it's time for you to pay up on what you owe me."

"What are you talking about?"

"I know it's been crazy around here, but a while back you and I had a discussion about the proper time and place we could explore the whole dating thing. Somehow, we skipped dating and went right to kissing. Not that I mind — I love kissing you, but I also would like to take you out on a date. A real date. As much as I like hanging out with my family, our friends, or all your coworkers, that's not technically dating. I want to take you out somewhere where you're not reminded of your job every other second — that rules out hanging with my family or your coworkers. Besides, I want to spend time with you and only you."

"Now?" I ask, as I look down at my tank top, flannel shirt and cargo pants.

"Yes, now. You look beautiful. What you're wearing is fine for what I have planned."

"Plans? You have plans for us? Why is this the first time I've heard about them? You should tell a person about stuff like that. If I'd known we were going on a date, I would've dressed entirely differently."

"Maybe I didn't want you to dress up for a date. Maybe I just want you to feel comfortable in your clothes. I just wish my old Harley was running. It would've been fun to ride to our date in style."

"I have fond memories of my dad taking me out on his motorcycle — his was a Honda. I remember the logo. My mom would pitch a fit because she thought it was too dangerous for him to take me on his bike. It probably was, but I remember squealing with delight and laughter whenever he went around a corner and the bike tilted." My heart hurts as I think about how much my dad would have liked Jameson.

"Maybe someday we can ride together. Unfortunately, my bike isn't in running condition. It's sitting in my dad's garage. Who knows what shape it's in? I would love to go riding with you — especially now that I know you're a fan."

"You know who else loves motorcycles? Denny and Gwendolyn go riding all the time. He likes to restore old cars and bikes. You should see if he could do anything about your bike. I bet you he can. He's quite mechanically minded and loves to tinker through problems."

"Next time we see them, I'll ask Denny about it. It would be fun to get the old bike up and running. I haven't had it in working order since before I was deployed overseas — so, you'll have to ride in my boring old rental car. Are you hungry?"

I shut down the computer, grab my purse and lock the front door. "Not really. I ate my lunch really late."

"Great! That works out even better," Jameson takes

his jacket off and drapes it over my shoulders.

"What will work out even better?" I ask when Jameson covers a sly grin like a mischievous child.

"It's nothing huge. We'll get to reward ourselves with dessert after our date, that's all," he says as he escorts me out to his car.

After he lifts me in, I quip, "I don't know if I trust you. You look a little too much like my brother when he's about to pull a prank on me."

"No prank. We're just going to have some good clean fun. What's wrong? Are you chicken?" he teases.

"You do realize that those are known as fighting words to sisters around the world?"

"The question is on the floor Ms. Kordes, do you trust me?"

I make the sign of the cross across my chest. "For reasons that escape me, I'm going to say yes. Although every instinct I have screams this is probably a really bad idea."

"Well, I guess that's not an undying pledge of love, but for today — it works."

"Why Mr. Payne, I had no idea you were so forward. After all, this is our first official date," I joke.

"No one has ever accused me of being shy. If I want something, I go after it with all burners on high."

I know Jameson probably meant that as a lighthearted joke, but I have no doubt as I study his intense expression that what he says is not far from the truth. If something or someone stood in the way of what he needed, it wouldn't take him long to figure out a way around the problem.

"I'm not sure if you meant that as a promise or a threat." I flash a playful smirk.

Without missing a beat, he responds, "Take it however you wish, darlin'."

Suddenly at a loss for words, I stare out the window. As we continue to drive, I start to recognize the neighborhood. "Hey, this is how we get to Aidan and Tara's house. I thought you said the goal of this date was not to hang out with my friends."

"Who said they're going to be there? Aidan has world-class digs. It'd be a shame not to put them to use."

I swallow a burst of laughter "They do, don't they? I about die of envy when I go into Tara's kitchen — especially when I found out she doesn't cook. It's just such a shame. She could host a whole cooking show in there."

"From what I've heard, between Kiera and her mother-in-law, they practically do whenever they have get-togethers."

"That's a true statement. I came here once with Colette when we were snowed in at Christmas and couldn't fly home. It was like a Hallmark card meets Julia Child. I've never seen anything like it."

"I bet. Even when they do casual stuff like chili and cornbread, it's amazing."

"Okay, color me confused. Why are we coming here if no one's here? If you say that you're going to watch football on one of Aidan's bazillion satellite channels, I'm going to take away your nice-guy card."

"I'm not even sure I want a nice guy card. Haven't you heard they always finish last?"

"Not in my book."

"Although, I might lose it by default once you figure out what we're going to do tonight. I swear it's fun."

"Oh Lawdy. I'm not sure I want to hear this."

"Relax, I'm just taking you on a date. We're just not doing it the traditional way. I swear, if you want me to be a gentlemen, that's what I'll be."

As we drive into Aidan's driveway I blow out an anxious breath.

"You all right over there?"

"Yeah, I'm fine. I like to be in control. It's hard for me to just go with the flow."

Jameson puts his hand on my knee. "Nothing is going to happen today unless we're both on board. I promise. This is supposed to be a fun, stress-relieving date."

I take a deep breath and shake out my hands. "Thanks. I need some space where I stop thinking about everything. My brain is tired."

"What I have planned is perfect. You won't have time to think about work stuff."

Trying to calm myself, I smile and try to just roll with whatever he has planned. "Sounds fascinating. I can't wait to see what we're going to do. It's like a weird twist on a blind date."

Jameson fishes a key out of his pocket and unlocks the front door.

As we step into the large foyer, I exclaim, "Wow! It's so weird to be here when it's silent. Aidan's parties are never quiet."

"I know what you mean. It's weird though; for such a big star, Aidan seems disarmingly normal. He's a guy I'd play pool with at the neighborhood bar."

"I wouldn't recommend it. He was a traveling musician for several years before he made it big. The guy is a pool shark."

"Thanks for the warning. That would explain the professional pool table in their basement. But, we're not here to play pool."

"So, why are we here?"

Jameson puts his arm around my waist. "Come right this way." He escorts me through the family room and across the patio. "Welcome to your mind clearing activities." We stop in front of the recreational center that Aidan built for the kids he hosts at his day camps.

"We're going rock climbing?" I squeak. "Oh my gosh! Every time I come here, I'm always tempted to ask Aidan if I could try the wall. I've never quite managed to work up the nerve. Are we seriously going to do this? I don't have any gear or anything."

"We are. Aidan and Tara have all the gear anyone would ever need. They have groups come through here all the time. They keep a warehouse of equipment and clothing in different sizes. The only thing you'll need to do is put your hair back and get some climbing shoes. The rest of what you're wearing is fine. Have you done any rock climbing before?"

"Only once. In a leadership class in college, we did it as a team-building activity. After I did it, I added weightlifting to my running routine. I had the weakest arms in the whole class. Maybe I'll do better this time."

"I'll let you get changed. The locker rooms are behind the wall. What size shoes do you wear?"

"I wear size eight and a half."

When I enter the room serving as the women's locker room, the only thing that resembles a traditional locker room is the name on the door. It looks like a spa inside. I notice there is a stack of clothing on a chair. There is a note on top with my name on it.

When I open it, I see Tara's elegant handwriting.

When you climb with a partner, it requires you to trust them with your whole heart, even when your brain may tell you to do otherwise. Life is a lot like that too. Enjoy your climb at Camp Willow Tree and in life.

P.S. Wear a shirt over your undershirt. You can tuck your ponytail into it.

Wishing you love and plenty of kisses on your date,

Tara O'Brien

I've heard rumors about Tara's ability to predict the future; I wonder if she's just being friendly or knows something specific about my life. I guess it doesn't matter much. Either way, I'm determined to make it all the way to the top of the wall. This is going to be an interesting test. Sometimes, Jameson and I work well together, and other times we seem at cross purposes. I hope we are on the same page today. If we aren't, it could be downright scary.

CHAPTER TWELVE

JAMESON

As I search the shelves in the "shoe shed" as Aidan calls it, I breathe a sigh of relief. I wasn't sure how Kendall was going to react to my unusual choice of date locations. Aidan was the one who suggested it. He said the experience really brought him closer to his wife when they first started dating. I'm hoping it helps us too. I have a lot of ground to make up.

I've dug myself a pretty deep hole with all my assumptions about Kendall's character. I watched her over the past few weeks as she's been dealing with crisis after crisis. I was flat-out wrong. Kendall is the most open, transparent and giving person I've ever met in my life. It is obvious Quinn's death affected her deeply, but I no longer believe it's impaired her ability to do her job or created a twisted agenda. I think Kendall Kordes is about as real and authentic as anyone gets on this planet. I may have found the one person on the whole planet who really isn't too good to be true.

When I return to the locker room area to deliver

her shoes, she is already waiting for me. "Excited?"

Kendall grins at me. "You have no idea."

"Scared?" I search her face for clues.

"Probably not as much as I should be. I trust you to hold the rope for me. You are ridiculously strong. Although, I am a little worried about my ability to do the same. I'm not as strong as you are, and you're bigger than me."

"It doesn't take as much brute strength as you think. It's a bunch of levers and pulleys. The weight thing is not such an issue."

"That's good, because I'd hate to drop you and break your heart — or something else."

"Don't worry about me. I can climb the wall without ropes. I used to do the real thing as part of my job. So, this is just good conditioning for me."

Kendall rolls her eyes. "Of course, you did. Now I'm going to feel like a big fool when I can't make it up the wall."

"I'll make sure you make it. I won't let you fall."

I hand her the climbing shoes. "Make sure you tie those securely and thread the ends back through the laces. I've seen loose laces complicate more than one climb."

"This is so cool. I've wanted to do this for a long time," Kendall sits down on the floor and puts her shoes on.

"I'm glad you approve. I worried you might want to do something more traditional."

"Anyone can take me out for a candlelit dinner, but

not everyone can offer me a chance to do something on my bucket list."

I blush. "I try." The next time I see Aidan, I'm going to buy the man a beer.

I take Kendall's hand and lead her to the climbing room.

I position us in front of the left-hand side of the wall as I hold up a safety harness. "You put this on like your pants. I can help you tighten it if you want."

"Yeah, I bet you can. I've worn one of these harnesses before. They land in some pretty private places. How about if I put it on and you check it for the proper fit?"

I shrug nonchalantly. "That works too."

Pulling on the safety rope, I test it for tension and slack.

As I step into my harness and buckle it, Kendall puts her own harness on and tightens her straps. "I think I've got it; but I'd feel better if you double check my work."

I run my fingers under the straps to make sure she doesn't have them too tight. "Everything looks good."

I take Kendall's hand and turn her around so she's facing the wall. "Let me tell you about Aidan's challenge wall. A wide variety of people come through here. Many of them are teenagers or preteens with no climbing experience. So, he's divided his wall up into four sections."

Kendall swallows hard as she gazes up at the wall.

"The one in front of you is the 'Getting My Feet

Wet' wall. See the black line of stones? That is the division that marks the medium skill level, known as, 'So Far, So Good' section. There are more mini-jugs and pinches in this section. On the wall behind us is his most popular climbing layout. He calls it the 'Hey, I've Got This!' section."

"Okay, that makes sense. What's next?"

"On the far wall is the expert level — otherwise known as 'Nope, Maybe I Don't'."

Kendall studies the walls carefully. "What determines the difference between the beginning wall and the expert wall?"

"If you look carefully, the hand holds and footholds on the beginner's wall follow a predictable pattern. Left, right, left, right. They are evenly spaced jugs. The jugs are larger and deeper than the ones on the other walls. On the expert wall, Aidan moves the handholds randomly and they are spaced further apart, with obstacles you must navigate to get to them. He uses several kinds of holds. Some of them are only big enough to stick a finger or two in. Others are like small ledges designed to use only your fingertips."

"I'm sure I'm not ready for that yet," Kendall says with wide eyes.

"The other day, I was over here helping Aidan with clean up after one of his day camps and we had a little friendly competition between former military and law enforcement types."

"Yeah? Who won?"

"Believe it or not, Katie Ashford did. She must've

kicked butt when she went through the police academy. She left the rest of us in the dust. Tyler did well too. For a big, tall guy, he can get himself up that wall with admirable speed."

"I've only met Katie a couple times, but according to Logan Anthony, Aidan's chief of security, Katie saved his life and took down the suspect."

"I can believe it. She out-climbed a bunch of us."

"Perhaps someday, you'll be talking like that about me."

"I have absolutely no doubt that you are going to be a natural."

"We'll see. I think I'd like to start on the beginner's wall." Kendall starts to walk toward the stone structure.

I put my hands on her shoulders to stop her. "Wait. Get a mental picture of the wall in your head first. Do you see the pattern of grips? This wall has three different ways to the top. They are all pretty straightforward. Just choose the line that makes the most sense for you."

"Okay, I think I see where I want to go," Kendall says after she stops and studies the wall.

"Hold up. I've got a clip this to you," I caution as I fasten the safety line to her harness.

She flushes. "Oh yeah, I probably don't want to forget that."

"Don't worry about anything; I've got you if you miss a grip." I show her the guide rope.

"I trust you. I know you won't let me fall."

"This may seem basic, but before you adjust a hold

either with your foot or your hands, make sure you have two other points of contact."

"Got it. Two on the wall at all times."

"Sounds like you're ready, let's go."

Kendall takes the first few jugs with ease. She has a huge grin on her face. I have a feeling she'll be coming back to Aidan's wall often.

She looks down at me with panic. "Which direction now? I forgot!"

"You can go either way. You've reached a fork in the road."

"I'll go right."

"Sounds good to me. You're doing a great job."

Kendall moves up three more jugs. "This is a great upper body workout. I wish I would've done more. My arms are tired. It's hard to balance with my legs this far apart."

"On this portion of the wall, the jugs are large enough that you can stand on them with both feet. See the ones that are bright green? Those are the widest. If you can make your way to one of those, you can stand on them with both feet."

"Isn't that against the rules?"

"Darlin' there are no rules. It's just you and the wall. It's all about emptying your brain of stress and finding a way to the top. It's knowing your limits and feeling brave enough to push beyond them."

Kendall turns her head and looks down at me.

"Whoa! I probably shouldn't have done that. It's a

long way to the ground."

"It is. But, look up. You are almost to the top of the wall." I hold tension on Kendall's safety rope.

She looks up. "Look at that! There's only three climbing holds left. I can do that."

"I know you can. Are you ready? I suggest you take the center jugs. It's the easiest route to get untangled."

"Got it." Kendall says as she moves from one climbing jug to the other. She pauses at the top jug. "What do I do now?"

"Give me a second," I instruct as I hook my guide wire to Aidan's spotting device.

"You need a rope? That's a little scary."

"I guess there's one rule. Aidan does not allow anyone to climb without a safety rope no matter how much experience they have."

I climb the wall nearest to Kendall in a matter of seconds. I stroll down the scaffolding walkway toward the area of the wall where she is and extend my hand to help her up. With the additional security, she swings her leg over the top of the wall and onto the platform.

"I know it's only a wall for beginners, but Oh my Gosh! that was fun. I want to do it again. Umm … how do I get down?"

"For that, I need to be at the bottom managing your rope, I don't want you to come down too fast."

"How will you get down? No one is there to hold the line for you."

"I'll go down the same way I came up," I answer as

I examine her carabiner to make sure it is secure. "Your way is more fun. You just lean back and frog jump against the wall to move down. I'll be at the bottom guiding your dissent."

"This is where the trust part comes in, right."

"What do you mean?" I ask, puzzled.

"Oh, it's probably nothing, but Tara left me a lovely note about trust."

"From what I understand, Tara's messages typically have a deeper meaning."

I pull on Kendall's harness to test it. "I think you are ready to rock 'n' roll. Let me get down the wall and I'll guide your descent."

Kendall gasps as I launch myself over the side of the wall and start to climb down. "Maybe I shouldn't have watched that," she says in a panicked voice.

"Don't worry about it, your way is much more fun."

When I reached the bottom, I unsnap the harness from my carabiner and walk over to pick up her guide rope.

"Okay, see the big green jug? Swing your leg over and place your body weight there. Right below it to your left is another green jug. Put your right foot there. Lean back against the harness. Don't worry. The guide wire will hold your weight. You just jump on the wall moving from jug to jug. This is my favorite part of climbing. It feels like you're flying."

"Okay, if you say so. Right now, my knees are knocking together like a Congo drum."

"Look at what you've accomplished. You made it

all the way up the wall without having to start over. That's spectacular."

I watch anxiously as Kendall follows my instructions. It's nerve-racking.

Kendall makes her first leapfrog and slides down the rope. At first, she shrieks in surprise. But then she laughs. "This is like the best fair ride ever!"

"I know! The feeling is addictive. Wait until you get to try the real thing. Climbing outdoors is a joy all of its own."

"You might want to wait to celebrate until I actually make it off the kiddie wall." She makes a few more bounces.

When she reaches the ground, she sways a little. When she regains her bearings, she does a little happy dance as she spins around. "I did it! I really did it. Not only did I do it, I loved it! I want to do it again. Do you think I'm ready to move up to the next wall?"

"You should probably climb the other two routes to the top first. On the next level, the jugs are a little farther apart and have different holds. I want you to be secure in making choices before you move to the medium level of difficulty."

"That makes sense. I need to take a rest. My arms feel like limp spaghetti noodles. Can I watch you climb the hardest wall?"

I shrug. "Sure. It looks like Aidan has rearranged things, so it will be a challenge for me."

"A challenge like 'Oh my gosh, I'm never going to make it up this wall' kind of challenge?"

"Nah, more like I'm going to have to put my thinking cap on to figure out his maniacal plan. I can normally do this kind of stuff in my sleep. The last time I was here, Aidan said he was going to build me a pattern of climbing holds that even I couldn't figure out."

"Was he lying? Do you see a path to the top?"

"Yeah, there are a couple. I won't get stuck, I promise," I assure her as I tighten my straps and hook my carabiner to the safety harness.

I start to retie the end of the rope to the automatic spotter, but Kendall asks, "Can I do that?"

"If you want to. I was going to give your arms a break."

"You won't actually be putting any weight on the line, will you?"

"I don't expect to need the rope. Aidan is clever, but he's not *that* clever."

"So, how do I use this thing?" Kendall holds the rope in her hand.

"You're serving as a counterbalance. If you feel tension on the rope, just lean away from it."

"I think I can handle that," Kendall bites her lip. "But, you're not going to need the rope, right?"

"I think I'm good."

Kendall walks up to me, plants a kiss on my lips and gives me a quick hug.

"Don't worry Jameson; I've got you covered."

"I know. I trust you," I answer. We might be talking about rock climbing, but I mean so much more.

With renewed enthusiasm that Kendall and I may be able to iron out our differences, I face down Aidan's new challenge and scramble to the top of the wall. With all the new finger grips and shallow holes, I know my hands will be sore tomorrow. There are more than a few awkward twists and turns required to make it up the wall. Aidan didn't renege on his promise to make it a challenge. Usually, if I want a challenging climb, I have to go outside.

When I reach the top, Kendall whoops with excitement. "I can't believe you made it up there so fast. I want to learn to do that."

"You just need practice."

I start to climb down the same way I went up, and Kendall asks, "Aren't you going to jump like I did?"

"Do you feel comfortable enough to hold the lead rope?"

"Yeah, I think so. I just take up the slack so the rope can stop you if you start to descend too quickly, right?"

"That's right."

Kendall widens her stance. "Go for it!"

I lean back and take a couple of frog jumps against the wall as I let my line out.

Kendall laughs out loud. "What I wouldn't give for a videotape of this. All the people in high school who said I would die alone in my bedroom because I was too scared to face the real world would never believe what I'm doing now."

I step out of my harness and give her a deep lingering kiss. "I would venture to guess they don't know the heart of the fierce warrior that you hide behind all your nerdiness."

"I like that. I *am* a fierce warrior, even if I don't look the part."

"Well, Warrior Woman, do you want to take a couple trips up the wall before we go get something to eat?"

"I do. There's nothing like conquering what scares you."

KENDALL

"NO! THIS WASN'T JUST something I read in a book. A lot of faith you have in me as your twin sister."

"Didn't happen if you didn't capture it on video," Will insists.

"It did so happen! If you don't believe me, you should come talk to Jameson. He was pretty impressed with how quickly I picked up my climbing skills. He even let me try out the other levels of difficulty. By the end, I wasn't scared. It was totally cool. It was like playing three-dimensional chess with my own body; I had to figure out where to go and how to stay balanced at the same time. Jameson was so great, he didn't even make fun of my rookie mistakes. He just showed me how to get out of my jam and move on."

"Well, I gotta give the guy kudos for getting you out of your comfort zone. That college professor you were going out with was a real snore."

"Okay, so Dr. Noff was a little more obsessed with naked statues than I felt comfortable with — but somewhere in the universe there's a match for him."

"What's wrong with this Jameson guy?"

"Nothing! He's been a perfect gentleman. I think you'd like him."

"So, when are Mom and I going to get to meet this guy who's swept you off your feet?"

"Mom has met him — over Skype at least." I sigh. "As for you … I don't know. It's complicated."

"See, I knew there was a 'but'. Do I need to have a heart-to-heart with this guy?"

"William Benjamin Kordes, don't you dare. Our issues have nothing to do with the kind of person Jameson is. It has to do with our situation. It's a work thing."

"You're sleeping with a co-worker? I didn't know you had it in you. I mean, there's living outside your comfort zone, and then there's living on another planet. I don't know if I should feel sorry for you or give you a virtual high five."

"Oh shut up! It's not like that," I protest. After I think about it for a moment, I have to admit, "Okay … so it might be a little like that. Or, it might be even worse."

"Kendie! Is the guy married?"

"No. Who do you think I am?" I reply indignantly.

"What am I supposed to think? You said it was complicated and then you said it might be worse than sleeping with a married guy. So what's up?"

"You're right. I'm making it seem like it's a lot worse than it is. Jameson and I are still trying to figure it out."

"You're so lucky. I've got all the time in the world. It sounds like this is going to be a long conversation. Start from the beginning."

"I'll tell you the story, but you have to not judge the situation until you've heard the whole thing. There are reasons behind everything that's happened."

"Am I still going to respect you after I hear this?"

"Of course, you are. We haven't done anything wrong — it's just awkward. You know that ransomware that's been going around? Locate My Heart got attacked. So, one of Logan and Aidan's friends came to help us out. He works for this company called Identity Bank and —"

"You're working with Identity Bank? Do you know how famous Tristan Macklin is for his video games? You don't even know! He's like a god in the gaming community," Will interjects.

"I suppose he probably is — but that's not how I know him. I know him because he helped out with a fundraiser for Locate My Heart. He helped us get computer equipment we needed to run our age progression software. Anyway, when he found out we were the victim of ransomware, he sent his most talented computer tech."

"The new guy in your life?"

"Yeah, Jameson used to be military, but now he's not."

"A cautious, careful person might want to know why someone is former military..." my brother lets his speech trail off.

"I do know why he's former military — and that is

at the heart of my problem."

"You have problems with this dude?" Will growls.

"I did at first. There's no doubt about that. He seemed to hate everything I've dedicated my life to, and he was convinced Locate My Heart, and all of its employees were out to fleece families everywhere."

"Yikes, that's not good."

"We had a rough start."

"Why would he even think that? There is nothing nefarious about what you guys do. Why would he think that you take advantage of people? He sounds like a jerk!" Will finishes in a huff.

"Although sometimes Jameson talks before he thinks things through, he's not a jerk. He's the older brother of a missing child, and his family was burned badly by conmen when they hired people to help them search."

"Oh … I see. Does Colette know you have the hots for this guy?"

"Bizarrely enough, she's encouraging the relationship. It's really hard to read her. Did I tell you she stepped away for a bit and gave me a shot at a promotion?"

"Are you going to finally be the director?"

"I don't know. Colette has some personal stuff going on, and she put me in charge for a while. During the time I've been acting director, we've had a few high-profile cases."

"You mean the one with the baby, right? I'm glad that the kidnapper was finally arrested."

"Me too. We've had quite a few cases in the last few months. We've been able to solve all the new cases except for Jameson's. I feel terrible about that. I hate to treat any case differently than any other in terms of importance, but this one breaks my heart."

"I know you. You get close to every single family. It's like you adopt them as your own. You stress over every development in a case."

"I know. But, this is entirely different. As near as I can tell, no one really bothered to look for this kid because they thought the parents had something to do with it. Nothing I've uncovered supports that theory. It was just the news media and the tabloids running with the story they didn't even know. As far as I can tell, Toby was just a good kid who had a passion for video games."

"Toby? Are you talking about the kid who was known as the Archaeologist? I remember that. I guess I was in college when it all happened."

"Are you telling me you know something about this case?" I ask incredulously. "Let me get some paper and a pen."

I take off my fluffy blanket and set my tea on the coffee table. I run to the kitchen table where I left my tablet. I'm not really sure how I feel about my little brother being the one to provide information on Toby's case. Still, I've been in this business long enough to know that any information is better than none — even if the source make me uncomfortable.

"I'm back. So, what are you talking about?"

I hear my brother sigh, and I can almost see him running his fingers through his hair as he always does when he collects his thoughts.

"You remember that I was big into multi-player role-playing games when I was younger?

"Yeah, Mom about had a cow over the cost."

"Hey! I earned that money washing cars," he protests. "Anyway, I was a member of a lot of gaming groups online. Most of them had chat groups. There was this player who suddenly showed up in all the chat rooms. He seemed to be able to conquer every video game as soon as it came out. He would shred the levels faster than anyone I've ever seen. There was a lot of speculation about who he was. He went by the screen name The Archaeologist of Pain. Although it seemed like he could play almost any game out there, he preferred the war ones. He said he had inside information about how military battles are actually fought. Whoever he was, he wasn't just talking smack. He could beat all of us."

"So, no one knew him personally? No one played with him from his school or something like that?"

"No. A lot of people believed he was a gaming insider who got the games before they were released. Other people thought he was probably a weird pedophile. Some established gamers who lost to the Archaeologist weren't happy he was around."

"Did he get kicked out of the gaming groups because he was a kid?"

"In the beginning, people didn't even realize he was a kid. My friend Galen, worked for the Badlands National Park in South Dakota as a park ranger at the dinosaur exhibit. Apparently, this kid is a huge fan of dinosaurs. So, he made arrangements with his teacher for Galen to remote into his classroom and do a lecture on fossils. Toby turned out to be a kid getting ready to go into the seventh grade. Galen didn't bust him on the gaming boards because Toby was actually making friends and being helpful to other players. A lot of people wanted to hate him, but he was just so darn nice people started looking up to him."

"Did Galen know that Toby wasn't even supposed to be playing video games?"

"I don't think so. Most people assumed the Archaeologist of Pain was a homeless person because his time online was so limited. Some members of the board researched his IP address because some people thought he was up to no good. Almost always, they came back to the public library. A bunch of us had a discussion about raising money for him and his family to get a place to live."

"Oh, wow! So, what happened with that?" I ask.

"He announced online that he was going to get to do something cool with his family that most people dream about and he had a countdown clock in his signature. I don't know exactly when he disappeared, but it was a few weeks before he was supposed to do whatever exciting thing he had planned, and no one heard from the Archaeologist of Pain again."

"Did anybody alert the police?"

"And tell them what? That a kid who was really good at video games suddenly stopped playing? Most people didn't have any idea who he was — or that he was a child. Galen tried to contact the school, but they told him that state and federal laws prevented them from disclosing any information about their students, and he wasn't able to get anywhere."

"Did Galen have any contact information for Toby's mother?"

"He did. But he was never able to reach anyone."

"I guess I need to speak to Galen. He probably has more details about the situation, and it's better for me to talk to him than to have you relay the story to me secondhand."

"I'm sorry. That won't be possible, Sis."

"Why? He won't want to be part of an investigation?"

"No. That's not it. If Galen were around, he would want to be right in the middle of the effort to find Toby. Unfortunately, he was killed serving overseas."

"I'm sorry you lost your friend Will. That's awful."

"Yeah, I am too. He was so excited about being in the military too. He tried to get me to enlist."

"A history of epilepsy and military service don't usually go together."

"I know that, but he was convinced I could get a waiver. Seriously, Kendall, can you see me as a soldier?"

"It would've been an interesting exercise at least. I don't know if it would've been more frustrating for you or the drill Sergeant. You don't conform well."

"That's the understatement of the year. I've been trying to convince you for years a little nonconformity would be good for you. It looks like Mr. Tall, Dark, and Handsome was the one to convince you to spread your wings."

"Oh yeah. Jameson is pretty good at that. He pushes my buttons and pisses me off — and then in the next heartbeat, he does something so generous and selfless I wonder why I was so pissed. It's kind of cool though because he doesn't mind arguing a point with me and it never seems to bother him if I'm right."

"That is worth its weight in gold right there because you, Kendall Kordes, like to argue. You need the right kind of guy to get a handle on your sass."

"I'm not all that sassy!"

"Uh-huh, if it wasn't you, then who was it who argued with me for forty-five minutes about the proper way to sort recycling?"

"Hey now! Oregonians are serious about our trash."

"I noticed. But the fate of the planet isn't going to be decided on one wrongly sorted yogurt container, I promise."

"Okay, I concede that I'm a little anal-retentive when it comes to all that stuff."

"I hate to remind you that you are fastidious and picky about everything. It's part of your charm. It's also why you're really good at your job."

"Speaking of my job, would you be willing to come out to see me in Oregon? I think you should speak to the investigators working on Jameson's case. It sounds like you have more first-hand knowledge than anyone else we've spoken to — even if it is only through the Internet. That's more than we had before."

"I don't see any reason why I can't. I'm between projects right now. This is a pretty good time. I just have to let Mom know I won't be around to check on her."

"There's one snag in the plan though. I can't send you an airline ticket. I just let go of my part-time job and things are tight because I won't get a pay raise until the new grant cycle. I'm so sorry."

"I'm not fifteen Kendall. I've got my own means. I promise."

"How could you possibly? Mom says you still don't have a job."

"I don't have a job she recognizes as work, but I have a stellar job."

"Oh, please tell me it's not posting ads to Facebook and Instagram or something like that."

"Now it's my turn to ask who do you think I am?"

"Sadly, I don't even know. I've been gone from home for so long. I probably won't even recognize you. These days, clearly, I don't even know what you do for a living."

"I do the same thing I used to do when we were kids. It's just on a bigger scale. I find a problem, and I fix it. I'm an inventor."

I'm glad my brother can't see me roll my eyes. I think they just landed on next Wednesday.

"I was hoping to have you here in person, but maybe it would be better to hold the meeting over video conference call instead."

"Kendall, listen to me. When I tell you I don't have to worry about it, I *really* don't have to worry about it. Did you see the Kickstarter campaign I sent you for power coil? The Power Coil — The Charger That Makes All Other Chargers Obsolete".

"Yeah, I saw that. It reminds me of what you used to do when you were messing around in class. Didn't Mom have to go to the principal's office because you were tearing apart pens? It's too bad you didn't get a patent on it back then."

"I did." Will answers.

"You got a patent?" I ask, thinking I must've misunderstood him.

"Yeah, I was sitting in my college class listening to a professor who didn't know anything about technology or the emerging-market of accessories. He was too busy telling me about ad models that were so old they could've come from a 1960s textbook. I decided I could do better than that on my own."

"That's why you dropped out of college? Mom thought it had to do with Dad's disappearance."

"It did — and it didn't. I dropped out of college for me. I was so bored that I wasn't learning anything, and my grades sucked. I'm sure it works for some people. For me, it just wasn't my thing. I figured if I could put all the energy I was wasting at college into my inventions, I could come up with a way to pay for private investigators to look for Dad."

"Wow! That was a risky strategy. From the outside, it didn't look like you had a strategy at all. It's funny. I spent all this time trying to stay in college and get scholarships to try to complete my degree. I patched together one class after another while I worked while you were trying to avoid college altogether. I don't know — I just think there's something ironic about that."

"I tried to explain, but you were busy trying to cope with Quinn's death. I didn't want to get in the way. I figured at some point I'd probably have the opportunity to explain why I made the choices I did. So, I guess this is it. Samsung, Apple, and Nokia started a bidding war for my patent and my prototype. It's fair to say we'll be able to send our great, great, great grandkids to college on what I earned from the sale of the patent."

"Are you serious?" I gasp.

"I swear on my signed copy of Goosebumps."

"I have one question for you — why in the heck is Mom still working? Her back and her knees are killing her."

"Believe me, I've tried! Mom is stubborn. She doesn't believe the money is real. She thinks the bank made a mistake. Dad spent time making furniture before he went missing. That's what Mom thinks people buy and sell. She doesn't understand intellectual property, and she has no idea how much my invention was worth."

"In her defense, I have no idea either. If you told me, it would probably scare me half to death."

"Let's just say I hope Locate My Heart has a fundraiser soon because it would make me so proud to be able to hand over a big old check."

"You don't have to do that, Will. I loved you when you were poor, and I'll love you if you're rich or anywhere in between."

"I know that. That's why I want to do it. Trust me,

my friends who showed up just because I've got money now have received nothing. You remember how they treated me in high school. It's amazing how popular I've become."

"I'm sorry, Will. It shouldn't be that way. My friend Tristan, who runs Identity Bank, knows about that. Maybe you should talk to him."

"I don't know if I'd be able to do that. The guy is revered in the gaming community. I'd probably sound like a shrieking teenage girl at a rock concert."

"From what I understand about Tristan, he'd probably be very confused but very gracious about that. I think you need to talk to him. Come to think of it, you two should discuss a few things. He's got an initiative within his company to make technology more accessible."

"That's cool. Some games cause me real issues."

"That's what I'm talking about. He's looking at making his games more user-friendly for people who have migraines and seizure disorders. However, the reason he started his company was to look for his sister. Identity Bank is renowned for its ability to find lost people. If you want the best to look for Dad, Identity Bank is who you need"

"I'll look into it, but I don't think you know what you're asking. Meeting Tristan and the people who work for him is like meeting royalty."

"Did you ever consider that he might think the same thing of you? Tristan is an inventor too. It's not often he'll run into someone who started a three-way bidding war over something they dreamed up in the middle of social studies. Seriously, I'm so proud of you. Not everyone would've had the foresight to apply for a patent. That was flat-out brilliant."

My brother clears his throat. "Well, I guess I have my moments."

"You do. Now, I need some of your brilliance to rub off on me. I have to figure out how to do one of the most difficult things I've ever had to do."

"What's that?"

"I have to break up with a guy I'm falling in love with to preserve the integrity of the investigation into his little brother. I don't know that there's any way on the planet to make that an easier process."

CHAPTER FOURTEEN

JAMESON

HEATHER TRIES TO DISTRACT Tyler from his pool shot by unbuttoning the top button of her blouse. He sinks two balls anyway.

"Should I really congratulate you for that?" she teases. "I thought chivalry was alive and well. You're supposed to let me win."

Tyler grins. "All is fair in love and war — or pool, Gidget."

Heather looks up at me. "When is Kendall coming? The women need more players on our team."

"I don't know. When I talked to her yesterday, she said she was really looking forward to it. It is not like Kendall to run late."

"You might want to look at your phone," Tara instructs.

"I didn't hear it ring."

"Check it anyway. Don't respond right away. Think about it for a while. You know Kendall well enough to know that she wouldn't do anything to hurt you," Tara says mysteriously.

Knowing Tara's reputation, my heart sinks to my toes as I dig my phone out of my pocket. Sure enough, there is a voicemail from Kendall. I plug my earbud in and walk outside so I can hear it.

Kendall's voice sounds clogged with tears as I listen to the recording. "Shoot! I was hoping to be able to talk to you about this, but maybe it's easier I don't. For now, I think it would be better if I don't see you. I need to talk to Tyler about this first before we make any radical moves … but for now we need to stay apart."

I stuff the phone back in my pocket and try to make sense of it all. I come up with nothing. I thought things were getting better between us since we started climbing at Aidan's place. Our relationship seemed to be moving in the right direction and she acted like things were getting back to where they were before we talked about her ex-fiancé and Quinn. I know I blew that conversation. I've apologized to Kendall several times. I thought we'd put that behind us. I don't know what this is about. I guess there's only one way to find out. I stride back into the pub and tap Tyler on the shoulder. "I need to talk to you."

"Right now? I'm kind of in the middle of something," Ty responds.

I mess with my baseball cap and bounce my weight from foot to foot. "I know — but this is important."

He looks at Heather, Tara and Aidan. "I guess I'll be right back. Order me some cheesy fries, will you?"

"Sure thing. If you're not back, we'll just eat without

you," Aidan replies with a shrug.

Tyler and I walk out to my rental car. "You've been here long enough that it might be cheaper for you just to buy a car," he says as he observes my tags.

"Yeah, I know. I've decided I like this car so much that I'm going to buy one just like it from their fleet sale. I'll just give it to my parents when I go home."

"I figured you might want to stick around. I thought you and Kendall were a done deal."

"We were until we weren't. When I met Kendall, all my priorities changed. Or, at least I thought they did, and then I got this message. Do you know anything about this?"

Tyler takes my phone and puts it up to his ear as he listens to Kendall's voicemail. "I swear, I have no idea what she's talking about. It sounds like she and I need to have a conversation ASAP."

"I appreciate that. If I'm going to be screwed over, I'd kinda like to know why."

"I'd wait to jump to that conclusion," he cautions.

"I've always had a hunch Kendall and Locate My Heart were simply too good to be true. This may turn out to be my confirmation."

"I hope not. I like seeing the two of you happy together."

<hr>

"Are you enjoying your visit home?" Tristan asks me as he spins a fidget toy.

I pull away from the camera on my iPad. "Most of

the time it's been great — right now I think I'd rather be in another state."

"What's going on?"

"Oh, just personal stuff — nothing you need to be worried about."

"Related to the search for your brother?" Tristan presses.

"Honestly, I wish I knew."

"Oh … one of *those* situations. Hopefully, it will resolve itself soon."

"I hope so too. Being in limbo is the pits."

"Hey, I wanted to run something by you. I met with my accountant yesterday. It's been a banner year for Identity Bank. The new software division John Ashford is leading is taking off like gangbusters."

"That's great! Doing the right thing isn't always the same as doing the profitable thing. It's cool when it is."

"You're right about that. I'm glad we were able to pull it off. That division means a lot to me. Identity Bank has grown so much that I'm thinking about opening a West Coast branch. I already work with Logan Anthony and Katie Ashford to protect Aidan and Mindy. We've expanded that coverage to include Jude and Tasha. It's a lot to handle remotely. I think Identity Bank would work more efficiently if we had a presence on both coasts."

"Seems like a solid plan to me," I remark. I'm not sure what Tristan wants me to say, but it makes sense.

"I don't think you're quite getting my drift here, Payne."

"What do you mean, sir?" I ask reflexively.

"I'm asking you if you'd like to be in charge of the operation," Tristan answers with a grin.

"Sir? I'm the just computer guy. You want me to be in charge of opening a whole new branch of Identity Bank?"

"You do realize that I actually read the background information about the people I hire to protect people's identity, right?"

Feeling foolish, I murmur, "Yes, sir."

"I may not have served in the military, but people around me have. Your job involved a lot more than just a few virus checks and computer programming skills. Without exception, all of your reference letters praised your ability to organize big projects and be a team leader. They told me what I already know about you which is you are a stickler for details, and not much escapes your notice. You are exactly the kind of person I look for when I start a new venture. I think you're perfect for the job."

"Thanks, it's a lot to take in right now — things are up in the air on every front here."

"It appears you're going to be in Oregon for a while. Why don't you find a place to rent? It seems like it would be far more comfortable than staying in a hotel. I'd rather pay for you to be in a place which suits you. Do you still have the AutoCAD software on your computer?"

"I do," I answer as I take a mental catalog of the software on my computer.

"If you decide you want to lead this project, let me know. We can have a video session dedicated just to the planning. There are a lot of pieces of the puzzle we need to put together to make this work."

"I know, I need to figure this out. Is Joe Summers good to stay in my place for a while longer?"

"Yeah, it is close to his son's school, so it works out great."

"I wonder if he'd be willing to take over my lease. I just signed one before I came out to Oregon. I can take the hit if I need to for breaking the lease, but if he likes it, maybe we can work something out."

"By the way, I think Scout may have adopted Joe's son. Scout seems to calm Brody down."

"Yeah, if I'd had the time, I was planning to run Scout through Mitch's therapy dog program. If you have a chance, tell Mitch thanks for kenneling Scout until Joe could move into my place. As much as I love him, I always felt awful when I was on the road and had to leave him behind. Maybe it's a good thing he has bonded with a real family."

"Correct me if I'm wrong, but it sounds like you've made your decision," Tristan ventures.

"Look, I'll be honest with you. If you would've asked me the day before yesterday, I would've been all over it. It seemed like I had a great girlfriend and I love being able to pop in and see my parents to make sure that they're okay. I don't know what happened in the last couple of days, but it seems like maybe things aren't going to work out between Kendall and me. She has cut off all contact, and I don't know why."

"Did you go badmouthing Locate My Heart again?

You know that place is her passion. She has big dreams for ways that she can make Locate My Heart more efficient. A person like you could really help her make those dreams come true."

"I know that. I've been working with her about how to streamline her process using the new equipment and software that you and Aidan were able to provide."

"Don't underestimate Kendall. She's crazy smart and learns very quickly."

"I know that! I know I was a jerk in the beginning, but I've learned more about who she is and why she does what she does. It all makes more sense to me now. Or, at least it was making more sense until she pulled the rug out from under me. She's not even returning text messages. It's like she disappeared into a black hole."

"That's weird. It seems very out of character for her. Did she give you a heads up?"

"All I got from her was a voicemail telling me that she couldn't be around me or talk to me until she talked to Tyler. Tyler swears up and down he doesn't know what's going on. I don't know what to think. You know I have a horrific past with places like this. I had to help my parents file bankruptcy because of what unscrupulous search agencies, psychics and private eyes that were anything but private did to them. My tolerance for this kind of crap is really low. I hope she's not pulling something on me. I really like her. I was starting to see white picket fences in our future."

"I wouldn't write that dream off yet. I've worked with Kendall before. What you see with her is what you get. Probably more than anyone else — except Mindy,

Kendall wears her emotions on her sleeve and all over her face. I have never known her to be anything but straightforward. If she says she needs to talk to Tyler before she can be with you, there must be a solid reason."

"I wish Kendall would tell me what is going on," I grouse.

"Maybe she can't. I think you need to wait this one out. Don't do anything rash — and that includes taking the promotion with me. Wait to see how this plays out. Spend some time with your family while you're in Oregon and take a real vacation."

⸺ • ⸺

"You don't have to keep bringing us food; I'm still capable of cooking," my mom insists as I come through the door with a large lasagna pan and a bowl of salad.

I stop to kiss her cheek before I put everything on the kitchen table. "I know Mom. I was pet-sitting for a friend of mine, and he has a kitchen that would make an award-winning restaurant jealous. I just couldn't resist whipping up a couple batches of lasagna just to try out his stuff. There is no way I can keep this in my little refrigerator at the hotel room. So, I brought it to you guys."

"How long are you going to stay at that place? It's just not right to have you living out of a hotel. I thought your job here was short-term. Are there more problems at Locate My Heart?"

"No, not computer problems. Tristan had me stick around. He was hoping I would take some time off, but I'm too antsy to take a long vacation — so I started working on a project for Silent Beats."

"You're going to think I'm silly, but could you get Tasha and Jude's autograph for me? They just seem like the sweetest couple. Are they anything like they are on television?"

"I think you'd really like them. Jude is shy and respectful. He loves Tasha like the air he breathes."

My mom clutches her hands in front of her heart. "Oh, you can't know how relieved I am to hear that. Sometimes you read that a celebrity is one way on stage; but when they're off-stage, they're the complete opposite. I didn't want that to be true about Tasha and Jude."

"You can put your mind at rest, Mom. Everyone that works with Aidan has been incredibly nice. Just like you would hope."

"I saw Aidan once. Your dad took me out for dinner for Valentine's Day, and we went to this little out-of-the-way bar. Aidan was there with Tara and he was serenading her for their anniversary. It was the sweetest thing."

"Please tell me you didn't bug them for pictures," I reply.

"Oh heavens no. I wouldn't interrupt a beautiful moment like that for pictures. They deserved to celebrate their anniversary just like everyone else. It was still neat to see though."

"I've had a chance to hang out with Aidan and Tara quite a bit now. They are the most normal stars I've ever seen in my life. Everyone around them is exceptionally friendly."

My mom's eyes light up. "Does that mean you've made friends here and you might actually stay this time?"

"Would that be something you and Dad would like?" I ask, choosing my words carefully.

"Of course, we would. Having both of you boys gone breaks my heart every day. I would love to have you back here."

"I'm looking at some options, I'll see what I can do, Mom. I miss you too."

"I don't want to pry, but is this about your relationship with Kendall? You know, there's an awful lot to like about that girl. I don't think I could've done better if I'd hand picked a match for you."

"Really? Some days, it feels like all we ever do is butt heads."

"That's good. It shows you both care about a lot of things and developed your own opinions. That's not a bad thing. It's not if you fight, but how you fight and how you leave it between the two of you."

"Mom, Kendall won't even talk to me or answer my texts."

"Did she tell you what's going on?"

"She said she couldn't have any contact with me until she talks to our friend Tyler."

"Well, Kendall seems pretty level-headed to me. If she says there was a reason she can't be in touch, I would take her at her word."

"I just wish she would figure this all out. I miss her like crazy."

"When you were a baby, I used to tell people you were born inpatient. I see not much has changed. Give Kendall some time to sort out what's going on. If she's worth hanging onto, she'll be back," my mom advises as she gives me a warm hug.

Chapter Fifteen

Kendall

Tyler brings me a styrofoam cup filled with tea and sets it down on the table in the interrogation room. After he takes a seat, he crosses his foot on top of his other knee and balances a yellow legal pad on it. "I have to be honest with you; I thought we'd meet and have coffee at the shop down the street. I was surprised when you said you wanted to hold the meeting in my office. Does this mean our conversation is professional rather than personal?"

"I don't know. It's a complicated question. Jameson and my professional lives and personal lives have been irrevocably intertwined since the first moment we met. I don't know how to separate them anymore. I thought I could keep my private life private and confine my work with Locate My Heart to business hours only, but that's not the way it's turning out," I admit in a tearful voice.

Tyler leans forward and hands me a tissue from the box on the table. "First, I need you to breathe. Whatever it is, we'll sort through it."

"I don't know what to think. This could be good news, or it could destroy everything between Jameson and me. Still, I have to share it. I can't keep it to myself even though I know it could destroy every bit of happiness in my life right now."

"It sounds like there's an important story here. Let's start at the beginning. What brings you in today?"

"Jameson said he told you about Toby. Is that correct?"

"Jameson mentioned it to me. He was concerned about getting his parent's hopes up again because the last search was so disastrous for them."

"See? That's exactly what I mean. I wonder whether I pushed him into searching for his brother because I wanted to show him that our services at Locate My Heart are not the same as the flim-flam artists he worked with before. What if I backed him into a corner?"

"And what if you didn't?" Ty presses.

I take a few deep breaths as I try to calm down enough to tell him the whole story. "Actually, that's why I'm here today. There's a potential new lead in Toby's case. But, for me it's complicated. I'm not sure how to proceed."

"I'm sorry, Kendall, you need to tell me more details than that."

"Ty, I'm so embarrassed. I knew better than to get involved with a client or even a potential client. I knew Jameson is in a vulnerable place and sharing things with me he doesn't ever share with anyone. I feel like I'm taking advantage of our relationship. I don't know how to back out of it. Now, this new complication has cropped up."

"Do you want to call if off with Jameson?" Ty asks me pointedly.

"No! I don't. I fell for Jameson hook line and sinker. I never expected it because I haven't been involved with anyone since Quinn died. I don't even know how to process all of this."

"Process all of what?"

"If I'm honest with myself, there hasn't been a time in our relationship where we haven't had some tension. As long as I am in this line of work, Jameson is going to feel uneasy about what I do. He's been burned too many times in the past. He's trying to protect his parents. I understand that. I'm not even questioning the way he feels about what I do."

"It could make it tough, for sure."

"If I were in his shoes, I'd feel the same way. I know how betrayal feels. After Quinn died, I joined a grief support group. I thought everything I shared in that group was private and confidential. Later, I ran across something that I'd written about Quinn's death posted on an Internet site without my permission."

"That's terrible. Anybody who's in a group like that expects that their thoughts will be private. I know I did when I was dealing with my post-traumatic stress disorder."

"You don't just get over it. So, I'm worried about whether we can ever have a good relationship if he always views me as the thing that reminds him of the worst time in his life."

"This is just a bump in the road. Y'all can fix this. But, this isn't a new issue between the two of you. What brings you in today?"

I bury my face in my hands for a moment. "You may change your mind about complications when I tell you my brother might actually know a lot more about it than any of us do. He apparently knows Toby from hanging out on the Internet. I guess they used to frequent lots of the same gaming sites."

Tyler whistles softly between his teeth. "That might be the biggest break this case has ever had."

"I know! What do I do about it? I don't want to be the focus of this — but I also don't want to have to break up with Jameson just because of my brother's online friends."

"That's understandable. You had no way of knowing Toby's life would somehow intersect with your brother's."

"But I don't want to taint this investigation. I had no idea that this case would involve my own family members."

"Kendall, you have solid instincts. You were right to keep your distance from Jameson until we get this all sorted out. I know it is less than ideal, but you're right. The investigation into Toby's disappearance should come first."

"I may be worrying for nothing. I love my brother, but he kind of floats through life. I don't even know what details he focuses on and which ones he ignores. He has a different sensibility about things than most people."

"Why don't you tell me what you know and we can go from there?" Tyler says gently.

In a rush of seemingly chaotic words, I recount the story Will told me and fill in the parts I learned from the original investigators findings.

When I finish, we take a break. Tyler brings me a hot cup of tea and a few cookies Heather made.

He sits down at his desk and looks back through his notes. "So, the next logical step would be to talk to your brother. Where does your brother live?"

"Lincoln, Nebraska," I answer.

"Okay … that's a little farther away than I expected."

"Don't worry about it. My brother is planning to come out for our birthday this weekend."

"That's good. We can always hold these things over a video conference call, but they never seem as productive to me because I can't read the person's body language as well on camera."

"Allegedly, William will be here live and in person to answer our questions."

"Why do you say allegedly?"

"William has been known to change his plans at the last minute without notice. So, I hate to promise anything. He and I operate on a different vibe. I am a planner by nature, and he likes to be spontaneous and make decisions based on his gut."

"I see," Ty responds as he finishes taking notes. "Jameson doesn't understand what's going on and he's jumping to all the wrong conclusions."

"Of course, he is. He is Jameson. It's part of his nature to be skeptical. His life experiences haven't given him reason to change his mind about things. But, you see my problem here — if I tell him that there has been a development with Toby's case involving my brother, he'll move heaven and earth to talk to William. You know good and well that if he does that, it might compromise the investigation. So, what am I supposed to do?"

"Let me handle that part. If you can, please avoid talking to Jameson until I've spoken with your brother. I need to get William's account straight from him before he encounters any more outside interference."

"I wish you luck. I've been stewing over this for a couple of days. I can't come up with the right answer. Anything I do is going to hurt Jameson. Maybe coming from you, it might not be so painful."

I grimace as I hear my phone ping again. I know without looking it's probably another text message from Jameson.

Brynley walks by my desk. "Are you ever going to put that man out of his misery?"

"I wish I could. But it's not that simple. There are huge stakes involved and they're bigger than just the relationship between us."

"Wow! Sucks to be you."

I laugh at Brynley's vernacular, but she's not wrong.

"Some days, it really does."

The phone on my desk rings. "Geez! Can the man not get a clue?" Brynley exclaims as she rolls her eyes.

I shrug as I answer the phone, "Locate My Heart, this is Kendall. How can I help you?"

"Umm ... Hi Kendall, this is Bethany Livingston."

"Bethany? How are you doing?"

"I'm good. No, I'm pretty great now that Asher is back. I'm one of the lucky ones. He picked up with nursing right where he left off. All that pumping was worth it, I guess. I have a freezer full of milk, but I'm still managing to nurse him through it. My pediatrician is amazed at my stubbornness throughout the process. He thought I would have to quit."

"That's great news!"

"I called to ask you a strange question."

"I get lots of odd questions in this job, don't worry about it."

"Did you ever get a chance to speak directly to Naomi Fitzgerald?"

"Briefly. She called after the whole event was over to apologize for her aunt's behavior."

"What'd you think of her? Did you get a good gut feeling? Do you think she was genuine or do you think she really wanted to take Asher?"

"This is only my opinion, but I believe she was an innocent bystander that was caught up in her aunt's delusion. I don't think she had anything to do with it. She was just trying to cope with an adoption gone terribly wrong."

"I'm glad to hear that because that's how I feel too, but Edwin thinks I'm crazy."

"Has she contacted you guys?" I ask as my stomach tightens with unease.

"Yes, I got a beautiful handwritten letter from her apologizing for the whole incident. She would like to meet me for coffee to apologize in person because she's going to be in Oregon for a conference. She's willing to meet me in Portland to talk."

"How do you feel about that?"

"I want to look her in the face and see what I think. I'm still trying to figure out why this happened to my family. Maybe she has answers."

"Would you like me to go with you?" I offer.

"No, you've gone above and beyond the call of duty to help us. I need to face this one on my own."

"Are you sure? Because it's no bother."

"Okay, I would feel better if you were there. Can you sit a couple of tables away? I can signal you if I need you."

"That sounds like a good plan. When is Naomi coming?"

"A month from today. She wants to meet at three o'clock in the afternoon because her conference ends at noon."

I open the calendar app on my computer. "I'm completely free that day, so I'll put you on my schedule."

"Now, I have to convince my husband I haven't

completely lost my marbles. Men can be so difficult."

My phone pings again twice in a row to indicate I have messages. I scowl at my cell phone before saying to Bethany, "I'll give you an amen to that!"

———◆◆———

I wait until seven thirty before I check my messages. As I suspected, almost all of them are from Jameson. But there is one from my brother announcing that he will be here early. My knees buckle with relief.

I text him back and tease, *Is there any way you can get here tomorrow?*

A message pops up immediately.

Do you need me there?

Honestly, I'd love it if you could come tomorrow. Things are really complicated here.

"Sis, all you had to do was ask," he texts back.

I tire of texting him, so I change to FaceTime and wait for him to answer.

"What happened to you? You look terrible — are you having trouble sleeping again?"

"Yeah, things are a mess in my life. I am officially asking for a favor. You might get rewarded with peanut butter and chocolate chip cookies when all this is all over."

"You know I'm always up for those. Mostly I've always wanted to walk into the airport and buy a first-class ticket to leave last-minute and not worry about the price."

I laugh out loud. "You're such a weirdo!"

"Yeah, but you're my twin, so what does that say about you?" Will responds, relying on a taunt from childhood.

"Let me know if you want me to pick you up at the airport."

"Are you kidding? Do you know what kind of car I can rent with a card that has no credit limit on it?"

"Careful, Will. You're going to spend yourself into the poor house again," I warn.

"You're such a party pooper. Maybe you'll change your mind when you get to ride in my cool set of wheels."

"Maybe, but I doubt it," I answer. "I'll see you tomorrow. I love you."

After I hang up with William, I read the text messages from Jameson. Each one is progressively less hopeful and his final text breaks my heart.

If you wanted off my brother's case, all you had to do was say something. You didn't have to destroy us. I feel like a fool for believing you were different from the rest.

Jameson, as much as I want to talk to you, I can't. Please contact Tyler. He can explain more. Hopefully, I'll be able to tell you the whole story soon.

I wait for him to respond and nothing comes. In a pattern that's becoming all too frequent, I cry myself to sleep.

Chapter Sixteen

Jameson

I place a cold towel around my neck as I guzzle a bottle of water. I take a moment to rest my head on the back of the couch as I cool down. I try to keep my thoughts on my job, but all I can think about is getting things resolved with Kendall.

Tara walks through the break room at Silent Beats. "I brought you something, I figured you might need it after spending the morning in the crawlspace." She offers me an Aidan O'Brien T-shirt emblazoned with the word crew on the back.

I gratefully take it from her.

"Aidan has showers upstairs if you want to take one. You're bigger than Aidan, but I'm sure Jerome has an extra pair of jeans you can borrow."

"Thanks, I appreciate that. Fiberglass is nasty. I've got all the wiring from the new system hidden now though. There should be enough power for both the recording system and the computer network now that you had the electrician put in a new box. Before I started working for you guys, I had no concept of what a complex process it is to record a song."

"I felt the same way when I first saw Aidan record a duet. I grew up listening to him play the piano, and that was complicated enough. When you add all the sound engineering and mixing of voices, it gets really technical."

"Says the ballet dancer," I tease.

My phone buzzes to indicate I have a text message and I eagerly check the screen. Unfortunately, it's just Joe Summers asking me if he needs to pay the bill for trash pickup.

After I respond to him, I scroll through my messages again to see if I missed anything from Kendall. I'm still trying to wrap my brain around what could be causing her to stay away from me. I need to take a break and go talk to Tyler.

"Hey, after I take a shower, I need to bug out for a while. I'll be back tomorrow to hang the last cameras and your new monitor in the rehearsal room. Is that all right with you?"

"Of course. Why do you think I brought you clean clothes? I'll put Jerome's jeans outside the bathroom door. I don't know what to tell you about Kendall. I've been in her shoes more times than I care to count. Sometimes, when you know more than you can disclose, it puts you in a no-win situation. Please listen to what Tyler has to say, and try to look at it from Kendall's point of view. I suspect you'll find that she is trying to work for your best interests — even if it might not seem like it right now. I know you have no reason to trust me, but I believe Kendall is trying to save your relationship."

"Why? What did she do wrong? Why is she trying to hide from me? If she wants to sort all this out, why doesn't she do it directly with me?" I demand.

"Sometimes, it's a matter of timing. Trust me. You're just going to have to wait this one out."

"You sound like my mom. That's what she told me."

"You might want to listen to her." Tara shrugs.

I yank my hat off and throw it on the couch along with the damp towel as I sit down and take my shoes off. "I don't understand why no one will be straight with me. Everybody keeps telling me I need to wait to find answers. I'm not the one who backed away. Why can't I just talk this out with Kendall?"

"I don't think you heard me. Kendall is trying to protect you and your relationship. You can go into the meeting with Tyler believing the best about Kendall or you can feed your own fears about the situation. It's up to you. I'm sorry, I've already said more than I probably should — but, I don't want you to throw away a chance at happiness just because Kendall is trying to do the right thing."

"What right thing?" I bellow. "I thought things were getting better between us, but now I don't know. If we can't talk through our problems or differences, what point is there in being in a relationship?"

After I take a seat in Tyler Colton's office, he doesn't even bother with polite small talk before he drills down on me. "Are you done being a jerk? I thought you were through with that phase of your relationship with Kendall. Either you trust her or you don't. If she tells you she can't talk to you, there's a reason why. I need you to respect that. Read between the lines here. As a law enforcement officer, I need you to understand that Kendall *can't* talk to you right now. It's not personal — at least not in the way you're assuming. So, back off and leave her alone until this is resolved. Please … you're complicating my life."

I sink back against the vinyl chair as I absorb the Sheriff's words. That's the most words I have ever heard Tyler string together in a row. Generally, he doesn't say much. He is pretty low-key and non-confrontational. For him to challenge me directly means this must be serious. "Kendall isn't in any danger, is she?"

Tyler looks startled by my question. "Not as far as I know. This is about an issue much larger than the future of your relationship with Kendall — which, by the way, you guys need to fix after this is over."

"How can it be bigger than the future of us?" All the pieces of some weird kaleidoscope in my brain suddenly come together with nauseating clarity. "Crap, she knows something about Toby, doesn't she? Is he dead? Is she afraid to tell me that she didn't get to him in time? She promised me that if we reopened the search, she would do her best to bring him back to my family. Now, she's ducking out. If he's dead, why wouldn't she just tell me? If this is how Locate My Heart treats families, their customer service needs a tune-up."

Tyler stands up. Even when I stand up and match his posture, his height is impressive and imposing. "You best think about the words that are flying out of your mouth. They won't taste very good when you have to eat them. Calm down and stop making assumptions. To repeat what I said before: Kendall told you that she can't talk to you at the moment. You need to honor that. What you decide to do with your relationship isn't part of my responsibilities as a sheriff. But, as your friend, I'm telling you not to jump to conclusions that are going to chip away at the foundation of your relationship with Kendall. It's just not worth it."

Tyler's curt tone with me reminds me of my days in basic training. Instinctively, I straighten my posture and fight the urge to salute as I turn on my heel and say, "Thank you for the advice, sir. Perhaps one day it will make sense."

"For your sake, I hope it does," Tyler tosses toward my back as I stride out of his office.

As usual, I find my father working in his wood shop. "What are you working on?" I greet.

"Oh, your mother nicked her favorite pair of knitting needles, so I decided to make her some new ones for her birthday." He holds one up for me to see.

"Dad, those are beautiful. Mom is going to love them. When you're done with that project, I brought you a piece of wood for your walking canes." I hold it sideways so he can see the wood pattern under the place

I stripped off the bark. "I love the grain on this one. There are little burls everywhere."

My dad takes it from me and examines it carefully. "Wow, isn't that something? Where did you find this?"

"Would you believe I found it just off the jogging path behind Kendall's house? It must've blown down in the big windstorm we had a couple of weeks ago."

"Where is that gal of yours? I love it when she comes to visit me because she brings the most delicious food. I never know what it's going to be, but I'm never disappointed."

"Well, you might be disappointed now. I don't know if Kendall is going to be around anymore."

"What do you mean, son?"

"At the moment, we're not exactly talking."

"Ahh … I see. Your mom and I have been there many times."

"Seriously? I always figured you guys never fought. I never remember seeing any arguments as a kid."

"We tried to keep it from you and your brother. When two strong-minded people get together, there's bound to be conflict. So, you've got two choices — you can try to talk through it, or you can give her some space to come around."

"I don't think I have much choice. Kendall's not even responding to my voicemails or text messages. She says she can't talk to me right now."

"So, space it is. I know that by nature you want to fix everything. But sometimes, time is the only tool you need."

I scrub my hand down my face in frustration. "Why does everyone keep telling me that?"

"Sometimes the answer we don't want to hear is the correct one."

"Dad, you sound like a fortune cookie." I chuckle.

"That might be true, but it doesn't mean my advice isn't sound."

"I just wish I had all this settled. I have decisions I need to make."

"What kind of decisions?" my dad asks.

"Tristan Macklin offered me a gargantuan promotion. I'm still trying to decide what to do."

"Isn't that a good thing?" My dad asks with a perplexed expression

"Normally it would be, but Tristan wants me to be in charge of developing a whole new branch of Identity Bank on the West Coast. I don't know if I'm ready for that kind of responsibility."

"Son, you were in the U.S. Army. You were in charge of keeping our men alive. I can't think of any bigger responsibility than that. If you can handle that, setting up a new business should be a total cakewalk."

My dad and I don't talk much about my military service. When I first joined directly after high school, my parents as lifelong educators were disappointed I decided not to go to college. Over the years, they've come to accept that the military was a good choice for me. Still, I had no idea my dad thought of my service in such glowing terms.

"The thing is, as homesick as I am, I don't want to

make a move all the way back here and regret it because Kendall and I keep running into each other in our mutual circle of friends — that would be purgatory. I didn't plan on it, but I've given Kendall my heart. I never realized how perfect she is for me until she disappeared from my life."

"When the time is right, make sure you tell her how you feel — and I'm not just saying that because I want you to get your butt back in Oregon. It might be hard at the moment, but it won't be hard forever."

"Dad, that's just the thing … I'm afraid I've blown it and I'm not sure what I did exactly. I thought we had worked through our problems and now I'm not so sure. I can't fix what I don't understand."

"Then you need to work harder on understanding what the problem is. Even if that means being patient until she can tell you what the real issue is."

"You may have noticed that patience isn't my long suit," I admit with a shrug.

My dad laughs out loud. "At what point in this conversation did you forget that you are my son? This is not a newsflash to me. I've known you since the day you were born. The interesting thing about being in a relationship is they allow us to work on our weaknesses. So, get to it, son. It may be the most important thing you ever do."

CHAPTER SEVENTEEN

KENDALL

BRYNLEY RUNS INTO MY office. She looks flushed and out of breath. "I don't know how you do it, but there's another cute guy sitting out in the parking lot asking for you."

I smile at her wide-eyed expression. "Is he there now? What is he driving?"

"I was so distracted by his looks, I wasn't paying too much attention to his car, but I think it's a brand-new convertible Mustang. He's a man after my own heart. I love the red ones. I wish I could take a spin in it," she adds wistfully.

"Let's go see who my mystery visitor is. If it's who I think it is, he'd probably be happy to take you for a ride."

Brynley rushes ahead of me to look out the window.

"Come on, I'll introduce you."

"You actually know this guy? He's hot!" she exclaims.

"If you say so. He's not really my thing."

"How can he not be your thing? All those luscious eyelashes and his dimples go on for days," Brynley mumbles under her breath as we get closer to the car.

I walk up to the driver side and lean over and kiss him on the cheek. "I see you didn't pay any attention to my advice. You should listen to your sister. Nice wheels though."

"It was anticlimactic, if you want to know the truth. The guy at the rental place just wanted me to sign the credit card receipt. Nobody seemed to care that I rented the nicest car on the lot."

"Of course, they didn't. The rental car company was just interested in getting paid. They don't care where your money came from." I let loose with a chortle of laughter. "Did you expect them to throw you a parade?"

Will looks crestfallen. "No, I guess not. I don't know what I expected — I just thought it would be a bigger deal than it turned out to be. I mean, the car is nice, but it's still just a car."

Brynley flips her hair over her shoulder. "Just a car? Bite your tongue. This is a cherry-red Mustang Convertible. If I don't miss my guess, it's this year's model."

"Sis, you've been holding out on me. Who is this vision of loveliness and brains?" Will asks as he steps out of the rental car.

I roll my eyes at my brother's antics. Before I can answer, Brynley steps forward. "Hi, I'm Brynley. I'm an intern here. I'm studying to be a social worker."

"Impressive," my brother comments as he flashes his most charming grin.

Brynley swoons. "Why, thank you. I try to be."

Will turns to me. "Do you think it's too late for me to talk to your cop buddy? I'd just as soon get this all over with."

"No, I think you're good. Tyler is usually in his office this time of day. Do you want me to run over with you so I can introduce you?"

Brynley silently mouths, "Cop buddies?" before she presses her lips together in disapproval.

"I'm sure Sheriff Colton is looking forward to what you have to say. It could be our big break in this missing child case."

Brynley exhales when she hears the explanation. "Don't worry about anything here. I'm helping Colette put together a slideshow for the charity auction, so we'll both be in the office."

"I appreciate that. I don't know how long I'll be gone."

"You want to ride with me?" Will asks. "It'd be a shame for this monster of a car to go to waste."

"Do you realize we are going to a Sheriff's Office? You can't act like it's the Indianapolis 500."

"Well, fine if you're going to be like that," Will pouts.

"I'm your big sister. It's my job, remember?"

"You're my big sister by like three minutes. I bet if I took Brynley for a ride in this thing, she wouldn't be telling me to be careful." Will winks.

"I don't know. I guess you'll have to ask me to find out, won't you?" Brynley challenges.

"Consider yourself asked," William retorts.

<hr>

I escort my brother into Tyler's office. There's a knot in my stomach because William looks scared to death. Will is known for being adventurous and spontaneous. This is not an expression I usually see on his face.

"I don't know, Sis. Maybe I don't remember all the details as clearly as I think I do. What if I steer everyone in the wrong direction?" he whispers as we wait for Ty.

"Look, Toby has been missing for almost five years. Your information is the closest thing to a concrete lead in years. Even if it doesn't end up being the only clue that helps us find Toby Payne, it's a place to start."

"Do you think the similarities between his screen name and his last name means something?"

"I can't tell you that Will; it's not my place. But Sheriff Colton will be able to put it all in perspective."

"You know, I wouldn't do this for anybody but you."

"I don't want you to do it for me. I want you to do it for Toby Payne. If I had a missing child, I'd want someone to come forward even if they didn't know for sure if their information was helpful."

Tyler enters his office and stands in front of us as he sticks his hand out for my brother to shake. "You must be Will. Kendall is one of our favorite people around here — and it's not just because she brings us yummy stuff to eat."

"Her cooking is the bomb, isn't it?"

"It is. I understand you're here to share some information with us on a missing persons case."

"I guess I am. I wasn't even aware what I know might be important until I talked to Kendall. She thought I should share what I know with you."

"Every bit helps — especially in a cold case like this. It may turn out to be nothing, or it may turn out to be the one thing that turns this case from cold to hot."

"I hope so. The Archaeologist of Pain was a nice kid. He was without a doubt the best gamer I've ever seen — child or adult."

Tyler turns to me. "You know how this works Kendall. Our office needs to do a formal, on the record interview with your brother. I don't want his account of the situation to be influenced by your presence. Since I know the parties in this case, I'm going to have Officer Garcia do the questioning."

I hold up my big tote bag. "Is the small conference room open? I'll just go do some work."

"There's a schedule on the wall, but I think it's free. Are you sure you don't want an officer to take you home?"

"Oh, don't bother anyone. Jameson set me up with a laptop that's far more functional than the desktop I used to use. I can be mobile now. I'll just go hide away and conquer some paperwork."

"You won't let them torture me with a rubber hose

or anything, will you?" Will jokes.

I wink at my brother. "It could be considered payback for the feather duster incident. I might have to think about it."

"I was seven years old! How was I supposed to know tickling you was going to make you pee your pants?"

Tyler laughs out loud. "Come on now children. It's time to let the past go and live for the future."

Will sighs. "I hope what I tell you today will help us find Toby. He should have the chance to live for the future too."

"I couldn't agree more. We promise we'll be gentle. We just need to put the facts on the table as you know them. That's all we're trying to accomplish today."

"That's why I'm here. Let's get this done." When he catches the pensive expression on my face, he says, "Relax Sis. I'm not a seven-year-old kid anymore. I know how to adult with the best of them."

"I can't help it. I'll always worry about you. I think it's in the job description of being a big sister. Thank you for stepping up. It means more to me than I can express."

⎯⎯⎯ ◆ ⎯⎯⎯

The clock in the conference room is unbearably loud. It seems to tick off the time in slow motion. I've done everything I can think of. I've cleaned out all of my email boxes, including the junk ones. I've corresponded with people I've been neglecting for far too long. I even updated the pictures on Locate My Heart's website.

Now it's just me, Pink, and Jewel to pass the time. Well, that's not exactly true. Jameson is inhabiting about every other thought I have. If it were a normal situation, I would've been able to call him up and tell him all my hopes and fears about this development and help him understand what it means to him and his family. Unfortunately, these are not normal circumstances, and I really don't know if I handled it the right way. I hope I didn't blow everything up between us. His last few text messages seemed extremely angry and had an air of finality about them. I never wanted that to happen. I just want to make sure that every T is crossed, and every I is dotted — so if we ever find out what happened to Toby, and it involves another person, that we can bring justice to his case.

Finally, there is a knock on the conference room door. To my total shock, it's Jameson.

"Hi … um … I'm sorry. I can't talk to you right now," I stammer as I catch a hint of his cologne in the air and almost lose my resolve.

"Tyler's going to be here in a minute. He cleared us to talk to each other, but not about what's going on with my brother."

"I had a feeling this might happen. I wonder if Ty wants Locate My Heart to pull out of the case entirely?"

"I hope that doesn't happen. Both of my parents adore you. They'd be devastated if you couldn't help us anymore."

"I'm not sure what to do. I'll talk to Tyler. Still, it might be better if Colette takes over for me."

"If you can, I want you to stay on my brother's case.

Your friendship with my parents has helped them in ways I can't even describe. My mom is back to planting flowers and reading books. She even cleaned out her craft room. I know it might not seem like much, but this is the first time that I've seen them care about what's going on in the world around them in several years. They've created their own little unit. It's a while since they've let anyone into their lives, including me — now they are."

"I don't know if I had a lot to do with that. It might just be that with the renewed efforts to find Toby they are also finding some hope that they lost along the way."

"Whatever it is, I don't want my parents to backslide. I like this version of them. It reminds me of how they were before all of this happened."

"I don't know, Jameson. Maybe I shouldn't be so involved. What if things don't go as well as we hope? Are you going to forever equate me with the darkest time in your life? That doesn't bode well for us."

"I don't have any answers. I just know that not having you as part of my life isn't working for me."

I practically sob. "It's not working for me either. This has been the toughest thing I've gone through since Quinn's death. I even begged my brother to come earlier so that we could get this all settled."

"Wait? Your brother is all tied up in this?" Jameson asks incredulously.

"See? This is exactly why I have to back away. We are not even supposed to be talking about this; yet, here we are. I don't know how we separate our personal and our professional lives."

"There has to be an answer," Jameson argues. "Sacrificing our relationship isn't okay with me."

Tyler walks into the room. "It shouldn't have to be. No one is asking you to do that."

"It sure feels like that to me. I was the one left in the dark — not only about my personal life, but the search for my brother. I don't know who put Kendall in a position where she felt she had to lie, but that's not right."

I place my hand on Jameson's forearm. "Please don't blame them. This was on me. I wanted to make sure that my presence in your brother's case didn't cause any problems. As soon as William became involved, there were no good choices. I chose to protect you and your family over my heart."

"So, do we have to stay apart until my brother is found, or the perpetrator is tried ... or when exactly?" Jameson replies with a hopeless look on his face.

Tyler shakes his head. "No, I don't think we have to entertain something that severe right now. Officer Garcia was able to do a comprehensive, videotaped interview with Will."

My brother peeks around the doorway and waves at Jameson. "Nice to meet you, I just wish it wasn't like this."

"Come on in, Will. Let's talk about this so everyone can clear the air. I don't want you to give the precise details of the statement you gave to Officer Garcia, but I do want you to give Jameson a brief overview."

Tyler and Will take a seat at the conference table and my brother cracks his knuckles like he always does when he's nervous. He looks at Jameson. "If I'd known this was going to cause problems between you and my sister, I might not have said anything. I don't know how helpful my information will be anyway."

"Oh, don't say that! Even if Jameson and I are going through a rough patch, having information is better than not knowing."

"Kendall is right. As tough as this has been, if it leads to finding my brother, it'll all have been worth it."

Will looks uncomfortable as he strokes his beard. "I hope what I have to say isn't disappointing. Maybe it's been a little over-hyped. Unfortunately, I never met your little brother in person. My only interactions with him were online. I thought he was a really neat kid."

"Did you know he was a kid?" Jameson presses.

Will twists a pen in his hands and starts to take it apart and put it together. "Not at first. He was so good at every game put in front of him that we thought that he was a homeless person who hung out at the library all day and played games. I knew him as the Archaeologist of Pain — that was his screen name online. One of his competitors was jealous of his success and researched the IP addresses he was using to access one of the gaming boards. When it was discovered that he was accessing the computers at a library, a bunch of us got together to talk about whether we could do something to help if he was homeless. But, he completely disappeared before we could do anything."

"Is that all you knew about Toby?"

Will shakes his head. "Toby became friends with one of my friends who worked at the Badlands National

Park in South Dakota. They specialize in fossils there, and Galen was a Ranger who frequently spoke in the visitor center. So, apparently, your brother worked with his teacher to have Galen do a remote lesson from the Badlands."

"This is unreal! I remember that. Toby was so excited about it he wrote me a seven-page letter. He was so impressed by your friend Galen, he wanted to grow up to be a park ranger."

"Jameson, I know this is a long shot, but do you still have those letters? If so, we could use them to collaborate details," Tyler interjects.

"Why don't you just talk to Galen?" Jameson asks.

"Galen was killed while serving overseas," Will explains.

"We've lost too many good soldiers," Tyler remarks.

"Yeah, Galen was one of the genuinely good guys," Will confirms.

"Will, I appreciate you coming forward. I don't even know if you know this — but did my brother ever tell you how he learned to play all these games? My parents were pretty strict about Internet access. When I was home on leave, he would come over to my apartment, and we'd play for a couple of hours, but nothing that would account for the type of expertise you're talking about."

"I don't know. Galen and I were part of a tiny group who knew that Toby was only a teenager. Everyone else assumed he was a gaming insider who had an unfair advantage by getting the games early."

"Did any of that rivalry seem extreme?"

"There's always smack talk going on — especially when big scores go up, and people progress through the levels of games more quickly than others. Accusations of cheating or gaming the system are pretty common."

"You saw how Toby played, do you think he was cheating?"

"No, I watched him go through a game he had never seen before — screenshot by screenshot — and he was scary good. He just had an innate talent for figuring out what the creators of the game expected of him."

Jameson takes his baseball cap off and bends the bill. "I just feel stupid. I had no idea my little brother had this whole other life. He seemed like a nerdy kid; he liked to read books and play chess. I never figured that he would find a way around Mom and Dad's rules and become some famous master gamer."

"If it makes you feel any better, the Archaeologist of Pain was a respected player. People sought out his advice, and he was a valued member of our gaming community. I was sad when he disappeared. I had no idea it was under mysterious circumstances. I just figured maybe his parents got a divorce or some weird home or school thing going on."

"I can assure you that's not what happened," Jameson asserts.

"I didn't say it was. I'm just saying what I thought might've happened to Toby. None of it made any sense, so I was trying to figure it all out."

"One day, he told my mom he had a project due he

needed to work on. He said he was going to walk to the library. After he left our front door, no one saw him again," Jameson recounts.

"Look, I'm sorry. I wish I could tell you more, but I only knew his online persona," Will explains.

Jameson shakes out his hands and arms. "I don't mean to take this out on you. I'm just frustrated with the whole situation. I appreciate the fact that you came forward. I can't believe you flew all the way to Oregon to give the interview. That was a real stand-up move. I can't thank you enough."

"Well, I figure if I accidentally opened a can of worms I needed to see it through."

"Maybe someone else can pick up the ball with the information you've provided. It's a lot more than we had before." Tyler continues to take notes.

"I can't believe I've been sitting on what could be a critical clue for all these years. I have every single letter that Toby ever sent me. I can tell the guy who is subletting my house where they are, and he can express ship them to me," Jameson offers.

Ty jots down some notes. "That would be great."

"That gives me an idea," Will adds. "I'm still friends with Galen's mom. Maybe he kept some letters or something else from Toby. I'll ask her."

"I appreciate your enthusiasm William, but I think that that is a task better left to the Sheriff's Office," Tyler cautions.

"Right. I need to keep myself separate from other witnesses. I suppose that includes dead ones."

"I know you want to help. However, we need to keep chain of custody. Evidence in the wrong hands is not helpful in court."

"Yeah, you're right. If I started reading Galen's letters, it'd be harder to remember just what I recall," Will replies.

"Exactly. So, let me get a team of people together to chase down these new leads." Tyler puts his pen down. He narrows his gaze as he points at me. "You. Go out to eat or something. Spend some quality time with your boyfriend. He misses you. Don't let this investigation interfere with your life. You've done all you can to separate yourself from the evidence."

"Does that mean that I don't need to pass the case off to Colette?"

"Ideally, it'd be better if you did, but I understand why you might not want to," Tyler responds.

"Can I request that she stay on the case? My parents don't trust very many people and they've bonded with Kendall. If she were to step away, it could complicate the investigation. My parents might back away and decide not to be part of the search. You have no idea the hell they went through."

"I will document your concerns in my notes and append them to Officer Garcia's report."

"I hate to sound whiny here, but I'm so hungry I am about ready to collapse. Airline food, even in first-class, isn't overly filling. Are we done here or can we pick up at another time?" Will pleads.

Ty smiles and then clears his throat. "I think we are

finished here. Thank you all for coming and hashing this out. I hope that all this pain and angst leads to some solid, concrete information we can use now to find your brother." Tyler pauses and looks directly at Jameson. "You'll never know how sorry I am about the way the case was handled when your brother first went missing. Unfortunately, I can't go back and fix that, but I can make sure that his case gets the attention it needs now."

"I guess that's the best I can expect at this point. I don't want to give up hope, but every day that passes makes it more difficult for me to hang in there," Jameson admits.

"We'll work as hard and as fast as we can. Your brother deserves to be found. It's happened in many high-profile cases, there is no reason to think it can't occur here."

Jameson swallows hard. "Thanks, this has been the very definition of hell for me and my family."

I'm clenching my teeth so hard they feel like they're going to crack. I've been struggling not to add my two cents to the conversation. I want to stay out of the way. That doesn't make it any easier not to speak up for both Jameson and William. I know they might feel like they are on two different teams, but we are all united in our mission to find Toby.

Jameson looks at me. "Are you still mad at me? You've been quiet."

"I never was mad at you," I assure him. Then I add more with a grimace, "Okay, that's not completely accurate. Some of your text messages were a little mean-spirited and over-the-top."

Jameson blushes. "Yeah, I get lost in my thoughts and get riled up. I apologize for that."

"I know that about you. I tried not to take it personally. I'm not saying anything because I want to be invisible in this case. My role here is to help your family deal with the whole process of having a missing child. I don't want to interfere with the efforts of law enforcement agencies — here or down in Cottage Grove."

"Are we clear here? If everyone's had their Kumbaya moment — I seriously need to eat," Will reminds us.

"I know this quaint little bakery that serves awesome deli sandwiches. Heather has a new line of soups this week. They are probably some of the best stuff I've ever tasted. That's sayin' a lot considering how well I eat," Tyler suggests with a grin.

Jameson pats his stomach. "Oh, I know. Joy and Tiers is my food-jam. They know me so well now they prepare my order when they see my number. Your wife is one talented pastry chef."

"Sounds good to me. Can we hit the road?"

"I know you too well, little brother. You just want to drive your fancy rental car."

"It's a true story — still, I'm starving," William responds.

I stand up and shake Tyler's hand. "Thank you for all your help with this. I know it's been a rough couple of weeks. I hope it will all pay off in the end."

CHAPTER EIGHTEEN

JAMESON

TYLER DOESN'T EVEN ASK me if I want a pastry, he just hands the plate over his desk. Without hesitation, I grab a couple of cream puffs and pop them in my mouth. "All I can say is you are one lucky man. I don't know what you did to deserve Heather, but you should thank your lucky stars."

"Hey, you're preaching to the choir. I don't go to bed at night without thanking God for that woman. She saved my life."

"Yeah? How so?"

"Before I met her, I was hiding from the ghosts of my past. I wasn't dealing well with my PTSD. I was burying it under a facade that everything was fine. The stress was slowly killing me. Heather gave me permission to admit I couldn't handle it all by myself and needed help."

"You guys do seem like a powerful team. I'm glad she was there for you."

"We are solid now. But it took us a while to get there. In the beginning, it seemed like we would be anything but partners."

"Sounds like Kendall and me. Some days, we're like mortal enemies."

"Maybe so, but when it works between you, it really works. Love is worth fighting for."

"I'm sure you didn't bring me down here to give me relationship advice." I take a drink of coffee and snatch another creampuff.

"You're right. I didn't. Our forensic teams have had a chance to go through the letters we received from you and Galen Eckhart. We have some questions we thought you might be able to answer a few."

"You were able to get letters from Galen?"

Tyler pulls out an accordion file. "Fortunately, Galen was a meticulous record keeper. His mom couldn't bear to part with his stuff, so she rented a storage locker and moved his whole house into it. Everything is pristine."

I sag back against the vinyl chair in relief. "I hope there's something of value in those files. I don't know how much of a relationship Galen had with my brother. I only know what Will told us. Toby didn't talk about it much, except for the one letter he wrote about the time Galen gave the virtual lesson to his classroom. As a budding paleontologist, he was over the moon about the fossil lesson."

"Not hard to imagine. I don't know many kids who aren't excited by dinosaurs."

I scrub my hand down my face as I absorb Tyler's words. It's so hard for me to hear my brother was not even thirteen when he disappeared. He was just a kid. He should have had his whole life ahead of him. Yet, he's gone.

"Few kids were as thrilled about dinosaurs as my brother though. It's not surprising he made friends with someone like Galen. He was obsessed with fossils."

"Did Toby ever write letters to you about his online life?"

I shake my head. "No, I think he wanted to hide that part of his life from me. He probably figured I would tell Mom and Dad. Occasionally, we'd play video games together; but even, then he never let on that he had anything but average skills."

"Did he ever talk about anyone named the BadassAvenger?"

"Toby didn't talk about his friends much. Other than a couple of neighborhood kids he grew up with, he didn't hang out with very many kids. He said other kids thought he was weird. He once said he wished he could be a soldier like me so he could kick the bullies' butts."

Tyler smirks. "I know more than a few guys who go into the military for that very reason."

"Me too. Still, I feel awful that I missed the point. Maybe it wasn't just a case of hero worship. What if he was trying to tell me something, and I missed the message? I mean, geez he created this whole other identity and didn't even tell me. What kind of sucky brother does that make me?"

"A very typical one. Many teenagers these days have multiple identities that their families don't even know about. There are whole apps designed just to fool family members and friends."

"So, why did you want to know about this BadassAvenger?"

"Apparently, Galen was concerned about this particular screen name. He couldn't trace it, and he felt like this particular player had it in for Toby. Galen took enough notice to track their interactions."

"He couldn't just look up the IP address?"

"I guess not. I suppose there was shielding software involved."

"That complicates things. Especially if your forensics folks have to go back and reconstruct the timeline dating back all those years."

"I know. That's why I hoped that Toby discussed his gaming habits with you and the screen name might ring some bells with you."

I shake my head sadly. "No, he never talked about any of that stuff. His online activities are a huge mystery to me."

"Well, the good news is your letters serve as corroboration of Will's account of the timeline. Galen's letters provide significantly more insight into your brother's online activities. We may be able to establish more relationships from Galen's records. It's going to take some more time."

"So, what you're telling me is we're in a holding pattern again? It seems like that's all I do these days," I grouse.

"I know it's frustrating, but for the first time in years, we are making progress on your brother's case. Something is better than nothing."

"I know, but it seems like we are moving at a snail's pace."

"We are moving. That's something that hasn't happened before. Do me a favor. Go take your girlfriend out on a date and thank her for giving you a shove in the right direction. It's the least you can do."

I think about Tyler's words for a moment before I admit, "You know, you're right. If it weren't for Kendall, I'd still be trying to tackle this on my own, and none of this new information would've come to light. I think I'm going to take you up on your suggestion."

<hr>

"Hi beautiful," I answer when Kendall picks up her phone and greets me.

"Oh, Lord! If you could only see me, you wouldn't even remotely say that," she responds with a laugh. "My ponytail hasn't been straight in about three hours, and I spilled my tea on my shirt when I came in the door this morning. I haven't even had time to fix it."

"You'll always be beautiful to me. You know that, right?"

"I know. I'm completely baffled every time you say things like that."

"I called to ask you a question. I feel terrible that our last few dates have been completely low-key. I'd like to make it up to you. When can you take a couple days off in a row?"

Kendall lets out a whoosh of breath. "Are you conspiring with Colette? She told me the other day if I don't take a break she's going to put me on an involuntary sabbatical."

"I guess great minds think alike. So, what do you say? Are you ready to be spoiled?"

Kendall moans. "Your offer is far too tempting. I can't remember the last time I've taken time off for myself. I'll call Colette and see if I can take a three-day weekend. I need to be back on Tuesday because I have a meeting with Bethany."

"Sounds great. Just let me know what Colette says."

Not five minutes later I receive a text message from Kendall. "Colette says to tell you that you've been elevated to hero status. I have her complete blessing. Plan away."

"All I can say is you might want to bring a little of everything. Who knows what I have up my sleeve?"

"Oh wow! Are you going to tell me where we're going?"

"Nope. This is your fantasy, stress-free adventure." I text back.

"You have no idea how much trust it takes for me to hand over all that control to you."

"I do understand. That's why it means so much to me that you're willing to do it. I won't take it lightly, I promise."

Kendall's eyes widen as I pull up to Locate My Heart riding one of Denny's restored motorcycles with an enclosed sidecar.

"No way! This is how we're getting to our date? I have never seen anything so cool. It's like we've gone back in time. There's only one problem. I don't know if my suitcase is going to fit," Kendall says as she examines the motorcycle.

"You'd be surprised. You can cram a load of stuff in these hatches. We can rearrange stuff in the luggage if we need to."

I take Kendall's carry-on bag and stick it in the storage compartment. It's a tight fit, but it works. "You ready to hit the road?" I ask as I hold out a motorcycle helmet for her.

Kendall does a little spin of happiness as she buckles the helmet. "I don't even care where you take me, I'm just excited to go on the trip."

"Don't say that too soon, I've got some epic plans."

"Normally, I'd demand to know each tiny detail, but I am just going to try to chill and take each adventure as it comes. I trust you to treat me right."

"I hope this weekend exceeds your every expectation." I check her helmet strap and give her a kiss before I help her into the sidecar.

My heart beats faster as I pull out of the parking lot toward I-5 South. Kendall isn't the only person who needs a break from life. It's been a long time since I've felt this much joy. There's just something about spending time in the presence of someone who calms your soul to adjust your whole outlook. Kendall does that for me. It's not something I ever anticipated — especially the way we began our relationship, but over time, Kendall has become a centering force in my life. I go to bed thinking about her. I wake up thinking about her. She puts a smile in my life.

As I weave in and out of traffic on the interstate, I relish the freedom. It's been a long time since I've allowed myself the luxury of appreciating my surroundings. Since leaving the military, I have been putting out one fire after another and lurching between jobs. I am lucky to work at Identity Bank, but the constant travel is a grind. I hit the ground running, and I haven't stopped since. I haven't stayed this long in one place since I can remember.

My mom is beside herself with joy because I've been here to celebrate both my birthday and Christmas. Despite my parents' joy at having me home, every Christmas without Toby is bittersweet because it was his favorite holiday. He and my dad would always work on the homemade train track they were building in the wood shop. It was always a tradition to add a new section to the elaborate village they've built in the corner of my dad's shop. Since Toby's disappearance, Dad can't even bring himself to look in that direction. It remains buried under tarps. I can't help but wonder if they'll ever finish their project.

Kendall's voice breaks through my sad memories as she speaks through the intercom system built into our helmets, "I forgot how cold the wind gets, I should've worn something a little warmer than jeans."

I glance down at the sidecar. "There is a blanket rolled up at your feet. I can pull over if you can't reach it." I glance up at the exit sign. "I've got good news. We'll be there in a few minutes, and you can get warmed up. I was expecting it to be a little warmer in March. I guess it's been a while since I've been home in Oregon in early Spring. I apologize. I hope what I have planned will make it all worth it."

"Now you tell me there's a blanket! Why didn't you say something earlier?"

"I should've. I'm sorry. I was just so excited about our adventure, I forgot abut it."

"It's okay. Now, I can guilt you into telling me where we're going?" Kendall teases.

"Nope. That's the whole definition of a surprise."

"My teeth are chattering. I'm just saying this better be good — "

***

Kendall runs her hand up the rich wood bedpost. "This is like something out of a fantasy. I've never seen anything like this. How did you find a castle in the middle of downtown Eugene? It has a four-poster bed! I could just sit and stare at this room all day. I've never seen a room with both a fireplace *and* a whirlpool tub. I guess you were right when you said I'd have an opportunity to warm myself up. I don't even know where to start."

"Am I off the hook for my misstep about the weather?" I ask as I hang our clothes in the closet.

"You are off the hook and so much more. I've

always wanted to stay at a bed-and-breakfast as enchanting as this. Lyle and I were planning to stay in a quaint little place like this for our honeymoon. Quinn's death changed everything."

I get up from my seat, walk over and hug her from behind. "I'm so sorry," I murmur against Kendall's hair.

Kendall shrugs. "It's actually all right. Lyle is content now and weirdly, I'm happy for him. Lyle and Pamela are very successful in real estate — just the way he always planned. He even has a couple of blonde-haired, blue-eyed kids complete with two well-behaved cocker spaniels. They are a postcard-perfect family. Sometimes I'm jealous of his ability just to pretend he never had another son."

"Do you ever think about starting over again with your own family?"

Kendall leans her head back against my chest. She shrugs. "In the beginning, I was in a state of shock. Everything I viewed myself to be was gone. Suddenly, I wasn't a mother, even though in my heart, Quinn was still there. I wasn't a fiancé. I had to call off all my wedding plans."

I wince. "That couldn't have been easy."

"It wasn't. My friends didn't know how to relate to me anymore. Even Will, who has always been just a heartbeat away, didn't know how to help me. In a blink of an eye, the whole of who I was changed. I had to discover a new me — a stronger me. The thought of moving on to someone new never occurred to me. It seemed as if that part of my life was a closed chapter. Finding kids through Locate My Heart is my passion now.

Every once in a while, I'll give into some well-meaning friend who tries to set me up on a blind date, just to counteract the loneliness. Trust me, it can lead to comical results. The last guy was nice enough, but he was a tad obsessed with sculptures of naked women."

"I hear you. I've been out with several interesting women myself." I chuckle softly and kiss the back of her neck. "How about we put away all this heavy talk and start our rest and relaxation out right? Why don't you take a bath and see if you can get warmed up? Then we'll grab some dinner. It's my understanding that the food here is award-winning. If you wish, after dinner, we can take advantage of the fireplace. I heard the concierge downstairs tell another guest the inn has an extensive lending library if you'd like to borrow some books."

"Wow, you sure know how to tempt a woman."

"I know the keys to your heart, and we are just getting started."

⬤◦⬤

Kendall nibbles on her French toast. Her lashes lower as she moans. "I don't know how you're going to get me home. I'm not going to fit into the sidecar, the way you're feeding me. I'm still recovering from last night's lobster ravioli."

"What I have planned today will take care of some of our indulgence from yesterday."

"Do tell?" Kendall challenges.

"Dress warmly and wear comfortable shoes," I instruct with a wink. "Oh, and bring your camera."

Kendall rolls her eyes at me. "You are such a tease. I can't even get a straight answer from you."

"I thought you found that to be one of my most charming traits. I always keep you on your toes, right?"

"Looked at in its most flattering light, I suppose that's true. Otherwise, it drives me a bit nuts. I like things to be a tad more predictable."

"See? We balance each other out well. I like to fly by the seat of my pants, and you keep me grounded."

Kendall feeds me a couple of bites of her brioche French toast. "I can't eat anymore. If I do, I will literally explode. Besides, I want to see what you have planned for us. I can't believe I was so tired I fell asleep reading in front of the fireplace last night."

"That's all right, we've both been working way too hard. Our bodies obviously needed the rest.

As I pull the motorcycle up to the entrance of Hendrick's Park, Kendall exclaims, "Look at all those rhododendrons. I've never seen so many flowers in one spot! No wonder you told me to bring the camera."

"We're going to have plenty of time to take pictures because this is our hiking destination for the day. I love this park. It's so peaceful. There are so many different varieties of flowers, you can't possibly see them all — but it's fun to try. The paths meander everywhere, and it's perfect for private conversation, especially this time of year. It's a little early for full bloom, but the flowers are already stunning."

"A few years ago, Will got me an uber-fancy digital camera to take macro pictures. I'm so intimidated by all the bells and whistles, I've never learned how to use it correctly. I kind of wish I would've brought it because it would take some amazing pictures. Unfortunately, all I have with me is my cell phone and a little cheap camera from Walmart. I didn't know I was going to be presented with a world-class picture taking opportunity. Next time, I'll know better."

"You have a good eye for artistic things, so I'm sure your pictures will be magnificent either way," I comment as I zip Kendall's hood up a little tighter. I drop a light kiss on her lips as I pull away. "Let's get this show on the road. I have more things planned for today."

"More than this?" Kendall asks with a stunned look.

"Absolutely. Prepare to have more of your fantasies come true." I slide one arm around her waist and cuddle her closer as we choose a path and start to walk. Her wide eyes and gasps of appreciation are all I need to know to affirm my choice of outing. This is going to be a very good day.

"I thought these boots were comfortable when I put them on, but I was wrong," Kendall wheezes as we sit down at a picnic table.

Her eyes widen as I remove boxed-lunches from my backpack. "How did you score these? When I asked him about it last night, the chef said he only makes these for special catering jobs."

"I doubt I had much to do with it. I've got a hunch that the chef is sweet on you — especially after you wrote him a handwritten thank you note for dinner yesterday. He seemed confused and a tad smitten."

"I was just being nice. It was fabulous food. You have to give me that."

"Oh, I'm not arguing. I'm just saying you've earned another fan."

Kendall flexes her ankles and rolls her shoulders. "I definitely earned something. I'm not going to be able to move for a week. I've been working at a sedentary job for too long. I forgot how much of a workout a simple hike can be."

"Don't worry. I'm in the business of taking away all your pain this weekend. I've got you covered." I promise with a mischievous grin.

CHAPTER NINETEEN

KENDALL

"WHAT'S WRONG? DID YOU lose your Polly Pocket dolls again?" Will asks when he finds me on my hands and knees under my desk. I hit the back of my head on the bottom of my desk drawer when I raise it in total shock. As far as I know, Will should be in Nebraska.

Rubbing my head, I look up at him. "What are you doing here?"

Will reaches out a hand to help me up. "I think the better question is: why are you down there?"

Brushing off the back of my pants suit, I explain, "Jameson got me a new surge protector and my charger is stuck. I've got a meeting on the road, and I need to take my computer."

"Where is your Prince Charming today?"

I smile to myself. "He is pretty princely. Sadly, all fairytales must come to an end, and we both had to go back to work after our fabulous weekend together."

Will grins and winks at me. "Had a good weekend,

did you?"

"One of the best I've ever had. I didn't know Jameson had such a tender, nurturing side. You should've seen all the things he did for me. We had the most delicious food I've ever eaten and then we went on a beautiful nature hike. Jameson was thoughtful enough to know I would get sore and scheduled a his-n-her spa treatment at a massage salon. I was more pampered than I've ever been in my whole life. After that, we went back to our room and ate in front of the fireplace and danced. It was beyond anything I could have thought up in my most indulgent fantasies of what a perfect romantic weekend would be like."

My brother's face softens as he takes in my joy. "Sis, I'm am happy to see you so content. You've been alone a long time. For a while I wondered if you would be sad forever."

I roll my shoulder. "I don't know what all this means in the grand scheme of things. There will always be a part of my soul that never lights up again. It died when Quinn died. Jameson makes me happy and hopeful in ways I haven't been. I'm realistic enough to understand we have giant obstacles in front of us and I don't know how we will tackle those. I am trying to just take it one day at a time and capture all the bliss out of each and every one. I'll just deal with anything else as it comes."

Will moves my desk a few inches from the wall, reaches down to unplug my cord, and hands it to me. "That's the best you can do. If there's anything I've learned, sometimes biding your time and being flexible can work out in the end."

"Yeah, I suppose they did for you. You didn't answer my question — why are you back in Oregon?"

"Turns out, I like it here. Besides, if I can't hang out with my sister, who can I hang out with? You're the only person who isn't weird around me now that I have money."

"Let me text the client and see if she minds if you tag along. It might be less awkward for this meeting if I have someone with me. Everything you might see or overhear in this meeting is confidential. You have to promise to stay in the background though, okay?"

"Don't I always?" Will counters.

I choke back a guffaw of laughter. "Umm ... like never. You must be terribly jet-lagged and confused."

"Bethany is tougher than I expected her to be, based on her TV interviews," Will comments as he takes a bite of his loaded mashed potato skin. "What she is doing today is beyond gutsy."

I stare across the restaurant at the two women sitting at a table several yards away. "Both women are stunning examples of courage. I don't know if I could do the same thing."

"Why are we here? It feels kind of like we're chaperones on a blind date."

"We're here for moral support. Bethany is afraid she might freeze up like she does in front of the television cameras. She just wanted to make sure that if things got weird, I could provide an out. I think she'll probably handle it fine. Even so, I want to make sure she feels as comfortable as she possibly can in such a bizarre situation."

"You're right. This is about as strange as it gets."

"On the drive up here, Bethany explained what this meeting was for. I was flabbergasted. If something like that happened within my family, I think I would want to disappear to the core of the earth and never reemerge. It takes a big person to try to right all the wrongs with that kidnapping."

"I agree. I hope everything goes smoothly with the meeting," I comment. Just as I add those words, I hear a sob from Bethany's table.

"Uh-oh, that can't be good," Will mutters under his breath.

Will stands up to go toward Bethany's table. I lay a hand on his forearm as I whisper, "Wait! She hasn't given the signal."

My brother glares at me. "The woman is sobbing. I think that's signal enough. I'm going to go check."

After a moment of indecision, I concede, "I guess I could use a trip to the little girl's room." I have to scoop up my computer and dump it in my bag and run to keep up with my brother.

I try to slow down and nonchalantly walk by Bethany and Naomi's table. Bethany catches me out of the corner of her eye. She motions me over to the table. Will and I stop in our tracks. Instinctively, Will steps back. "You too. We need your opinions," Bethany says.

"Both of our opinions?" Will asks skeptically. "You

don't know me."

Naomi nods. "That's what makes your opinions so valuable. You don't have any preconceptions about what's going on."

"I know about your case because I saw it in the news," Will cautions.

Bethany rolls her eyes. "Hasn't everyone?"

"Yeah, viral media has changed everything. Everybody has an opinion even if they don't know all the facts." I reply sympathetically.

"You're telling me. I've never seen anything like this. People hate me. I didn't have anything to do with Aunt Latrice's craziness. But, I'll never convince anyone of that," Naomi replies tearfully.

"That's not true. You convinced me, and that's all that really counts. The rest of those people can take a flying leap. Opinions are like belly buttons. Everybody's got one, but they don't really matter much," Bethany replies.

Inwardly, I breathe a sigh of relief. I was afraid that the meeting had broken down beyond repair and turned into Bethany's every nightmare. Yet, that doesn't seem to be what's happening here. The women appear to be developing some sort of friendship.

Will and I borrow chairs from the next table and sit down with Naomi and Bethany.

I barely have a chance to place my computer back at my feet before Will speaks up. "I know I'm supposed to be hiding in the background, but I can't help being the curious little brother in this situation. Why were you all crying?"

"Oh my, we did create quite a scene, didn't we?" Naomi blushes.

"It's okay, I wasn't paying attention to our surroundings either. I was crying as much as you were," Bethany admits.

"About?" Will presses.

"Well, every day I look at Asher, and I think how lucky I am to be blessed with him. It makes me sad to think that Naomi and Seth don't get to have that same joy. So, I started thinking about ways I could help with that. I decided that God must've put Naomi in my life for a reason, even if it started out in the craziest of ways. I offered to be a surrogate mother for her. I want her to have the same feelings of happiness from motherhood I get to experience."

The incredible generosity at that statement takes my breath away. I gasp. "No wonder you guys were bawling in the middle of a restaurant. I feel like crying right now. Are you guys sure about this? Both of you have been through an incredibly emotional few months. This is a huge decision, even under the best of circumstances."

"Yeah, we know. We know it's crazy, and people will think it's weird. Some people are going to believe it's some sort of strange publicity stunt but to us, it feels right — like it's our destiny. If it hadn't been for my aunt's weird fixation with making my life perfect, Bethany and I would've never met."

"I hate to be a pessimist here, but that surrogacy stuff is brutal — not to mention expensive," Will says quietly.

Bethany's shoulders slump. "There's the weakness in our plan. All of our women's intuition and our heart's bonding over this idea isn't going to fix our realities. That's the first thing my husband is going to say."

"Mine too — right after he has me undergo a thorough psychological exam. If he thought that my flying out here for this meeting was the definition of stark raving mad, this idea is going to blow his mind." Naomi adds.

I smiled wryly. "You have to admit that this approach is a little unorthodox. It's going to make people scratch their heads. Bethany, your offer is incredibly generous, but you don't need to feel guilty that you have a baby and Naomi doesn't. Sometimes bad things happen to good people. I lost a son too. Eventually, you build a new life that's different from the one you expected, but life does go on."

"But what if the life Naomi was intended to have includes a baby I helped her create? I know it sounds weird, but I have a real sense of peace about it. What if I'm the one to help her move on from her loss?"

"Is that what your gut is telling you? Are you sure it's not just a knee-jerk reaction to the kidnapping? You really don't blame Naomi?" Will asks with a contemplative expression on his face.

"No! This was never Naomi's fault."

Will pulls out a business card from his wallet. "I have a charitable foundation set up with my financial advisor. If you decide to do this, and you need some help with your medical bills or anything else to make this happen — call him. We'll call this 'Project Whole

Hearts'."

I look at Will with wide-eyed astonishment. I am rendered speechless.

"Wait? What? Did you just offer to pay for the whole procedure? You don't even know how much it's going to cost," stammers Bethany. "Why would you do that?"

"Because my twin sister lost her child and no one can make her heart whole. If I can help heal yours, I'd like to help."

"Just like that?" Naomi pushes. "We don't have to prove anything to you?"

"Why should you have to prove that you and your husband would love and provide for a child?" Will counters.

"That's funny! I kept asking that question the whole time we were going through the adoption process the first time. It would've been so much easier if we could've just done it the old-fashioned way," Naomi answers with a low laugh.

Bethany reaches out and squeezes Naomi's hand. "I'm so sorry. I don't know why things are easier for some people than others. But, now it seems we might be in this fight together. The next battle is to convince our husbands we are not two certifiably insane women. That may be the toughest battle of all."

———•———

Tears gather in the corner of my eyes as Will drives me back to Locate My Heart. "I'm sorry I ever prejudged the way that you might spend all of your money. That was the most generous thing I've ever seen in my life."

"I'm so glad that I've finally made you proud."

"I've always been proud of you, but this goes above and beyond. I hope those two can work something out. It would be a beautiful outcome to what could've been a very tragic event."

"That's why I came on board. I think they really mean it. I believe somehow, on a soul level, the trauma bonded them in a way that they can't separate from each other."

"I'm just blown away that you care enough about strangers to get involved."

"I remember when we were eating tomato and mayo sandwiches, and I was mowing lawns to keep the electricity on. I swore that if I ever got any money, I was going to make sure that people could afford not only the necessities, but things their hearts could only wish for."

"I'd say you're well on your way to accomplishing that."

Will parks his car in Locate My Heart's lot. He looks over at me. "If I am the grantor of wishes, what do you wish for?"

"Pie-in-the-sky? I want no more missing children. I want to be able to sleep at night knowing every child is safe in their bed."

"Well, that's a no-brainer," he answers with a dismissive shake of his head. "I meant personally. What does your heart wish for?"

"I don't know. I guess I just want normal. I want to

be happy. I want to love again with my whole heart. Watching Naomi and Bethany try to patch together something beautiful out of something so ugly makes me wonder if maybe I could have something more. My heart wish is to believe in love again. I want Jameson."

"You know I'm just a heartbeat away if you need my help, right?"

"I do," I answer as I give him a hug.

"Remember, you're the strong, logical one. If I can make a miracle happen, so can you. I'm proof that heart wishes do come true. Go get yours."

CHAPTER TWENTY

JAMESON

The shrill ring of my phone interrupts my concentration, and my fingers slip from the hand-hold as I'm two grips from the top of the wall. "You all right?" Aidan asks as he glances over to make sure I've caught myself. "I think you should grab that. I know that ringtone. That's the one Tyler had us set up to receive updates on Logan's shooting case involving Katelyn. He's calling on official business."

Before I can process those words, an incoming call arrives from Tristan. That's enough to spur Kendall off the wall. She is the first to reach the ground. Even out of the corner of my eye, I can see she has turned deathly pale. I quickly reverse direction and rappel down the wall.

Kendall says nothing, but places her arm around my waist and briefly rests her cheek against my chest before we jog over to my duffel bag and retrieve my phone.

Tyler has left a stark text message. "Meet me at the station ASAP. This is it."

Kendall draws in a quick breath as she reads the message. "Holy cow! Toby?"

"I can only assume. Let me call Tristan back. Isaac probably has inside information." All the oxygen seems to leave my body.

I don't even get a chance to say hello when I reach Identity Bank. "Don't argue. Aidan's plane waiting for you at the Salem airport. It will fly you where you need to go."

"I'm not arguing. What's going on, Tristan?"

"I don't have very many details, but your brother has been located in West Virginia. He is understandably traumatized and only wants to meet with you. He is too frightened to meet with anyone else. At the moment, he is refusing any medical treatment — although he is accepting food — which is a positive."

"Where is he?" I ask incredulously.

"Barboursville, West Virginia. We are still trying to backfill the details, so I don't have much. I'll keep you informed as we find out more. We'll keep Tyler in the loop."

"Thanks, Boss. I appreciate it." I sway as I try to absorb it all.

Abruptly, my legs buckle, and I collapse to my knees.

On the way down, Kendall tries to catch me, but I stop her. "I'm going to hurt you. Just let me go."

"Let me help you, please. I love you," Kendall

pleads as she wipes my forehead with a towel. "What's going on?"

"It's my brother. Toby is alive!" I frown as a wave of dizziness passes over me. "He only wants to see me; not our parents. Now what? Should I even tell my parents he's been found? Should I go check him out to see if he's okay first? Do I need to call a psychologist? I don't know what to do next," I stammer as I try to stand.

Aidan leans over and helps me up. "I don't know about you — but I'd start with a shower. No matter how luxurious my plane is, the shower leaves something to be desired for a guy your size. Take a moment to collect your thoughts. I'll send Tara over to Joy and Tiers to put together a care package for your brother. I know from working with the kids at camp, food can bridge gaps words sometimes can't. Kendall can drive you over to Tyler's office in a few minutes."

"I'm taking your plane?" I ask as my overworked brain struggles to keep up with everything being thrown at me.

Aidan nods. "There are perks be being successful, but they are worthless if I can't help my friends?"

"Okay, I guess that makes sense. I can drive to the airport, though," I protest.

Logan pats me on the shoulder. "Technically, you can… but… hold your hand out, buddy."

I do as he asks, and I'm embarrassed to see I'm unable to keep it even remotely steady. My drill Sergeant would be horrified.

Logan quirks his eyebrow at me. "Question is,

should you?"

"Shower it is," I mumble under my breath.

"I'll be here for you when you're ready," Kendall says as she gently kisses me.

"I know." I pull away, then brush a kiss against her eyebrow as I head toward the dressing room.

———•◦•———

Tyler stares at me over the top of his coffee mug. "You want to explain to me why the woman who is directly responsible for the fact that we were able to locate your brother is sitting outside of my office instead of by your side?"

I shrug. "This all seems surreal. I need to deal with one issue at a time. Right now, all I'm thinking about is Toby."

"This is what Kendall does. She helps people through these kinds of ordeals. Last I checked, you are a member of a family going through the trauma of having a missing family member. I think you're missing the point."

"Look, it's not like I'm not grateful, but my brother is in crisis and I need to get there. I don't have time to sort out all of my romantic issues with Kendall. I've got to stay focused on Toby."

Tyler throws up his hands in the air. "I think you're making a huge mistake, but it's your life."

"Can you stop pretending to be Oprah Winfrey for a moment? What about Toby? What do we know?" I demand.

Tyler consults his notes. "Rapture Borges has been detained on suspicion of kidnapping. She is being held without bail after someone recognized Toby shopping at a local Walmart in West Virginia."

"She?" My mouth goes slack. "My brother was kidnapped?" My vision goes gray as the implications of that sink in. "He wasn't even thirteen! Oh, Sh —! This is gonna break my mother's heart. My dad is truly going to want to kill somebody now."

"Before you jump to any conclusions, this is very early in the investigation. We don't have any evidence to determine the nature of their relationship. We are going to have to wait and see how all that plays out."

"What do you mean we don't have any evidence?" I bellow. "My brother doesn't even want to see my parents? That's proof enough that something is completely screwed up. She kept my brother for five freaking years. That's the definition of twisted."

"I'm not saying it's not, Jameson. I'm just cautioning you not to get ahead of what we know. We are treading very carefully because your brother is almost an adult. We don't know what he's been through. At this point, he is refusing any help and counseling. We must proceed with caution not to make the situation worse than it already is. That's all I'm saying."

"How in the world am I going to know if I'm making the situation worse? We thought he was dead!"

"If I was your CO right now, I would remind you to put a lid on it. You've got the time it takes you to fly across the country to pull it together. Your brother needs to see the calm, serene logistical soldier he knows and remembers. Behind-the-scenes, be as angry as you want to be, but your public face must give nothing away. Your brother needs to see only love and support."

"Point taken. Anything else?"

Tyler walks around his desk and shakes my hand as he pulls me in for a hug. "Man, I don't get to tell people news like this very often. I'm so happy for you. Go tell your brother how much you love him. Not very many people get another chance."

"Your brother won't look anything like you remember. I just want you to be prepared," the grizzled detective with the handlebar mustache, who is driving me from the airport to the hotel room, remarks off-handedly.

"Sir, my brother has been gone so long, it's nearly impossible for me to determine whether my memories are real or just wishful thinking. Even before that, I was serving in the military, so I was deployed for much of his childhood. My memories of him consist of cheesy school pictures and scarce video calls on holidays."

"That's too bad, Son. I'm sorry it worked out that way. Things could've been worse, I suppose. Just the other day, we found a family of four that had been missing goin' on twenty-seven years. Somebody stuffed them in a big ole' abandoned silo. The world is a really sick place.

"True enough. I'm not afraid to say a part of me is not looking forward to finding out the exact details of what my brother's been through."

"Try not to press the lad too hard. The details will

come out in due time."

I sigh. "I know. That'll be one of the most difficult things for me. I'm one of those guys who needs to know all the pieces to the puzzle, so I can start to reconstruct them and come up with a logical answer. I have a feeling there won't be logical answers to this problem."

"I can guarantee that there ain't no logic to kidnapping a child from a library and keeping him for half a decade. You're gonna need to let go of that idea."

"Thanks for the reminder. I need to leave the puzzle solving to you guys and just support my brother."

"Just keep that thought in the front of your mind and you'll be fine. Just remember your brother is alive. Not the same person he was, but alive."

As I wait for the law enforcement agents to check my ID before allowing me to enter Toby's room, I have to clench my jaw to keep it from trembling. Honestly, I doubted I'd ever see this day.

The first thing that strikes me when the door opens and I come face-to-face with my little brother is that he is not so little. He towers over me. His hair is long and curly like our mother's, and his eyes are turbulent with grey suspicion, just like dad's.

"What happened to your hair?" Toby asks incredulously as he scrutinizes me.

"Turns out fighting terrorists is a little intense and stressful. My hair started falling out, so I decided to shave my head and get it over with."

"It looks righteous. All I've got are these stupid Goldilocks curls." He grimaces as he runs his fingers through his long mop.

"Hey, don't knock it. Girls go crazy for that kind of thing."

Toby shudders. "Thanks, not interested. Don't know if I'll ever be."

"No problem. I can take you to go get your hair cut right now, if you want me to. You can even get a high and tight. It would make Mom cry because she always loved your curls, but it's your body. You can do what you want with it."

Toby rolls his eyes. "Like she would care. She never bothered to look for me."

"Why would you think that?"

"Rapture told me they never went on TV or had any big search parties for me. They were just happy I was gone and not embarrassing them anymore."

"Well, 'Rapture' was missing a few key facts. In fact, all of her 'facts' were wrong. Mom and Dad have tried everything they could to find you. At first the media was interested in your case, but after they couldn't find any dirt on Mom and Dad, they quickly moved on. We couldn't get anyone to feature your case after that. Dad even gave up his teaching career, so he'd have the time to devote to searching for you."

"If that's true, why did it take you so long to find me?" Toby challenges with a dark look on his face.

I grimace. "We didn't have much help. The world is a big place, and you seemed to vanish from it without any explanation. Local law enforcement agencies never seemed to believe you were taken. They thought you were just a moody teenager. The authorities seemed to think you had some long-standing beef with Mom and Dad and just split on your own."

"I didn't! I was minding my own business." Toby goes over to the hotel bed and flops down. He props himself up against the headboard and glares at me. "Go on."

"I was stationed overseas and couldn't help much. Mom and Dad hired a bunch of people to help, but they were not very honest and fed the media negative news stories about our family. It just snowballed. After we lost public support, no one seemed to care that you were missing. We couldn't get any news outlets or social media sites to share your story to get the word out."

"So, basically what you're telling me is Rapture was right? It was all just a show for the media? No one really looked for me? Your soldier buddies never launched an operation to find me? Mom and Dad's church friends or all their coworkers at school never gave a rat's butt about me?"

"We looked — for years, we looked. But we had no idea where to begin. Dad would drive around for hours. He hired private investigators, psychics and anyone else he could think of. He even tried hiring a publicity team to revive your story in the news."

"Lip service, nothing but lip service," Toby spits.

One of the agents watching my brother steps forward. "I don't think this is productive. I think you should step out of the room, Sergeant Payne. You are upsetting your brother."

"Enough!" Toby yells. "I will be eighteen in

seventy-four days. You don't get to decide what happens to me. I'm done with that. I don't need a babysitter. I've managed just fine on my own. I'm alive, aren't I? No thanks to any of you. Haven't you all seen brothers fight? He might be a stranger to me, but he's still my family. I can argue with him if I want to."

"Son …" the agent starts to argue.

"The name is Tobias Payne. Don't forget that. Right now, I'm gonna go get some food and get my haircut with my brother. I'm done with you and everyone like you."

"We still need you to come down and be interviewed by our forensic folks," the younger agent insists.

I step forward and place my hand on the guy's shoulder. "With all due respect, you're not going to find out anything from my brother in the next two hours that he won't remember in two months or two years. Give him a break."

"This is not your area of expertise, so just back off," the agent growls.

"Apparently, it's not your area either. Let us handle it our way. We've got this covered. I've got more layers of security clearance than you've ever dreamed of. I can keep my brother safe."

The argumentative agent looks toward the officer who drove me to the scene for guidance. The older officer merely shrugs. "It's not like we have a better plan. The kid has a point. He hasn't done anything wrong, and he's free to leave. Sure, we'd like him to cooperate in the investigation, but we can't compel him to seek medical treatment because he's not in any immediate danger."

"I don't know. What if the kid has been brainwashed or has that Stockholm syndrome or something?" the officer pushes.

"Dude! I'm not stupid. Rapture was mental, but that doesn't mean I am." Toby rolls his eyes.

I look over at Toby. "So, what kind of vibe are you feeling here? You want to see people or slide under the radar?"

"Not really feeling social right now. Outside and private sounds good."

"Okay, give me a couple, and we'll bug out of here."

"For real?" Toby questions with hopeful eyes.

"I promise," I reply as I fish my phone out of my pocket.

Toby looks up at the agent. "Now that my brother is here, can I go to the bathroom without you watching me like a hawk? I swear I'm not going to off myself."

The agent reluctantly steps away and waves Toby toward the restroom. "Help yourself. I'm going to go back to watching the game."

The older agent grabs some soda from the fridge and comments, "I think I'll join you. These two seem to have it handled. Now, we just have to figure out how to do the paperwork."

While Toby is away, I text Tristan. **Urgent SOS. I need a male hairdresser and a few changes of clothes — about your size and size 12 shoes at plane ASAP.**

Bigger than you? Tristan texts back immediately.

Yeah. He's a giant.

Toby okay?

Maybe. Working on it.

Give me 20. Stuff will be there.

Need discretion on hairdresser. Former military good.

No worries. Isaac has lists for this kind of thing.

Really?"

Not kidding. Anything else?

A Jeep would be cool.

Got a friend with a dealership nearby. Might take thirty. Can you stall?

Do my best. Sorting out egos might take that long.

Okay, talk to you later. Love playing Santa Claus.

Me too.

As I tuck my phone in my back pocket, Toby sticks his head out of the bathroom door. "Are the 'minders' distracted?"

I nod toward the other room. "Yeah, they're watching the game."

"Going to take a shower, but they creep me out. I feel like the cops are going to take pictures for evidence or something. Stand guard, will ya?"

"No worries. Nobody takes pictures of you without your permission. You are in charge. You hear me? I'm right here.”

“Thanks, man.”

<hr>

“Sweet! Is this like the one you drove in the Army?” Toby exclaims with wide eyes.

“Well, not exactly. This is quite a bit more upscale than I used to drive — but the concept is the same.”

“Still, these are bodacious wheels.”

“I figured you could use a little privacy.”

“Yeah, don’t know much about that. Where are we going?” Toby asks as I drive toward the private airport.

“It turns out the most isolated place I know is the plane I flew in on. I brought some food. With any luck, there is a barber waiting for you there.”

“That’s just sick. You’ve been out living life hanging out with rich and famous while I’ve been stuck in hell,” Toby snaps at me.

“I know it looks bad, but that’s not what’s happening here. I have great friends and I work for a very generous boss, but I’m just a computer technician. They are lending me their resources to help you. I’m nothing special, I promise you.”

Toby wipes tears from his face with his sleeve as he turns his face away from mine. “Would’ve been nice if you could have had a boss like that a few years ago.”

My stomach sinks to my feet as I see the search through Toby’s eyes. None of my decisions are ever going to make sense to him. Heck, they make little sense to me. There are so many things I would do differently now. I don't even know if I deserve Toby's love and forgiveness.

"I'm sorry we didn't find you sooner. It doesn't mean we didn't love you every second of every day."

"I missed you too. I still don't know what that means. It's not like I can go back to being thirteen."

"I can't tell you how many times I've wished that we could turn back the clock and change history. But, we can build new memories," I suggest as I pull up to the plane hangar. "You want to eat or get a haircut first?"

"Chop this crap off. Rapture said it was going to make as world-famous. It's a pain in the butt, and I'm smart enough to know she was just using it as a disguise."

"Works for me. Looks like there's already somebody here," I comment as I see someone standing outside of the plane.

"Your friends just let you borrow this thing — like whenever?"

"You'd have to know him, but Aidan has a thing about planes. This is only the second time I've ever taken him up on it."

"What did you do on the first trip?"

"Oddly enough, I helped return a lost baby boy to his worried parents."

"Is this a weird hobby for you now or something?"

"No, just came up in the course of my job."

"You may be my brother, but I gotta say, you're weird."

I laugh. "Not even the first person to make that observation, Toby."

I jump when someone knocks on the driver's side window. "Excuse me, sir. Are you Sergeant Payne? Isaac Rogan told me to report here, but I'm not sure I'm in the right spot."

"That's us."

"Okay. I would hate to think I was standing in front of the wrong plane. I'm Domingo Curley." He steps aside to allow me to jump out of the jeep.

"Seriously? That's a great name for a hairstylist," Toby says with a smirk.

"Yep, not so good for a sharpshooter."

"Imagine not. You still in?"

"Nah, I was involved in an incident with the 'not so friendlies' that messed me up for a while, so Uncle Sam and I parted ways. I am strictly civilian now."

Toby lopes around the Jeep and shows Domingo his hair. "I don't care what you do. You can even shave me as bald as my brother here. I just want this hair gone."

"I can do."

"I brought you a bunch of clothes too. By the time we're done, you won't even recognize yourself."

Toby draws in a deep shuddering breath. "I think that's the point."

———— •◦• ————

As we park alongside the tarmac watching planes take off, Toby takes his finger and licks the last dredges of cherry topping out of the container just like he used to do when he was little. It's as if focusing on breathing fresh, clean air is enough. We haven't said much to each other. Even so with every stilted word and every offhand joke, my brother seems to be shedding the weight of the world.

Toby's favorite discovery amongst the clothing and accessories that Tristan provided is the brand-new state-of-the-art cell phone, but he still appears cautious.

"Are you sure Rapture doesn't have anything to do with this? She's pretty well connected online," Toby frets as he turns his phone over and over in his hands.

"I am one thousand percent certain she doesn't have anything to do with this. Whoever this 'Rapture' person is, she is safely tucked away in jail with no Internet access."

"This thing is like a computer in my hand. It's wild."

"I don't want to press, but — how did she keep you away from stuff like phones? They're everywhere."

Toby sighs. "I thought the bad guys had Mom too. Rapture understood all about this military stuff like you did. She said Osama bin Laden had been killed and that the terrorists blamed you. Rapture claimed they were after me and my whole family. She said if I told anyone who I was, everyone I knew would be killed, including you." He shrugs. "I was little. I knew you killed bad guys, and I recognized the name Osama bin Laden from your letters and videos. I knew Rapture from the video-game world. She was the real deal there, so I didn't know if she knew stuff in real life too."

I pinch the bridge of my nose as I try to process his words.

"I never in a million years dreamed being a soldier would put you at risk like that. I thought I was keeping my country safe. I am so sorry she used my military experience against you. For my own sanity, I have to ask — did she ever hurt you?"

"You mean, did she torture me like a prisoner of war or beat me?" Toby asks sourly. "No. She was too weird for that. For a while, she tried to pretend like she was my family — like some weird mom or big sister figure. But, I think she eventually got tired of that too."

"Did she ever say why she took you?"

"Yeah. Rapture was the BadassAvenger. Until I came along, there was nobody better at video games than her. She was mad because she'd spent several years becoming the best there ever was — or at least that was true in her own mind. When I leveled up on her, she was pissed off. She figured that if we joined forces, we could take over the entire video game universe."

"Didn't people recognize you from the gaming sites?"

"In the beginning, Rapture didn't allow me anywhere near the Internet. She had me programming some weird military game. She told me she had contacts within the Pentagon and she was going to revolutionize the way drone strikes were done in real life warfare and that she was going to use my skills to change the way military combat was done. She said it would make her a millionaire and that we would be able to buy out Microsoft, PlayStation and all the other big players in the industry."

"You knew how to program computers at thirteen?" I ask, trying to cover my shock.

Toby rolls his eyes and shakes his head. "Did you

forget that Mom and Dad were both teachers and I was a terrible athlete? What else was I supposed to do with my time? I read books stupid fast. Computers interested me. Dad was always messing around with that kind of stuff. I could only whittle so many sticks in the woodshed with him. I started doing the computer stuff instead."

"Wow! I never knew you had all those skills. If she trusted you with computers, why didn't you message someone?"

"It was a while before Rapture let me use the computer without being supervised. In the beginning she watched everything I did. When she started being blitzed from the drugs, I use to sneak and watch the news. But, there was never anything about me. So, I figured she was right. Either Mom and Dad weren't looking for me, or something terrible had happened to them. I didn't want the terrorists to go after you."

"I'm sorry you ever had to worry about that. So, how did you guys hide out in plain sight for so many years?"

"We moved around a lot. Rapture worked from home as one of those call-in computer tech people. She would remote into other people's computers and fix their problems. We didn't have to leave the house much. She eventually got bored playing house with me and started taking drugs. They made her super paranoid when she was awake. Fortunately, she slept a lot. But, she had cameras everywhere. It was like I was under lock and key. Prisoners have more rights than I did. So, I did my thing. I started doing her job because she was too strung out to do it. The people on the other end of the computer screen didn't know who was helping them — so, it didn't really matter. As long as the paychecks kept coming in, I had food and a place to sleep. It beat moving around all the time. It became my new normal. "

"What changed?" I ask.

"I don't really know. Rapture got ticked off because the delivery service overcharged her for her Walmart order. So, I guess she had me go along as her 'muscle' to convince the management to fix the problem. The next thing I know the store security people are all over us, and they're asking my name. I was freaked out. I gave them the name Derek Dobie."

I raise an eyebrow.

"Yeah, that's the stupid name she gave me. I never want to hear it again. I'm done being that person."

"I bet you are. There's some stuff you need to clear up at the police department to make sure Rapture doesn't have the opportunity to do this again. But, there's a whole group of people who are anxiously waiting for you to come back and be Tobias Payne."

"I'm sorry, Jameson. I can't do that. I've spent too many years pretending to be somebody else. I gotta figure out who I am. I gotta start over from scratch. I've lived in so many states I might as well start here."

Chapter Twenty-One

Kendall

I SWALLOW A FEW curse words as I get another paper cut. I grab a tissue from my desk. I glance over at Kiera and Tara who are helping me put together the packets for the charity auction and grumble, "I still can't believe he didn't take me with him. This is like Lyle all over again. What in the heck is wrong with me?"

Kiera wheels over and hugs me. I have to bend down so she can reach me from her wheelchair. "There's nothing wrong with you. Sometimes when guys get scared, they run. Sounds to me like Jameson is trying to protect his heart from a world of hurt and you got left out of the circle. It doesn't mean you'll always be left out. It's probably just the circumstances. Jeff tried to do that with me when we first got together. I got a severe case of muscle cramps, and my husband didn't handle it well. He closed down and wanted to end our whole relationship. He was just afraid of getting hurt."

"Wow! That seems a little drastic," I remark.

Tara nods. "Some guys are prone to overreact. Remember when Aidan hit a bump in his career and thought he would never be good enough for me? He swore he'd be the one holding me back, so he considered splitting."

My eyes widen. "Aidan O'Brien? Mega superstar, owns an incredibly successful recording studio, mentors several other artists, the love of your life? That guy? I thought he's been in love with you since he was five years old?"

"He has. But that doesn't keep him from having crazy ideas about us. Every guy I know has insecurities that come roaring back to life when things are stressful. You can let it destroy you, or you can figure out how to work around it."

I slump back in my chair. "That's just it. I'm not sure that there is a work-around here. Jameson left without explaining why. It's like all of those months we worked together to find Toby didn't count for anything. I mean … come on! I don't have a bunch of fancy credentials for my job, but I worked hard to put all the pieces together to find his brother. I help families with reunification plans all the time. *He didn't want me.* Why am I even here? I'm not just pretty window dressing. I won't do that again," I whisper harshly.

Kiera pats me on my knee. "I don't think that's what Jameson wants either. He's proud of what you've done here at Locate My Heart. You should have heard him the other day when he was pitching an idea to Madison about how she should feature you weekly on her lifestyle show. He was not speaking as a man who lacks faith in you."

"It's nice that he's proud of me — but there seems to be a wall there. It's like he doesn't really trust me on some level. He's sweet and romantic, but he doesn't trust me with his heart. I'm his girlfriend and I want to be there for him when he's hurting. If he always shuts me out, what can I do?"

Tara puts down the packets she's been assembling and looks at me directly. "Nothing in your relationship has been easy from the start. Everything has been formed under fire. Don't expect that to change anytime soon. It's not necessarily a bad thing; it just makes it harder to sort through what's important and what can be let go. Right now isn't the best time to make decisions about your relationship. You're too busy putting out fires."

I laugh softly. "Putting out fires is a pretty good description of what we've been doing. Some of them are more fun to put out than others."

"I understand. Aidan and I have been there too. Nothing like making up after a big fight."

I throw my hands up in frustration. "I like fireworks. I may look all cotton candy and dimples, but I've got some heat behind me. But Jameson and I are not even fighting. We're not anything right now. It's like Jameson has dropped off the planet. I don't know —" I let my speech trail off as I look at my friends.

Kiera studies me carefully. "I hate to tell you this — but I don't think Jameson is intentionally being the villain here. As uncomfortable as it is, I think you should wait for life to settle down on his end. Maybe work on a few ghosts from your past — it may make it easier to deal with whatever is coming."

I wad up a piece of scrap paper and throw it at Kiera. "Darn it! Having super-smart friends is such a double-edged sword. You're probably right. Still, that doesn't make me less likely to bury my face in a package of Oreo double-stuffed cookies tonight," I confess tearfully.

Tara walks over and hugs me from behind. "Hey,

there's nothing in the Girlfriend Posse code that says you can't do both. That's what we're here for. If you need backup, let us know."

I curl up in the big leather chair that used to be my dad's and tackle the mission of facing my ghosts. With trembling fingers, I pull up Lyle's number on Skype.

"Hey, do you have a few minutes to talk?" I greet when I see his toothy grin.

"Yeah," he answers in a startled voice. "The kids are in bed, and Pamela's out at one of those makeup or Tupperware parties somewhere. What's up?"

I pause for a moment as I try to gather my thoughts. This is so awkward. As I think back, I don't know if we've ever talked about this. We just tried to move on with our lives. Maybe that's the problem. "Can we talk about us for a minute?" I ask haltingly.

Lyle swallows hard. "Kendall ... We've been over for years. I've moved on with Pamela. I have a whole life and family here. You understand, right? I love her. Whatever you and I had is over."

I gasp. "Oh my gosh! I didn't mean like you and me as a couple — I meant like what we had as a family. Or what we could have been ... I don't know. I guess I'm trying to figure out how you were able to move on. How did you get unstuck? Did you just forget about Quinn?"

"No, how could I? I was there when he died. I'll never forget about him. No matter what I accomplish in life, he will be my biggest loss. The son who never gets to drive his first car or kiss his girlfriend or get married and have children of his own. I know what the medical records say, but I'll always wonder if things would have been different if I'd only checked on him one more time."

"Why didn't you tell me this? I thought I was the only one who thought those things. I drove myself crazy."

"Are you kidding? You were so strong and put together. You handled everything like a champ. Not only did you clean up all the messes in our lives — you were out helping other people. You didn't need me. You didn't need anyone. I just stepped back and let you lead your life. You were full of goodness and hope. I was full of rage against the world. I wasn't doing you or anyone else any good, so it was better if I just left. I support what you do, but I can't be part of it. The pain is just too much."

"So, you just made a conscious decision to choose a different life?" I push.

"Sometimes you have to choose to put one foot in front of another and walk toward what makes you happy — even if you know that it will cause some pain along the way."

I take a gulp of hot chocolate before I look through the camera lens at the man I once thought I loved more than life itself. "What if it's all just an illusion? Maybe I'm just a fraud."

"What do you mean?" Lyle asks with a concerned expression.

I shrug. "Every day I go to work at Locate My Heart, and I pretend I have all the answers for all these grieving, hurting families. Yet, I can't seem to move past Quinn's death. I'm like the great pretender."

"Ken … it's not moving past. It's going forward despite. Quinn will always be there. Neither one of us can 'un-love' him. Loving someone else or having more children doesn't mean we didn't love each other or love our firstborn son. It means the world moves forward and we have to go with it."

"You make it sound so easy," I accuse.

"I don't know what to tell you. It is easy and hard all at the same time. The new stuff eases your pain some — but the memories never go away. You have to give yourself permission to be happy. That's probably the hardest part."

"Permission? I don't know if I've ever done that. I might have to give it a try. Thanks for the pep talk. For the record, I still think you're a pretty good guy. Give your wife and kids a hug."

"Take care yourself, Kendall. You deserve it. Whoever this new guy is, he deserves you too. Don't forget that."

"Bye Lyle. Sweet dreams."

"I'll try." With those two words, the screen goes dark and my past recedes into the background. Now, if I could only fix what's wrong in my future, I'd be set.

⎯⎯⎯▶◀⎯⎯⎯

Deciding that some communication is better than none, I hit the FaceTime button for Jameson. I'm a bit taken aback by his surroundings. "Are you sleeping on Aidan's plane?" I ask when he groggily picks up the phone.

Even in the dark shadows, his fatigue is evident. He looks broken. My urge to comfort him is a tactile thing. I reach out and touch the picture of his cheek. I'm heartbroken for him.

Jameson holds up his finger to his lips. "Yeah," he whispers harshly. "This seems to be the place Toby is the most comfortable. So, we're just hanging here for a while."

"Everything okay?"

"No. I don't know when it will be," he answers succinctly.

"Anything I can do to help?"

"I don't see how, unless you can rewrite time." Jameson sighs heavily.

"Sadly, I can't do that. I wish I could. It would be easier for me to help you if I was there with you."

"Maybe, but I don't think so. Everything is complicated. I don't need to deal with the mess of us."

"Is that how you see us? A mess? Is that all I am to you?" I ask indignantly.

"No! Look, I can't talk about this right now. I've got bigger issues. My parents still think my brother is dead. I've got a brother who needs a world of help who doesn't believe he needs anyone, including me. We've got to collect evidence on some deranged woman who thought she was going to take over the military with a video game. I don't have time to figure out my personal life right now. I've got too much other crap to sort out. I figured you of all people would understand that. I've got to go. I don't think Toby has slept in five years. He sleepin' now and I don't want to screw that up."

I stare at my phone with Jameson's photo shining up at me as the phone goes dead. The picture is one the proprietor of the spa took of us after our massages on our magical long weekend. Jameson had just kissed me breathless and I was literally weak in the knees. His adoring expression seems to mock our current reality.

I blink away tears as I cram a couple of Oreos in my mouth and wash them down with insipidly cold hot chocolate. I make one more phone call.

My brother picks up right away. I take a shuddering

breath before I sob, "I did it this time. I ruined everything. Oh, Wills, I need help."

"Professional or personal?" he asks. "I guess it doesn't matter. I'm making reservations as we speak. I'll be there in the morning. Don't do anything. Go to bed. If you eat any more cookies, you're going to throw up. Back away from the Oreos."

"How did you know I was eating cookies?" I reply guiltily, covering the bag with my blanket.

"You always eat Oreos when you're upset. Besides, I can hear the crinkle of the bag. You hate throwing up with a passion. This Jameson dude isn't worth all this. Whatever is wrong, we can work through it. Hang tight."

"I don't know if this can be fixed. Jameson's words sounded pretty final. He doesn't seem to want me in his life right now."

"Kendie, I've seen the guy. He's head over heels gone over you. He may be the strong, silent type, but the man has a thing for you. He is your heart wish. You don't give up on heart wishes that easy. You just find another way to make them come true."

"That's easy for you to say. Your world isn't collapsing around you."

"Take a shower and go to bed. I'll see you in the morning. Things will look different in the fresh light of day. I love you, Sis."

"At this point, I'm lucky somebody does," I grouse.

"Well, if your twin can't love you, what's the use?" He gives me a big loud air smooch and hangs up the phone.

CHAPTER TWENTY-TWO

JAMESON

Toby pours a third kind of breakfast cereal into his bowl before he pins me with a direct stare. "Go home. As ridiculous as it is, we can't live on this plane forever. I've got to move on with my life, and so do you."

"I'd like to go home — but I can't. We've got things to settle here. I can't just leave you."

"Why not? I do fine on my own."

"For one thing, you don't have any ID. I need to get your information from Mom and Dad. To do that, I've got to tell them something about what's going on. At this moment, they suspect you might be dead. I feel guilty being the only person who knows you're alive. Don't you think we should change that?"

"Rapture said as soon as people knew that I was with her, the world would know I was her sex slave and my reputation would be ruined forever. I'm sorry, I don't want that crap. I just want to go on living my life. So, if I don't tell anybody I've been found, does anyone have to know?"

"You said it yourself. Rapture isn't exactly sane. The world of social media is a strange place. People are going to believe what they're going to believe. You can't stop that. You can't make your decisions based on something someone might speculate about you. The bottom line is you had to do whatever you did to survive. You survived. That is an accomplishment all on its own. It's not fair to you or to Mom and Dad for you to have to continue to hide out because of public opinion. You deserve the love of your friends and family."

"That's easy for you to say; you've got everything you've ever wished for," Toby counters as he rolls his eyes and takes another bite of cereal.

I shrug. "Don't know about that buddy. I might've just thrown it all away."

"Why would you do something like that?"

"Because sometimes I'm just stupid."

"So … you give good advice, you just don't take it?"

"Something like that —" I grimace.

"What do you think would happen if I took some of your good advice? Do you think all hell would break loose?"

"Honestly? It might. But I know someone who could help with the process."

"Let me guess? Your 'richer than God boss'?"

"Yeah, Tristan will probably be involved along the way too, but the person I'm talking about is my girlfriend,

Kendall Kordes. She is the director of a nonprofit agency called Locate My Heart. She helps reunite families who have lost children."

"Was she your girlfriend before you started looking for me?" Toby asks suspiciously.

"It's a long and complicated story, but I actually met Kendall because her organization had a malware attack. Based on all the craziness that happened when you first went missing, I was reluctant to have anyone else become involved in your case. I thought every organization like Locate My Heart was one big scam. So, Kendall and I got off to a rocky start. In the end, she showed me that not everyone who tries to help is out to fleece families. In fact, it was her involvement that directly led to your rescue."

"Dude! Why isn't she helping us now?"

"Did I mention I'm an idiot?" I answer with an awkward chuckle. "I figured it'd be easier for us to sort through our issues without her here."

Toby crosses his arms in front of himself as he studies me. "Guess you might have a point. Chicks can be weird."

I smile. "Yeah, but they can be the best kind of weird too. Don't let one bad experience poison you for life." I pull up a picture of my girlfriend on my phone and show it to him. "Wait until you meet Kendall. I think the two of you are gonna hit it off well."

"So, how can this Kendall chick help us?"

"Are you ready to talk to Mom and Dad?" I ask solemnly.

"Do you think they're going to be disappointed I didn't rescue myself earlier?" Toby runs his hand through his newly shorn hair.

"Of course not! They are going to be so proud of you for using your wits and surviving all these years."

"Mom is probably going to bust a gut when she finds out I enrolled under five different aliases to attend various online academies and have GEDs in several states. Even Rapture doesn't know about it. Whenever she wanted to upload my programming to her server, she was paranoid our personal IP address was being bugged by the government. She'd make us travel where ever she thought we'd be more anonymous, like conference centers, colleges or libraries. Rapture had me make up a bunch of random IDs. She didn't know I kept a couple for myself. While I was waiting for all those huge files to upload, I uploaded my coursework."

"How did you do all this without her noticing?" I ask, impressed by my brother's ingenuity.

"I was careful to do school stuff while she was sleeping off her drug binges. I wiped my history every time. Mostly, I did it just to prove that I could. Some days, I had to convince myself I hadn't gone as nuts as Rapture. It kept me busy. Still, it'd be fun to prove to Mom I didn't lose my knack as a good student. I don't know if I can ever go back and prove I was actually all those people."

"It's definitely something we can work on. If you did the work, you should get the credit."

Toby is quiet for a few moments. "You're right. It's not fair for us to keep the secret. Mom and Dad need to know. Do you trust your friend? She won't spill the beans just to become famous?"

"Kendall? Oh no, the opposite is true. She has her own painful past and has been betrayed. She knows what it feels like."

"Okay, tell her we need her help. I want Mom and Dad to know I'm alive; but I don't want to become a national joke. I just want to start my life over again."

I seem to have been holding my breath for several days and now I draw in a deep breath. "You want to do this in person or on a video call? I can have this plane ready to fly to Oregon in a matter of minutes."

Toby blanches. "No, I'm not ready for that yet. What if they hate me? I think I'll just stick to a video call for now. I'm not really ready for the video part either, but I know that they'll probably want to see me, so I think I can kick up the courage to do that."

"I can guarantee you they're not going to hate you. Give me a few minutes to get it all set up. It's still early in Oregon, so we might be rousing a few people out of bed. However, something tells me no one is going to mind."

"I hope not. Just to be on the safe side, I'm going to go take a shower and shave. You know what a stickler Dad is for good grooming. I want to make a good impression."

"I think Mom and Dad would be willing to let it slide, when they find out you're safe." I collect his cereal bowl and stack it with mine.

<hr>

I pace around the plane for a few laps before I settle into

the Jeep to make my call. I almost lose my nerve when I notice that Kendall is wearing one of my favorite Portland Trailblazer shirts as a nightshirt. We may have left things in an awkward place, but at least part of her must still miss me.

"Did you forget about the time zone difference?" Kendall mumbles as she pushes her hair out of her face.

"No, I didn't forget. I called to eat some humble pie and ask for your help. Actually, Toby wants your help. No, that's wrong too. We both need your help. My whole family needs you."

Kendall sits straight up in bed. "Oh my gosh! What's going on?"

"Toby has decided he wants to let our parents know he's alive. But, he doesn't want anyone else to know. The creep who held him captive convinced him that if anyone found out that he was held by a woman, the whole world would believe he was some sort of perverted sex slave. He is afraid of his story becoming public. He's hoping to blend back into the world without anyone noticing."

Kendall is gulping air. "Wow! Just wow. That's a tall order. Let me think about that for a minute."

After a few moments, she says, "Okay, I have an idea, but it's going to take me about four hours. I've got to go get your parents — tell them a tiny fib and get them into a secure environment. After I do that, I'll be in touch. I'll use Tristan as the intermediary. He is less likely to arouse suspicion than Tyler."

"Sounds good. Have I told you recently that I think you are a rock star?"

"Not really. Recently you told me I was your mess."

I flinch as my own words come back to haunt me. "I probably shouldn't have said that. I can't juggle all the balls I have up in the air. I'm trying to be everything to everybody, and sometimes I'm not great at that. I have a hard time asking for help when I need it."

"Like you told me once before. We've got bigger issues to deal with right now. Let's focus on those first. You just gave me a task list a mile and a half long and I haven't even had a shower yet."

"Lord knows you can't properly face a crisis unless you smell like peaches and cream," I tease.

"Oh shut up! You're just jealous because I smell better than you do."

"Truthfully, I wish I was there to hold you in my arms. I was a fool."

"I wish you were here too. But given the circumstances, you might be a distraction I can't afford today."

I smile as I hang up the phone. That was less excruciatingly painful than I expected it to be. Given what a jerk I was the last time I spoke to her, I anticipated worse.

I make a quick phone call to Tristan. He answers on the first ring. "Things getting better?" he shoots.

"Actually, for the first time in days, I think I can say yes," I reply.

"Good. Headed back to Oregon?"

I sigh. "Not quite that good. But, we're closing in on a video call."

"I suppose that's something."

"We need the help of Identity Bank to make sure there's a complete media lockout. My brother is spooked. He doesn't want the meeting to be discovered by the media. He told me that he looked up kidnapping cases of kids his age hoping he would find that people were looking for him. He got spooked by the nasty comments on the news article he read. To him, it confirmed every warning Rapture had given him."

Tristan leans in toward the camera. "I have to tell you — your brother's pretty smart. After some of the experiences I've had with Rogue, I don't blame him."

"What he's asking for might be impossible. He doesn't want any media attention about his rescue. He wants to blend right back into society."

"Like the witness protection program?" questions Tristan.

"I don't think he's thought about anything that formal. I believe he intends to just dissolve back into the world as if nothing ever happened to him."

"If that's his plan, he must not have had much exposure to the Internet or reality television over the past few years."

"I don't know. The bits and pieces he shared with me are pretty unusual, to say the least. On the one hand, he seemed tightly supervised; on the other, his captor left him with almost administrative type computer clearance."

Tristan shakes his head at me. "Remember, you can't judge. Fear and mind control played a big part in Toby's choices."

I nod tightly. "You're right. I keep judging the situation as if Toby were an adult and had every piece of the puzzle. He was just a kid. He still is. Anyway, I called to see if you could help us lock down as much security as possible. We don't want any media outlets getting wind of this if we can help it. Kendall will be contacting you with any developments. We are leaving law enforcement out of it for now because of the potential for leaks."

Even through my phone, I can see Tristan raise his eyebrow. "About time you pulled your head out of your butt about Kendall."

"I'm aware I screwed up. Working on it," I admit with chagrin.

"As for the rest of it, consider the assets of Identity Bank deployed. I'll read Isaac in. Remember, this is the long game. Video call this time, in person meeting next. It's been a long few years for your brother. Normal is not going to happen overnight."

"Thanks for the reminder. You know me, patience is not my favorite thing."

"Life has a way of teaching us lessons we don't always want to learn."

CHAPTER TWENTY-THREE

KENDALL

"Hey, Bonnie. would you be willing to help me out with a project for Silent Beats recording studio today?" I ask in a conspiratorial whisper when she answers the phone.

"You mean with Aidan O'Brien, Tasha and Jude?" Her excitement shines through clearly, even over the phone. "Will I get to meet Tara too?

"Exactly! We would like to do a music montage honoring Aidan's influence on music. I thought it'd be fun to show a broad spectrum of fans. I wondered if you and Wesley would like to be extras in the audience."

"Oh honey, I'm such a mess, no one would want to see me."

"Nonsense! Besides, that's half the fun of this. You get to be made over by Aidan's hair and make-up people. Isn't it great?"

"Like they do on those talk shows?"

"Uh-huh, Only Aidan's folks are better because they do it more often."

"Oh shoot! I just have to do this — I mean who gets to do this kind of thing? My girlfriends will never believe this. Where would we meet you?" Bonnie asks, sounding flustered.

"Don't worry about it. I'm getting ready to come down and get you. I have access to the studio."

"Wesley better not be a party-pooper about this. I'll never forgive him," Bonnie threatens.

"I'm sure he'll be fine. As soon as he sees how excited you are, he'll be supportive." Even as I say those words with a smile, I'm crossing every appendage I have, hoping against hope, Mr. Payne understands how important this opportunity is to his wife.

━━━━●●━━━━

My brother has made the perfect foil to Bonnie and Wesley's nerves all morning. Whether it was talking autos and woodworking with Wesley or music and arts with Bonnie, he's been spot on. I never knew my brother had such an affinity for fashion until he started helping Bonnie pick out her wardrobe.

The hairdresser picks up another can of spray and Bonnie holds up her arm to block it. "I think that's enough. Will, what do you think? Don't I already look twenty years younger? I don't want to look plastic."

Will takes a closer look. "Mrs. Payne has a point. She supposed to look like a fan, not one of the stars. She looks radiant. You've done a great job."

"Oh, hasn't she? Look what she did with my Wesley! He looks like he did when we were dating," she gushes.

"Let's go check out the recording studios. It might be fun to record a couple of little pieces about how much Silent Beats music means to you," I say as my heart beats in my throat. This subterfuge doesn't come naturally to me.

"Wow! It's like being a real music star!" Bonnie says as she tags along behind me.

Wesley lays his hand on Bonnie's shoulder. "Honey, please calm down. You're going to cause yourself to have another spell. This isn't such a big deal. See, those are the monitors Jameson was telling us about. He installed those a while back and got fiberglass in his beard, remember? These people are human beings just like everybody else."

"I know, dear. They seem like such nice people. You'd never guess they are big stars."

"They are great. Jameson said so. Still, you need to put it all in perspective."

I pivot back toward Will, who has been quietly following us. "Thanks for your help. We've got it from here. I'll call you when we're ready to go."

"It was a pleasure to meet such avid music fans, Mr. and Mrs. Payne." As he turns on his heel to leave he adds, "I hope all the wishes of your hearts come true today."

Bonnie tilts her head toward my brother as he walks down the hall. "What an odd young man. I bet he was a fascinating student."

I can't cover my smirk. "Oh, you have no idea."

I usher the Paynes into Aidan's favorite recording studio and situate them in front of the cameras which are hooked up to the private servers Jameson just installed. I close the doors to the soundproof room and nervously take a seat.

Mr. Payne observes my demeanor and abruptly crosses his arms.

"We're not here for any music video, are we?"

I bite my bottom lip. "Well, technically, you could be. But that's not the primary reason you're here. I'm sorry I had to bring you here under false pretenses. It was for security reasons."

"Security reasons?" Bonnie asks with alarm.

"I needed to implement some safety precautions to make sure we didn't attract any media attention."

"Why would there be any media interest in us? They hate us," asserts Wesley.

"I think I'll let Jameson explain this one," I reply as I flip on the video feed.

Bonnie's eyes go wide as she sees Jameson's face on the screen. "Where are you? I thought it was strange you weren't at dinner the other night."

"Mom and Dad, I have a lot of stuff to explain, and some of it may not make any sense. Please remember that overall, it's great news. Even so, it's a bit shocking and hard to understand," Jameson stammers.

"What are you talking about, son? Just spit it out," Wesley demands.

"I'm calling you from West Virginia. I got a call the other day that someone had seen the flyers Kendall developed with the sketch artist through Locate My Heart. Toby has been found. He is fine. He is scared people are going to twist and turn his story into something it shouldn't be. He is reluctant to come forward and make his story public, but he wanted to let you know he is doing well — as well as can be expected given the circumstances."

Bonnie collapses against the leather stool and fans herself.

"Mom! Are you okay,?" Jameson shouts through the monitor. Wesley jumps up from his seat and checks his wife's pulse. I sprint over with a wet washcloth and lay it on her forehead as I try not to panic.

Bonnie immediately yanks it off. "Just tell me one more time that my baby is okay and let me see him. I'll be fine."

Toby appears on-screen. He fiddles with his collar and clears his throat before uttering one, simple syllable. "Hi."

"Oh thank heavens! I am afraid to believe my eyes. You are alive and in one piece. Is this real? You look just like your uncle, Micah. You're so grown-up — I can't believe it!" She lets out a sobbing breath. "I hardly recognize you!" Bonnie gets up from her seat and walks over and touches the monitor with her fingers. "Your mole is still there." She shakes her head in disbelief. "My brother would get such a kick out of this. You look exactly like him!"

Wesley's eyes tear up. "I missed you so much, son. I never thought I'd see this day. Are you okay?"

Toby shrugs. "I guess. I just wanted you to see I'm

alive — but I want this all to be over. I just want a regular life. ”

"I wish we could give that to you, but that option was taken away from us years ago. I don't think regular is a choice anymore," Wesley answers sadly.

"I deserve a chance to just live. I had to pretend to be someone I'm not for years. I want to be Tobias Payne — some anonymous dude from nowhere."

"But you're *not* a nobody," Bonnie protests. "You are Toby Payne, beloved son, and brother from Cottage Grove, Oregon."

"No Mom! I don't think you understand. I can't be that kid anymore. I mean, it's been cool hanging out with Jameson, but it's not the same as it used to be. It's not really like he's my brother."

Jameson reacts as if Toby physically punched him. "That's not true. I'll always be your brother."

"I was kidnapped and you all went on with your lives as if I never existed. It's not as if anything will change if I go on with my life without you guys in it. You all have done okay without me. So, y'all know I'm fine now. I'm sorry it has to be this way. I don't want to be known as some weirdo."

Wesley's expression hardens as he absorbs his son's words. "That's not true. We missed you every single day. I understand there are no easy choices — but, I think you should consider your options a little more carefully. What about a place to live and a job? How are you going to handle it when your kidnapper goes to trial? We're your family. We should be there for you —"

"If you care so much about being a family, where have you been all these years?" Toby looks away from the camera and bristles. "Screw it. I'll just do what I always do — figure it out. If you knew what I have gone through, you'd know I can pull it together and deal with all that crap." Toby turns to Jameson and says, "I'm done here." He looks into the camera and adds "Later."

Bonnie lets out a horrified gasp as the monitor turns black. She sobs and runs toward Wesley's chair. She buries her head in his chest. "This is a nightmare, right? Our son was here, and now he's gone and he hates us and —"

"*Bonnie Bella*," he coos softly. "Tobias is alive." Wesley gently embraces his wife. "That's what we found out today. He's been through the ringer. He's only a teenager. That kid can't be relied on to make solid decisions. No one could in his shoes. We're teachers, remember — we know this. Even under the best of circumstances, kids his age say irrational things when they are scared. That boy was more frightened than he'd want to admit, despite what he says."

"You think so? What if he never makes contact with us again?" Bonnie looks up at me with pleading eyes. "This is almost worse than not knowing. When I didn't know anything, I couldn't know he hates us and doesn't want anything to do with our family. What was I thinking? Of course, he hates us. We let him rot in the arms of the monster for years." Bonnie collapses against the studio wall and begins to sob. "Now, Toby has to go through a trial and his life might as well be lived straight out of the tabloids. He's willing to turn his back on anybody he's ever known to avoid the exposure. How tragic is that?"

"It's pretty tragic," I agree.

"Bet you're not going to put our little testimonial in your company's brochure," Wesley remarks bitterly.

"I'm sorry, I wish things had worked out differently."

My teeth chatter as I rinse the soap from my hair. Even my fragrant candles have given up the fight as they start to flicker out. I examine the shriveled skin on my fingers — it seems my 'tub therapy' session has run excessively long, even for me.

After Will tried his best to patch the Paynes' up and put a positive spin on things, he drove us home and retreated to the den as he muttered something about needing to get ideas down on paper. I don't blame him. I'm not much fun to be around right now.

Out of the corner of my eye, I see the whimsical sunflower candle Bonnie Payne gave me during happier times. I smile as I remember how tickled she was when she gave me the little ceramic candleholder. She joked that I could finally "grow" my beloved sunflowers anywhere, even around books and fences.

Happier times.

Today was supposed to be happy. My mind is spinning. I'm still not sure what went wrong. I've gone to training sessions where they've told stories about reunifications that didn't go well, but in all my years of working at Locate My Heart, I've never personally seen it. It's heartbreaking. It makes me question everything I've done over the years. What if happy really isn't happy?

"Are you decent, Kendie?" my brother yells into the master suite.

I look at the fleece robe I'm wearing as I stuff a tissue in the pocket. "Yeah."

Will comes around the corner and sits on my bed. He quirks an eyebrow at my Rudolph the Red-nosed Reindeer robe. "Cute and warm."

"White elephant gift exchange at work — but no one realized I'm so weird I actually like it," I explain.

Will seems unusually hesitant as he digs something out of his jeans pocket. "You have to solve this. You fix everything — you are the logical, calm one. Everyone listens to you."

He hands me a black credit card with my name on it. "Anything you want, put it on this card. It comes with all sorts of fancy travel benefits too. Just let them know what you need."

"Wills, it's a good thought. But, I don't know if I can change anything. This is all emotional gut reaction."

"But you don't know you can't change things. Give him more to react to. All he has right now is the word of his kidnapper. Go tell Toby the truth. All the truths — Bonnie's truth, Wesley's truth, your truth... I don't know … our truth even. Let him know what it all means."

"What about Jameson?" I ask, as I suck a breath and start to make plans. It's scary how much William and I think alike. I was already considering talking directly to Toby. Of course, going to speak to him face-to-face wasn't even on my radar.

"I don't think that's going to be a problem. Wesley just called me and asked if I could go and pick up Jameson at the airport tomorrow night. Jameson is going to go check in with his job in Florida and then he'll be back in Oregon. Wesley doesn't think Bonnie is up to driving to Portland."

Will checks his phone. "It's five forty-seven now. There is an eight fifty flight that lands in Huntington, West Virginia."

"Is this crazy? We don't even know where Toby is! Jameson is going to be pissed at me for going behind his back," I protest.

"Face it, Sis. Things are already rocky between you and Jameson; they can't get much worse. We're going for the greater good here. The rest of it can be fixed later. We might not know where Toby Payne is, but Tristan Macklin knows everything about everyone at all times. I'm sure he knows when Toby Payne brushed his teeth last. If you explain to him what you're doing, I'm sure he'll help us."

"I guess the only question is, are you coming with me?"

"No, I better stay behind. I need to go pick up Jameson at the airport and help him with his parents. For some reason, I remind Bonnie Payne of every incorrigible student she's ever taught over the years. It has endeared me to her. Who knows? If I had teachers like her when I was in school, I might've liked it better."

"Go on, get your bad self out of here so I can get dressed and packed."

When I text Tristan Macklin with the plan, along with Toby's location, his only reply is "Thank goodness not everyone is giving up. Godspeed!"

<hr>

The surprised expression on Toby's face is comical when he opens his hotel room door. "If you're looking for my brother, he's on his way back to Oregon. If you're not, I'm not into that kind of thing. I don't poach."

I wrinkle my nose. "Eww! Nobody was asking you to."

"Barboursville is a long way from Duck country. Can't tell me you were just in the neighborhood. If you're not here to play kissy-face with my brother, why are you here?" Toby asks as he steps aside to let me in.

I hold up the shopping bags I brought. "I got you some stuff. I was hoping we could talk for a while."

The first thing I notice when I look around the hotel room is how compulsively tidy it is. Even Toby's belongings are folded with military precision. Jameson is neat, but not that neat.

After I set the bags on the bed, I remove an object from the largest one and hand Toby a box. "I have to tell you, I had to think hard about this. Jameson has turned me into a Mac fan — but, I chose Windows for the Xbox thingamajig. My brother tells me you'd like the Windows platform better because of the game thing — so, I picked that —" I ramble breathlessly.

"Hey! Wait a second … umm … was your name Kensie?"

"Close. It's Kendall."

"Kendall, why did you get me a computer?"

"I figured you probably need one to look for a job. Wait until you see what else I got you. There's a sweet little printer, so you can do resumes and cover letters too."

"Why do you care what happens to me? You're just my brother's girl."

I look down at my feet and trace the design of the carpet with my toe as I admit, "I actually don't know where I stand with Jameson right now. That's not why I'm here."

"Can we get on with it? Stop trying to pretend like you're Santa Claus and presents are going to make it all better. Because trust me, presents don't fix anything. You can skip right to the part where you tell me that all my decisions are garbage and I can't possibly be old enough to understand the consequences of my choices," he challenges as he glares at me.

"Believe it or not, that wasn't my plan. I just came out here to tell you some things you probably don't know. I'm an outsider. I don't know all the information law enforcement or even your brother knows. He hasn't shared much with me. What I do know is that a person kidnapped you and held you hostage for a number of years. She had influence over what you saw, what you read, and who you had access to. You've only heard one side of the story. Chances are, whoever this person is, she's probably pretty unbalanced. If she was healthy and whole, she would've never kidnapped you to begin with. So, that leads me to believe that all the information she gave you is suspect. It stands to reason, right?"

"Unbalanced. Yeah, that pretty much sums up Rapture Borges in a word."

"That must've been frightening — but, that's not all of it, is it? If it were, it would be easier. You had to learn to count on this Rapture lady. For better or for worse, the two of you became a family, whether you wanted to or not. It probably makes it hard to just hate her and everything about her. It also makes it hard to decide what's fact and what's fiction."

Toby scowls at me. "What makes you think you know anything about anything?"

I shrug. "I might not."

"So, what do you want to tell me? What do you know that I don't?" Toby challenges.

"You seem to be under the impression that your parents and your friends lives just went on without a blip after Rapture kidnapped you. I want to tell you about the chain of events she unleashed."

"Oh great, you're going to blame me like everyone else?"

"No! I don't blame you for anything. This is all Rapture's fault. You seem to believe because of what Rapture told you that no one cared, no one looked for you, or it didn't have any impact on anyone's lives except you and her. I'm here to tell you the other side of the story."

"I bet you and Jameson are playing some sort of weird game of good cop/bad cop. He probably thinks I need some freakin' babysitter or something."

"Jameson has no idea I'm here. This is on me."

"Why bother with me? Why do I matter to you? Does your agency get some sort of kickback or money from YouTube videos or something?"

"Nope. Locate My Heart gets nothing from reunions, successful or otherwise. We're only trying to help families."

"So, what's in it for you?"

I take a deep breath and share my truth. "Once upon a time, I had a son." I choke over the words as a fresh wave of pain hits. "His name was Quinn. I went to the grocery store one day, and I didn't take him with me because he was sick and I was exhausted. I left him with my fiancé. Quinn went down for a nap and never woke up. I'll never get a chance for a reunion with my son. Ever. I regret that I was tired and cranky. Every day I question my decision about whether I should've brought him to the grocery store with me or whether I should have gone to the grocery store all. Every day, I want to take back the thought I had on the way over to the store about how great it was that it was quiet. To this day, I can't walk into a quiet room without my heart hurting."

"I'm sorry. That's sad — but what does that have to do with me?"

"You asked me why I care and what's in it for me. That's my answer. I do it for Quinn. If I can help other families not have to say goodbye forever, it feels like a win against evil. Quinn would be starting kindergarten this year, and I miss him every single day."

"Not all parents care as much as you do," Toby argues.

"It's true. Some don't. But your family doesn't fall into that category — not by a long shot. Do you know the reason your mother doesn't teach school anymore it's because she developed broken heart syndrome after Rapture kidnapped you? The news of your kidnapping literally fractured her heart muscle."

"When I didn't believe that terrorists took my parents anymore, Rapture told me the reason my mom wasn't out searching for me was because Mom didn't care that I was missing," Toby admits. "Is she going to be okay?"

"I don't know all the details, but I understand there was some damage to the heart wall during the incident. If your mom was not out actively searching for you, it was because she couldn't. Your mom had to withdraw from all of her social circles and retire from her job because she couldn't handle the stress of everything. She had to focus on getting better."

"What about my dad? Rapture said if he wanted to, Dad could call up all of his ex-military buddies and they would've formed a posse to come get me. But he didn't."

"Your dad did just about everything short of that. The only reason he didn't do that is because that stuff only happens in the movies. Your dad took out second and third mortgages on his house to finance people to go search for you. He drove around for hours and hours searching every single place he thought you might be. If he heard a rumor or saw an obscure news report, he went chasing after it no matter how far-fetched. He finally had to give up his teaching career because it made him too sad to see children who were not you," I explain.

"What about Jameson?" Toby asks. "Why didn't he do anything with his military connections? Rapture said if Jameson wanted to, he could've found her through her connections at the Pentagon."

"I don't know anything about that. But I do know your brother left the military to take care of your mom and dad. After your mom felt better, he worked hard to land a job at Identity Bank which specializes in searching for people. Because he knew opening another search would upset your parents, he quietly learned the surveillance techniques of Identity Bank and tried to apply them to your case."

"So, basically what you're telling me is Rapture is full of it, and I shouldn't believe her about the sex-slave thing either?" Toby asks me pointedly.

"I'm not telling you anything. I'm just laying out the facts. Your mom has a broken heart without you in her life, and your dad sacrificed nearly everything he had. Jameson gave up a career in the military to take an active part in the search for you. Your family has never turned their backs on you. Even if you can start over anonymously, there won't be a single day when your family doesn't wake up with awful, searing pain in their hearts. Your disappearance wasn't some blip on the radar for them. It wrote on the souls of who they are and changed them forever."

"It changed me too," Toby argues.

"It did. It most certainly did," I concede. "That's why you need your family around you to help you remember what's real when you have to go up against Rapture Borges."

"I watch YouTube videos. I know what happens when kidnapping victims get reunited with their families. All sorts of false stories get spread around."

"Before I leave Locate My Heart, I'll work with Tristan at Identity Bank to come up with a plan to make sure your exposure to negative press coverage is minimal."

"Leaving? You're leaving your job because of me? Jameson told me you were the reason I was found," Toby asks as his jaw goes slack.

I sigh as I shake my head. "It's not as simple as that. It doesn't have anything to do with you personally, except for the fact that I'm in love with your brother."

"Does Jamie know you love him?"

"I hope so, but that's a good question," I admit.

"If you love him, I don't understand what your job has to do with that —" Toby interjects.

"Right now, every time I go to work it reminds Jameson of the saddest time in his whole life. Every case is a reminder of what he should've, could've, or might've done in yours. It takes him back to all the pain your parents went through. If we have any hope for the future, I have to move on from my job. It's time anyway. I think I've been using other peoples' happily-ever-after's as a substitute for my own because I was afraid if I let myself be happy it would mean I loved Quinn less. I'm ready to lay that burden down and find my own bliss. Quinn would've wanted that."

"That's a pretty brave thing you're doing for my brother."

I swallow hard. "Love sometimes makes you do things you didn't think you were capable of doing."

"Do you think love is strong enough to get me back to Oregon?"

"Definitely! Especially when it's backed with a good credit card."

"Kendall … you gotta make me one promise."

"Yeah?" I ask as my heart beats out of my chest.

"Please don't leave until all this is over. It's not just my brother who needs you."

CHAPTER TWENTY-FOUR

JAMESON

WHEN TRISTAN SEES ME walk into the break room and throw my carry-on bag on the couch, he whistles through his teeth. "Gotta hand it to you, man. Your girlfriend is a force of nature."

I roll my eyes. "What did Kendall do now? Last time I saw her, she was breaking my parents' hearts like dry kindling."

"What on earth are you talking about?" Tristan asks with a befuddled look.

"She was the one who pushed for my parents to search for Toby again. It's like she had some big point to make about Locate My Heart. I'm worried about my mom having another episode because she is so upset that Toby won't come to see her. He wants to pretend we're not even family. How is that progress?"

Tristan sits ramrod straight and looks at me. "Allow me to point out the obvious. First, it was because of Kendall that you even know your brother is alive. If she had not pushed you to search, you would've never known. Second, your brother's reaction to finding the rest of you and the trauma he's been through is not her fault. Got that?"

"Affirmative," I mumble.

"Why are you being such a jerk about this? It's almost as if you don't want things between the two of you to work out."

"I don't know," I confess. "It's like Kendall is a reminder of all the things I should have done differently with Toby. I know that's not fair, but that's my gut feeling. I understand she's not like all the rest of them, but it's like a visceral reaction for me."

"You won't have to worry about all that stuff much longer. After she gets Toby situated with your parents and develops a media strategy with Identity Bank to make sure that your brother and parents are protected, she's stepping down from Locate My Heart. I'm telling you, if you're not careful, she will march right out of your life, and you'll regret it forever. Women like Kendall don't come along very often."

"What do you mean situated with my parents? Last I talked to Toby, he was watching HBO on the TV at the Hampton Inn in West Virginia. I couldn't get him to budge an inch."

"Do you ever check your phone? I sent you like a dozen text messages about all this. Your girlfriend is a hero. She flew out on her own dime to talk to Toby. Whatever she said convinced him to go back to Oregon and to give up his plan to strike out on his own."

"She went to West Virginia?"

"Jameson, I gotta tell you — you're missing the headline here. Kendall Kordes is planning to leave Locate My Heart. Think on that for a minute."

"I can't check my phone because the TSA conveyor belt malfunctioned and busted it beyond recognition. Who knows, she might've told me all about this, but I don't understand why she would leave her job."

"I don't know — maybe because you've criticized her and held her at arms distance nearly every step of the way. You accused her of being a liar and a cheat. Then, after she helped you find your brother, you shut her out of the process completely and told her that what she did wasn't even worth so much as a moment of your time."

"That's not true. I asked her to help coordinate the video call with my parents," I stammer.

"And then you promptly blamed Kendall when the call did not go well. Smooth move, Romeo."

Although Tristan's words were said with casual ease, there is no mistaking the fact that my boss has a point to make. Although my first instinct is to defend my actions, I know they are indefensible. He's right. I have undermined Kendall's every move. I let my anger and insecurities about the past color every decision I've made about her. You would think I would've learned my lesson after my assumptions about Kendall had been proven wrong time and time again. I don't deserve the generosity Kendall has extended.

"Did she tell you why she wants to leave Locate My Heart?" I ask, still trying to digest all the earth-shattering news I've been given in the last few minutes.

"Something about loving you so much that she

doesn't want to cause you any more pain. I know I'm officially your boss, but I'm also your friend. As your friend, I'd advise you to figure this stuff out before it's too late."

"Looks like I'll probably be needing a job in Oregon. Your offer still on the table?"

"It is — after you take some time off to get reacquainted with your brother."

"Consider it accepted. For once, I'm not going to argue with your logic. I just want to go home and tell everyone how much I love them."

<hr>

If looks could kill, I'd be dead. William is here to pick me up, but he looks like he would rather be anywhere else in the universe. I slide into his car and buckle my seatbelt. "Good to see you too," I greet.

"My sister may love you and think you're Mr. Tall, Dark, and Handsome, but I think you're a chump."

"Fair enough. I suppose I deserve the traditional 'grilling by the brother' routine."

"I don't think you understand. I'm standing in because our old man couldn't be bothered to stick around. The fact that Kendie trusts you enough to let you into her life and see her pain should fill you with shock and awe."

"It does," I reply solemnly.

"Really? That's not what I see. From here, it looks like you're just going through the motions with my sister. It's fun for you to have a girlfriend when it suits you. She's a great pal when you want to go rock climbing or flex your Prince Charming chops. I get it. My sister is gorgeous. It's probably fun to show her off to all of your friends.

I start to respond, but Will holds up his hand as a car behind us honks. Will pulls away from the curb and into a parking space.

"Kendall is so much more than that. The thing that burns me is that you know that. You've seen her work with families and the press. You've seen her grace under fire — yet, you still try to place her in some imaginary box in your head. It's as if she can take part in only so much of your life. Guess what? That's not the way love works. If you love someone, they are part of your life. You don't get to qualify it."

"That's not what's going on between us," I insist.

"Uh-huh. So, completely disrespecting her professional training and expertise and leaving her behind in Oregon while you reunited with your brother — the one Kendall helped you find — was an example of a fully supportive relationship?"

I roll the suddenly tense muscles in my shoulders and pinch the bridge of my nose. "No. That was me being a numbskull."

"So, if you know you made a mistake, why are you pushing Kendall out of Locate My Heart?"

I jerk in surprise. "I swear I had nothing to do with her decision to step down. I didn't even know about it until Tristan told me."

"She reached out to you for advice, and you blew

off her phone calls. That's way up there on the jackass scale."

I groan in frustration. "I couldn't answer my phone. The screening machine at the airport essentially ate it for breakfast."

Will smirks at me. "What the heck is that? The grown-up version of the dog ate my homework?"

I hold up my hands in front of me. "Look, it's the truth, okay. I looked for a screen repair kit at the airport and couldn't come up with one. Even if I had, my phone was likely too far gone to function."

"Plausible. But, that doesn't explain why my sister feels if she wants to have a successful relationship with you, she has to give up the most important thing in her life," Will challenges.

I turn and place my back against the car door as I address Will, "I don't know how much Kendall has told you, but I have spoken words to her that should've never been said — to anyone, let alone someone I love. Maybe I haven't been clear that I was the one in the wrong."

"You don't want her to quit her job?" Will clarifies.

"No! Why would I want her to do that? I have watched her perform near miracles with families and the media alike. She has brought so much healing to my family it's almost as if all those bad nightmares from before are gone. My mother is back to organizing coffee clutches to knit little hats for kids in the NICU. It's something I never thought I would see again. We haven't even had the best reunion yet, and already Kendall has changed our lives as a family. I'm certain every family she deals with feels the same way."

"This is going to seem like a pretty obvious question, but does Kendall know how you feel about all of this? When I last talked to her about it, she seemed to think her job is mental torture for you."

I scrub my hand down my face as I admit, "Yeah, it's hard in some ways because I have to relive all the things I wish I would've done differently in Toby's search. In every mother and father she helps, I see my parents. That doesn't mean that she shouldn't help people. I need to deal with my guilt over how I handled Toby's disappearance — Maybe I could've done things differently, or maybe not. Either way, those are my issues to sort. I don't want Kendall to quit her job over it."

"I'm not a relationship expert or anything, but I really think you guys should sit down and talk about this. Do you know that you are Kendall's heart wish?"

"Heart wish?" I ask, confused by the term.

"The thing you want the most, but you're afraid to ask for because you would be devastated if your wish never came true," Will reveals.

I let out a slow breath as William's words sink in. "Are you sure Kendall wished for me? I haven't treated her very well lately."

Will confirms, "Not just once — multiple times. I've got one question for you. Is my sister your heart wish too?"

I wipe a tear away from my face as I say in a strong clear voice, "I've done a poor job of expressing myself and my feelings, but yes, Kendall Kordes is without a doubt my heart wish."

Will nods tightly and grins before he turns the car on and pulls out of the parking lot.

"Jameson Payne, all I can say is it's a good thing I am filthy rich now because we are going to have to move heaven and earth to dig out of the hole you've made for yourself."

"William Kordes, I am glad you're on my side. You would make a formidable enemy."

"Keep that in mind. Mess with my sister again, and I can easily change your status."

CHAPTER TWENTY-FIVE

KENDALL

TOBY PLACES THE SILVERWARE next to the plates as he helps me set the kitchen table. "I guess this house seemed bigger when I was growing up. Are you sure this is okay? Mom and Dad aren't here."

"I know. Your mom wasn't planning for anything extraordinary to happen today. So, she's taking a flower arranging class at the local craft store."

"I wonder if she still makes caramel apples at Halloween?"

"I bet she does. Maybe you guys can make them together this year."

"I don't know what I'm going to say to them. I was pretty rude before."

"I find a sincere apology goes a long way," I suggest.

"I always thought so too, but it doesn't seem to be working with Jameson," Toby observes. "I mean, it's not like he's my best buddy or anything, but we hung out for a while. Now, he's not returning my calls."

I shrug and try to look nonchalant. "I don't know what's up with him. I've stopped trying to figure it out. I left Jameson a voicemail about today. If he shows up to our party, great. If not, I guess it's his loss."

Toby raises an eyebrow as he gestures toward the counter where all the deli containers are arranged. "I don't know. Could be a stretch to call rotisserie chicken 'party food'. Rapture didn't care if I watched the food shows on PBS, so I've got years' worth of party ideas in my head."

"A man after my own heart. Someday, we'll do the party thing proper justice. There's one thing I've learned about Bonnie and Wesley. They love this kind of stuff. I was confused at first too, but I've just learned to roll with it."

I hear the garage door open and Bonnie's voice floating into the kitchen. "Kendall, is that you? I wasn't expecting you today. You'll never believe all the stuff I got from the craft store. Wait until I show you." Her arms are full of bags as she rounds the corner into the kitchen. "Who on earth are you talking to? Is Will here?"

Bonnie stops in her tracks when she looks up and notices Toby. "Wesley, get in here!" she shrieks as she drops the bags on a nearby chair.

Wesley runs through the door wielding a shovel from the garage as if it were a weapon. "What? What's wrong?"

Bonnie places her hand over her mouth as she shakes her head. "Nothing. Nothing is wrong. For the first time in forever, things are right. Look who's here!"

Wesley drops the shovel on the kitchen floor and sprints over to Toby. As he wraps Toby in a tight embrace, he says, "Thank God you are finally home." Tears roll down both their faces as they stand there absorbing each other's presence.

"You are home for good, right? You're not just visiting?" Bonnie asks tentatively.

Toby moves away from Wesley and walks over to Bonnie. He pulls her toward him and hugs her. The expression on her face as she takes the measure of her son up close and personal is priceless. "Yeah, Mom. I'm home for good. Kendall convinced me that it's going to be difficult to start over, regardless of where I live. The only person I was punishing was me. If I didn't come home, Rapture would win."

"That woman is never getting another thing from the Payne family unless it's a good, long jail sentence," Wesley vows.

"It might not be so easy, Dad. Rapture had a plan in place in case we were ever caught. She's got documentation dating back years to show she is not mentally stable or responsible for her own actions."

"Well, she can just take those plans and shove them. She's never been up against you before. You are the strongest person I know," Wesley growls.

"I don't know if I can fight her all by myself," Toby admits.

"You don't have to. You've got a whole army of people fighting for you."

"Speaking of the Army, have you heard from your

brother? I've been trying to call his cell phone, but nothing is happening. I'm starting to get worried. Jameson is always so good about returning my messages."

A feeling of dread settles in my stomach. "So, it's not just me? None of you can reach Jameson?" I ask.

Everyone in the room shakes their heads.

Toby pulls away from his mom and sits at the breakfast bar. He buries his head in his hands. "What if Rapture was right and something happened to Jameson because I'm in contact with you guys?"

"I'm sure there's a logical explanation," Bonnie asserts. "Maybe he's working on something military related for Tristan Macklin. Some of those jobs are highly classified."

"I suppose so, but it's weird for him to be out of contact with everyone. The guy is all about technology — I don't think I've ever seen him without his cell phone in his hand," I reply.

We jump in surprise when the front door latch clicks with a loud metal scrape. Like a conquering hero straight out of a scene from a movie, Jameson strides through the door.

For a moment, all of us just stare at Jameson as if he is some sort of apparition. As usual, my heart beats faster at the sight of him. After days of no contact, I am afraid to believe he's real.

"Sorry I'm late. I got here as fast as I could." Jameson stacks his bags at the front door. He glances over at Toby. "Hey bro, I heard you were in town. Welcome home!"

William slips in the front door with no one noticing until Bonnie says, "There are fresh chocolate chip cookies in the cookie jar. Help yourself, Will."

Will blushes. "Thanks Mrs. Payne. I'm always up for a homemade treat. I'll never believe eating cookies before dinner ruins your appetite," he responds with a wink.

Toby clears his throat abruptly. "I hate to be the clingy little brother, but, Dude … a phone call would've been nice." Toby gives Jameson the teenage version of a guy hug.

Jameson pulls a mangled phone from one pocket and a phone I've never seen from the other. "Would you believe I've got two phones and neither of them work? The airport screening device destroyed one of them, and I can't get the other one to activate on my account. It's lost somewhere in cyberspace. Even I can't fix it."

"That explains so much," I mutter, as I breathe a sigh of relief.

Jameson puts his phones on the kitchen counter and ambles toward me. "It explains some things, but not nearly enough. You and I need to talk after the home-coming party."

The smile slides off my face. "I'm not sure I like the sound of that."

———•◦•———

As we wind our way up rough Forest Service roads, I'm filling the awkward silence between us with stories from Toby's trip back to Oregon. "I don't think anyone recognized us from the campaign to find Toby, but I did get some odd looks. He is too young to be my boyfriend but a little old to be my child. One guy in line actually muttered to himself, 'Stupid cougars'. Of course, that meant I had to explain the term to Toby. He hadn't heard it before. It's hard to say which of us was more embarrassed."

"My little brother has grown up to be a handsome guy. Who knows? You might be tempted," Jameson quips with a wink.

I shake my head vigorously. "No thank you. One Payne brother is enough. To make matters worse, the ticket agent was gushing over his passport picture. I thought he was going to dissolve into a puddle of humiliation by the time she was done."

"Here's a little secret about guys — we act all embarrassed when something like that happens, but inside we're all puffed up like sage grouses."

"Toby didn't look very puffed up to me. He looked miserable."

"Any problems getting through TSA?"

"No! I was surprised that Tristan could help him get a passport so quickly."

"Truth be told, the way things go at Identity Bank, that was probably more Isaac's doing. But I'm glad he was able to help out."

Jameson pulls into the parking lot at the Umpqua National Forest. I glance at my lightweight summer dress and sandals. "I'm not really dressed for a hike today," I protest.

"That's okay, I'm just going to take you to Spirit Falls. It's one of my favorite places. I always come here to think and to make important decisions. I want you here with me."

Jameson places his fingers through mine as he tucks me close to him. Together, we walk along the path to Spirit Falls. Finally, the silence begins to get to me. "Do you mean that? Do you want me in your life?"

"I do," Jameson proclaims squeezing my hand.

"Honestly, some days I can't tell."

"I know. I put you in a terrible situation, and I'm sorry. Instead of reaching out to you when I was feeling overwhelmed, I closed in on myself and tried to handle everything alone. As you know, that strategy didn't work very well, and it caused you a lot of pain. That wasn't my intention, but I still regret it."

"I'm going to try to make it easier for you. I'm looking around for another job. It won't be right away because I promised Toby that I would see his case through until the end. We'll have to see what happens once the media discovers that he has been found. Hopefully Tristan and I can mitigate the impact with our plan."

"You don't have to leave Locate My Heart for me. In fact, I would be heartbroken if you did. I see what a great job you're doing there every day. I wouldn't want to rob another family of your skills and ability just because I regret my own choices. Toby has been found, and he is reunited with my family. I need to let the past go and move on with life."

"Move on with life?" I ask, my voice raising in pitch as bone-chilling fear hits me. "Does that mean going back to Florida and leaving me?"

"No! This is the opposite of that conversation. I brought you out here to tell you I've made some monumental decisions in my life, and you are the reason I made them. I want to make sure you approve of what I'm doing, and that you will be by my side."

"This sounds a little frightening," I quip as if it's a joke, but even I'm not certain how much truth is in that little statement.

Jameson leads me to a flat, moss-covered rock he takes off his coat and then his button-down shirt. He lays his shirt on the rock before motioning for me to sit down.

Jameson straddles the rock and sits behind me as he cuddles me to his chest. "I've said a lot of things during our relationship that should've been left unsaid."

"I can't argue with that."

"All this drama with Toby reminded me of something else too." Jameson runs his fingers through my hair. "There are a lot of things that I've left unsaid that I definitely should have told you."

My heart skips a beat or two. "Sounds ominous."

"I hope you don't think so. I forgot to tell you the simple things."

I shiver. "Simple things?" I ask softly.

I feel Jameson's beard on the top of my head as he nods. "Yeah, the simple things like — I'm glad you're in my life. I love you. I'm proud of you. I never want to leave you."

My heart gallops as I listen to Jameson say the words I love you. After the past few weeks, I wondered if I would ever hear them. But even as happiness surges within me, the practical voice in my brain insistently whispers questions.

Hesitantly I ask, "How is that even going to work? You work in Florida, and I live in Oregon. Although, I guess I don't have to live here. If I don't work at Locate My Heart, I'm free to move."

"That's the other thing — you don't have to leave your job to protect me. I'm a big boy and I can cope. Those families need you."

"As relieved as I am to hear that, your reaction to my job is not the only reason I am planning to leave. I've been hiding behind the happy endings of other people for too long. I need to figure out how to move on after Quinn's death and find my own happiness."

Jameson strokes my cheek. "This might be selfish of me, but I want you to find happiness with *me*. I love you, Kendall Kordes. You are my heart wish."

"My brother doesn't know when to keep a private conversation private!" I exclaim as I roll my eyes. "I love you too — but I don't understand how we're going to make this work; we are on opposite ends of the country."

Jameson wraps his arms around me. "I can't tell you how relieved I am to hear that. I was afraid I had wrecked everything. If you love me, we have a chance to work everything out. Tristan has offered me a dream job here. He wants me to set up a branch of Identity Bank on the West Coast. Before I do any formal work with him, I want to make sure that that's what you want me to do."

"I'm not sure I'm in a position to tell you what to do about something so huge in your life," I answer tentatively.

Jameson spins me around in his arms and places my thighs over his so I'm facing him. "We've been dating for several months and the fact that you question your role in my life tells me I've been doing this relationship thing all wrong. I've been pushing you to the sidelines during times I should be treating you like my partner. I'm sorry I made you feel less than. I want to be different — if you'll give me another chance."

I place my hands on Jamison's shoulders. "It's not really about giving you another chance. I've made mistakes too. This is about giving *us* a chance. As hopeless as things have seemed lately, I never gave up on the idea of us. As you've obviously heard from Will, you, Jameson Wesley Payne, are my heart wish. I can't imagine life without you."

Jameson takes his baseball cap off and pretends to wipe the sweat off his forehead. "I was dreading this conversation. Your brother seemed to think I messed up beyond all belief and you might have given up on me."

"My little brother doesn't know everything. I'll be honest; there have been times I wasn't sure where I stand with you. Sometimes, our relationship feels like a dramatic fairytale. When it's good, it's really great, and when it's bad, it's scary for my heart. It was all I could do not to call Tristan every day and ask him when you had to go back to work in Florida. I worried you might go and never come back."

"I won't lie. This new position will require a lot of concentration and energy. I'll be putting in tons of extra hours to get this up and running. I don't just want to open Identity Bank here, I want to make it the kind of organization Tristan would be proud of."

"I wouldn't expect anything less from you. I think Tristan made the perfect choice. I understand things may be difficult for a while." I lean forward and kiss Jameson thoroughly. "That's what love is for. It seeps into the holes and cracks in our souls and replenishes our spirit when times are hard. As long as we're together, we can handle anything."

Jameson pulls me close. "Together. That sounds like the best plan I've ever heard."

"A normal life filled with love is my heart wish. I never thought I'd be happy again. I love you so much."

Jameson brushes my hair out of my face. "When I first met you, I was prepared to despise you. But, you didn't let me do that. Not only that, you didn't let me hate myself for my flaws either. You helped me love the people in my life too and accept the people they had become. I had all but given up on my parents, and the prospect of finding Toby alive and well. I never expected to fall in love with you. Kendall Kordes, you are the best thing to ever happen to me. At first, when Will explained heart wishes to me, I was confused, but now, it makes perfect sense to me. You are my heart wish and I can't wait to spend forever with you."

As I hug Jameson tightly, I smile. My twin is on to something. A heart wish is a compelling force.

EPILOGUE

JAMESON

I STAND BEHIND KENDALL and wrap my arms around her as we sway with the music. Tasha and Jude are singing their latest hit for a huge benefit concert for Locate My Heart. My mom is beside herself because Tasha is wearing one of the sweaters she knitted. "Look at my mom. I never thought I would see her this happy again," I shout into Kendall's ear over the music.

She nods. "I know! Isn't it great? Your brother seems to be having a good time with Hayden too. Her amputation doesn't seem to faze him. The two of them have been inseparable since they met."

"I was working on Tasha's case through Identity Bank when she first met Hayden. Hayden has turned Tasha's fan club into one of the most popular blog sites around. If I know my brother, I bet he is talking strategy with her."

Kendall shrugs. "If you say so, but I have a hunch there is a lot more going on than that."

Tasha and Jude finish up their set and leave the

stage. I watch Toby and Hayden for a few more moments. I realize Kendall is right; my brother is flirting. Toby catches me staring at him, and he gives me an awkward wave as he blushes.

"Toby has come a long way in a few months. He has turned his kidnapping into a message of online safety for other kids. It makes me happy to see him just be like a regular teenage boy for a change."

"It's fun to see him come out of his shell. Things are still hard for him. He has a difficult time explaining to his classmates what he's been through the last few years, but he has made some new friends at Lane Community College."

"He talks to you about this stuff?" I ask incredulously.

"Well, we might've been in the middle of a marathon apple pie baking session when it came up. Not much to do while you're peeling apples other than talk. So, it works."

"You are not claiming enough credit. You really impressed Toby when you made all those pies and delivered them to the homeless shelters around here. I guess for a time Toby and Rapture were homeless, and they relied on shelters and food programs. He told me he felt a lot better knowing he wouldn't be judged for doing that."

"Judge him? Never. Your brother's actions were downright heroic. Every time I find out another horrific detail, I have to bite my tongue and not say anything. I'm afraid if I overreact, he'll stop telling me what happened to him."

"At least Rapture Borges decided to plead guilty and save us all the trouble of a trial. It should help Toby move on. He doesn't need to have his emotional scabs picked at by defense attorneys."

"I'm relieved too. Little by little, it seems like our lives are becoming normal for once."

Aidan O'Brien hops on stage and taps the mic stand and clears his throat. "Can I have everyone's attention, please? Thank you all so much for coming out to support Locate My Heart. There was a time in my life where the person I loved disappeared for several years. It was incredibly painful. I can't imagine the anguish of having a lost child. So, I'm happy to support Locate My Heart as they help reunite families. Please help me welcome Colette Stephens, founder of Locate My Heart to the stage."

Colette looks embarrassed as the audience breaks out into thunderous applause. When the applause dies down, she addresses the crowd. "Thank you so much for being part of today and supporting Locate My Heart. You all have made this the most successful fundraising effort we have ever had. I am so grateful. When I started Locate My Heart, it was just a small dream. I wanted to help the families not have the same experience I had when my son was taken and killed. Through the generous efforts of people like you, Locate My Heart has grown exponentially and beyond all of my wildest dreams. I am pleased to announce today that I am stepping down from Locate My Heart."

A wave of sound goes through the crowd as people gasp and voice their protests.

"No, wait. It's a good thing. I have been at this for thirty-two years. I'm tired and stuck in my old technology. I have spent several months reviewing applications for the position of director of Locate My Heart. Being the director of a nonprofit agency is a challenge. It's made even more difficult by the delicate nature of our mission. I hired the one person I knew had the heart, smarts, and passion to carry on my dream."

Kendall is holding as still as a statue in my arms as she listens to her supervisor. I wonder if she really doesn't know what Colette is going to say. There's no doubt in my mind that Kendall is the most qualified person to lead Locate My Heart. I am confident Colette made the right decision. However, Kendall seems less certain.

Colette clears her throat and fights back tears before continuing. "In making my choice, I worried about whether Locate My Heart was going to be a burden to the next director. The job can be all-consuming and throw off the balance of your life. Over the past year and a half, I watched with pride and happiness as the new director fell in love and found another person who is as passionate about life as she is. I'm sure Kendall Kordes will be able to find the proper balance and lead Locate My Heart for years to come."

Kendall melts into me a little more as she whispers, "I thought this might happen, but I was afraid to hope."

Colette puts her hand up to shield her eyes from the stage lights. "Kendall, are you here? Come on up on stage and introduce yourself."

Kendall nervously straightens her skirt as another thunderous round of applause fills the venue. She steps up to the mic. "Thank you so much, Colette. I hope I can step into your shoes and do the legacy of Locate My Heart justice. When I started as a college intern all those years ago, I never dreamed I would one day be the director. You've given me so many opportunities and chances to succeed. I am so grateful. I'm thankful to the families who have trusted Locate My Heart to help you find your children. We take pride in treating every missing child we represent as the most important. We've had some wonderful victories recently and hope to continue the trend in the years to come." Kendall stops to take a drink of water. "Most of all, I would like to thank the public for supporting us financially and sharing all of our missing children posts. If it were not for you, our efforts would be much less successful. Thank you."

Kendall steps back from the mic, expecting Colette to resume her speech. Instead, Bethany and Naomi enter from the other side of the stage. Bethany makes her way over to the microphone stopping briefly to hug Kendall. "I know you all want to get back to the business of having a great party. I promise my speech won't be long — but I wanted to share with you all how much Kendall Kordes means to my family and me. With her help, we were able to find Asher alive and well. Now that he's been home several months, he's thriving beyond our wildest expectations."

Bethany grips Naomi's hand as she announces, "I feel like I'm amongst friends here and the news I'm about to give you will soon go viral. You guys are the first people in the entire country to know."

An excited buzz goes through the crowd as they look at each other trying to figure out what Bethany might be announcing.

Naomi Fitzgerald stands nervously in front of the microphone. "Many of you know me from online stories and other media coverage. Some of you might have formed opinions of me based on what my aunt did. The one person who didn't is Bethany Livingston. She not only didn't judge me, but she also offered to be a surrogate mother for me. Her act of generosity was made possible by the efforts of Locate My Heart, and I will be forever grateful. Despite all the crazy circumstances that led to us meeting, I have to believe there was a bigger purpose. I'm happy to announce that Bethany Livingston is pregnant with our child and she is giving me a chance at motherhood I've never had before. I am so grateful to the Livingston's and Kendall Kordes for all of their help to make my dreams come true."

Naomi and Bethany leave the stage as the room erupts in cheers.

Kendall's eyes are teary as she steps back up to the mic. "Isn't that wonderful? What started out as a story of love lost has been completely transformed into a story of hope, determination, friendship and family. With all of your help here tonight, Locate My Heart can continue to have happy reunions like the Livingston family. Thank you so much for your support and donations."

Kendall backs up as Colette returns to the stage. "Perhaps I should've mentioned this before I gave you the job, but the job of director just got more complicated."

"What do you mean?" whispers Kendall, but Aidan's high-quality microphones pick up every word.

"Locate My Heart received an anonymous donation tonight. It is enough to move us to a new facility. It'll be nice to have offices and an air-conditioning system that works. We'll be able to add staff and expand our services. It will be quite the challenge, but I have no doubt you will rise to the occasion."

"Wow! We've been trying to move for years. This is like a dream come true," Kendall comments, sounding breathless. "If you don't mind Colette, I'm going to go sit down before the reality of all this hits me."

I walk up to the stage to help Kendall down the stairs. As I do, I pass Will and raise an eyebrow in question.

He meets my gaze and shrugs. "A heart wish is a powerful thing."

When we reach the back of the room, Kendall throws her arms around my neck and kisses me enthusiastically. "I can't believe it! Did you have anything to do with this? It's like Christmas, my birthday and New Year's Day all rolled into one."

"I wish I could take credit for all of this, but I didn't have anything to do with it. I'm just the guy who is in love with the new director of Locate My Heart. I am so proud of you and can't wait to see what we can accomplish together."

"We get to do this celebration thing again in a couple weeks. I can't believe they are already breaking ground on Identity Bank's new facilities. Tristan must be thrilled that you guys are actually ahead of schedule."

"He is, but I think he is more excited to come out and talk to Toby. If I don't miss my guess, Tristan's probably going to talk him into joining his software development team."

Kendall grimaces. "I don't know how I feel about that. It's a great opportunity for Toby, but it would break your mom's heart."

"Tristan is pretty good about making deals which make everyone happy. I have a feeling he's already got a work around figured out."

Suddenly, the noisy environment starts to close in on me. I reach into my pocket and palm my gift for her. I place my arm around Kendall's waist as I escort her out of the concert hall. I spot a couch in a secluded corner of the lobby and head toward it.

"Is everything all right?" Kendall asks.

I sit down and tuck her close to me. "I guess I am feeling a little overwhelmed. When I first met you, I was merely functioning. I was going from job to job and crisis to crisis. I think I did it on purpose to dull the pain from Toby's disappearance. If I was too busy to think, I was too busy to miss him and realize all the love I had lost. I was keeping myself separate from my parents because I didn't know how to deal with their pain."

"That must've been awful. I'm sorry you had to go through that," Kendall comments as she squeezes my hand.

"Then you came along and shoved me out of my comfort zone. You showed me I could risk showing people how I feel without being weak."

"That's funny. I always think that you're the one pushing me out of *my* comfort zone. After all, you turned me into a climbing addict."

"Well, maybe we push each other," I concede.

"I think that's true," Kendall places her head on my shoulder.

"The point is, you've shown me how to trust and love again. I've never been this happy in my life. I love you Kendall Kordes, will you marry me?"

She stares down at the solitaire ring I am holding near her right hand. She looks up at me with wide eyes. "Yes! Yes, a thousand times, yes."

With slightly less than steady hands, I place the ring on her finger. I take a deep breath as relief washes over me. "You know, your brother's right. A heart wish is a very powerful thing."

Kendall stands up and pulls me up next to her before she gives me a passionate kiss. When she pulls away she says, "I argue with Will all the time, but I won't argue with him this time. I love you Jameson Payne, and I can't wait to be your wife."

If you want to follow Mindy on her journey to love, Tempting Fate is the next book in the Hidden Beauty series.

NOTE FROM THE AUTHOR

Thank you so much for reading *Heart Wish*. I hope you enjoyed it. The series continues with *Tempting Fate*.

Tempting Fate is the complex, emotional love story between Mindy Whitaker and Elijah Fisher. It's sure to be a fan favorite.

Everyone always expects perfection from Mindy Whitaker.

After all, she rescued her baby sister from a life of horrific abuse when she was just a kid. Mindy has always been too smart for her own good.

If she is so smart, why is she feeling so dumb?

Since leaving home for college, nothing is going right. She has no friends and even her gift of precognition seems to be on the blink.

The world is expecting greatness from Mindy, but all she wants to do is go home.

Mary Crawford

Elijah Fischer hasn't been home since he can remember. But a family tragedy interrupted his carefully laid plans.

Elijah was sure he had left behind the awkward, shy teenager he once was. When takes one look at the grown-up version of Mindy Whitaker, every insecurity comes rushing back.

Can Elijah and Mindy rediscover who they are in the face of insurmountable odds?

It doesn't take any precognition skills to determine you'll love *Tempting Fate*, a New Adult romance.

~Mary

Because love matters, differences don't.

ACKNOWLEDGEMENTS

Heart Wish started with the simple idea that words could change the world. Okay, maybe not the whole world but a small corner of it.

This book is meant to honor the organizations and volunteers who show up every day to do the tough, grueling work to serve families in need. It is hard, thankless work which often doesn't get recognized, but I want you to know your work is valued immensely. Thank you.

I want to give a shout out to Kathern Watts, Kathy Faltinson, and Becca Draper-Ristanovic who always give me honest feedback even when it's tough.

A special thank you to my family. Leonard, I love you. You always support my dreams — no matter how crazy they are. Brandon, I'm so proud of you. Just think, you are almost six months into your residency. Way to make the world a better place! Justin, thanks for your technical assistance on video games.

ABOUT THE AUTHOR

I have been lucky enough to live my own version of a romance novel. I married the guy who kissed me at summer camp. He told me on the night we met that he was going to marry me and be the father of my children.

Eventually, I stopped giggling when he said it, and we've been married for over thirty years. We have two children. The oldest is a Doctor of Osteopathy. He is across the United States completing his residency, but when he's done, he is going to come back to Oregon and practice Family Medicine. Our youngest son is now tackling high school, where he is an honor student. He is interested in becoming an EMT.

I write full time now. I have published more than thirty books and have several more underway. I volunteer my time to a variety of causes. I have worked as a Civil Rights Attorney and diversity advocate. I spent several years working for various social service agencies before becoming an attorney.

In my spare time, I love to cook, decorate cakes and, of course, I obsessively, compulsively read.

I would be honored if you would take a few moments out of your busy day to check out my website, MaryCrawfordAuthor.com. While you're there, you can sign up for my newsletter and get a free book. I will be announcing my upcoming books and giving sneak peeks as well as sponsoring giveaways and giving you information about other interesting events.

If you have questions or comments, please E-mail me at Mary@MaryCrawfordAuthor.com or find me on the following social networks:

Facebook: www.facebook.com/authormarycrawford

Website: MaryCrawfordAuthor.com

Twitter: www.twitter.com/MaryCrawfordAut

www.ingramcontent.com/pod-product-compliance
Lightning Source LLC
Chambersburg PA
CBHW032058180726
48284CB00002B/335